AN UNARMED WOMAN

AN UNARMED WOMAN

a novel by

JOHN BENNION

SIGNATURE BOOKS | 2019 | SALT LAKE CITY

To Karla, for educating me

The opinions expressed in this book are not necessarily
those of the publisher.

Cover design by Haden Hamblin.
Maps and *Rachel* illustrated by Amy Bennion.

FIRST EDITION | 2019

LIBRARY OF CONGRESS CATALOGING-IN-PUBLICATION DATA

Names:	Bennion, John, author.
Title:	An unarmed woman : a novel / by John Bennion.
Description:	Salt Lake City : Signature Books, 2019.
Identifiers:	LCCN 2018045640 (print) | LCCN 2018053789 (ebook) | ISBN 9781560853534 (e-book) | ISBN 9781560852766 (pbk.)
Subjects:	LCSH: Mormons—Utah—Fiction. | Murder—Utah—Fiction. | Utah, setting. | Nineteenth century, setting. | LCGFT: Historical fiction. | Detective and mystery fiction. | Novels.
Classification:	LCC PS3552.E547564 (ebook) | LCC PS3552.E547564 U53 2019 (print) | DDC 813/.54—dc23
	LC record available at https://lccn.loc.gov/2018045640

ACKNOWLEDGEMENTS

I thank the many readers of the drafts of this novel, especially the writing group—Donna and Bruce Jorgensen, Valerie and Dennis Clark, Althea and Levi Peterson, Charlotte and Gene England, and Karla Bennion.

MAPS

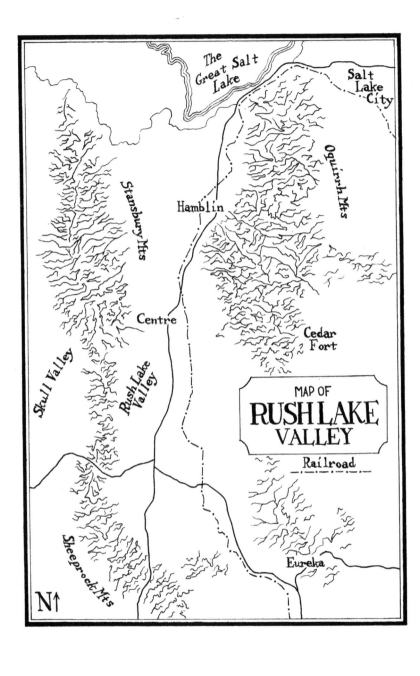

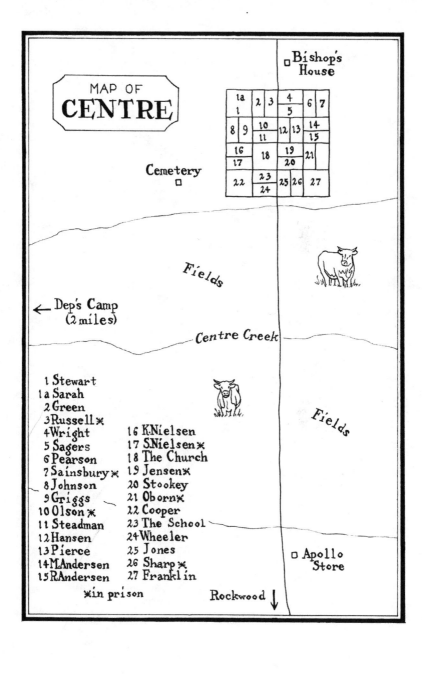

AN UNARMED WOMAN

Rachel by Amy Bennion

CHAPTER 1

Since dawn J. D. and I had taken turns driving north across Rush Lake Valley. It was my turn, but my hands could hardly grip the reins because I was a frozen block. Any minute the Angel of Death would seize me with ice tongs and drag me down to hell, where I would finally be warm. I just wished he would stop dawdling.

If heaven was as cold as Utah territory, the angels could have it.

The desert was silent except for the thud of the horse's hooves, the creaking of the rig. Even J. D., my stepfather, had finally shut his yap, for which I was damn grateful. He had wrapped himself in a rug of sheep pelts stitched together. All that showed was the end of his nose.

"I know you're play acting. You snuffle and grunt when you're really asleep."

He uncovered one eye, and I could tell from the way it crinkled that he was grinning.

"You have a tripping light tongue." His salt-and-pepper beard was narrow, well-trimmed, but his hair was shaggy. He was a Mormon patriarch in the carcass of a winter-starved bear.

"Bollocks!"

"Swearing's not becoming in a lady."

"Hell if I'm a lady!"

He sat up, and his eyes grew hard again.

"It's all of a pattern, Rachel, your swearing, stubbornness, and

3

sharpness of tongue," he said. "In many ways you're mannish—more full of mind than heart."

It was almost what a calf-eyed boy had stuttered to me just the week before—that I had the "b-b-body of a b-boy and the b-brain of a m-m-m-man." *Then why come sniffing after me?* I had asked him. He had no answer for that.

"I am not a man!" My voice came out louder than I wanted.

"Then become a woman. You'll be eighteen next month, and it's time to take up the reins of your life. Nobody can abide in childhood forever."

Damn his changeable hide. He believed that men and women moved in separate spheres but had trained me to ride, shoot, track, hunt, and work cattle. Now he wanted me civilized. Wanted me to marry our neighbor, Ezekiel Wright.

"So if I am an adult, let me work with you as a son would." I dropped the reins and rubbed my gloved hands together. "We did all right catching the thief who took Brother Apollo's horse." I glanced at the black gelding tethered to the back of the surrey. "I'm not as good a tracker as you, but with time—"

"You did help. You held the horse's reins while I rode the thief down. But that doesn't change the truth: when a woman marries, she leaves her parents' home. Much as I'll be sad to see you go to Ezekiel's household, it's proper for you to join with a husband."

It was as if I was talking to a cedar post, for all he heard me. "Whatever kind words you use, they still mean the same thing—you want to boot me out."

"You'd be just across the lane."

"If I could find a man suitable to me, I *would* marry him."

"Suitable to you! What kind of man do you want? Clearly no one from Rockwood."

I squelched a smile. "How mannish can I be, if five men have been interested, huh, J. D.? Lecture me that."

He waggled his head. "This is the pathway to vanity. Your beauty is of no use if you won't marry. How long will you keep saying no?"

"They were stupid, addlepated boys or lecherous men old as you."

"Ezekiel is none of those. He's barely forty. He's the best man yet to offer for you."

"I agree: that he is."

"But you want a man all to yourself?"

"I don't know."

"A man who wants only one wife wouldn't have the ambition to take you to the highest kingdom of heaven."

I showed my teeth like a wolf grinning. "It's perishing ironic, you a sworn justice of the peace and an agent of Wells Fargo but a criminal according to federal statutes. What's worse is you want me to join in your law-breaking."

"Obedient to God's law," said J. D., who would *not* be teased about the grand Principle of Celestial Marriage, "not to a false law that takes away our divine rights."

"That heavenly law will not give me expanding agency. It will send me and my future husband and my sister wives into hiding from federal deputies instead of roaming God's good earth."

J. D. wiped one hand across his face. "This good earth is a passing illusion. Heaven is the firmament. What we suffer here only adds to our eternal glory."

I grinned again. "Here it is approaching the turn of the twentieth century, and you're talking like the Old Testament. Heaven is not the firmament. The earth travels around the sun."

"I was speaking metaphorically."

I rolled my eyes at him, but he had covered his face with the rug again and could see nothing but his own thoughts.

The left-hand mare faltered. She was young and green, pretending to be weary, nothing like the other mare, steady and seasoned. The two were unequally teamed, just as I would be with Ezekiel.

I flipped the reins, calling the green mare a *"sleakit* beast." It was what my Nevada father, Irish-born, called me—a creature too cunning for its own good.

We traveled the edge of a wide, flat valley. Low mountains to our left hand, larger peaks twenty miles away on our right. The soil drab gray except where alkali lay thick as snow. The only plant that would grow was shadscale, squatty and pale. No human settlement survived in the whole valley except where streams trickled out of the hills onto skirts of fertile soil. One such town was Rockwood, our home; another was our destination, Centre, which had all morning seemed as distant as the hope of heaven, but was now close enough that I could see the steeple. Down in Brother Apollo's Underground store there would be a hot stove, a bowl of bread and milk, a long talk with his daughter Naomi, who was my best friend in either of the two villages, and later a bed piled high with quilts. I might even get a thick slice of roast beef or a hunk of cheese, maybe a slab of pie with thick cream to pour over it.

"I'm hungry as a wolf with pups."

"'Tis good for you to wait for a meal. Gives an edge to your appetite."

"I always have an edge to my appetite."

"'Tis true, Rachel, 'tis very true. I've never seen your likes for eating so much and remaining so thin. A man prosperous enough to already have a wife or two might think you sickly and unappealing unless you get a little meat on your bones."

Same tune, different lyrics.

When he was being a bastard to me—only a few times in the years since he had adopted me and my mother—the earth seemed ready to rip in half, the sun and sky fall away, as if I was back in Nevada with my drunken father, who would change from tears to kicks between one breath and the next.

I pulled up the horses and we stopped in the road. J. D. turned to frown at me.

"It's insulting for you to keep talking about how thin I am."

He muttered something I couldn't hear.

"Come on. Cough it up, get it out of your belly, 'cause it's making the both of us sick."

"Cough what up?"

"The wad of sermonizing you swallowed for breakfast. I've had enough for a decade."

That shut him up. All he could do was cover his head again and pretend he was hibernating.

A gong sounded ahead of us in Centre. The sound was not sweet like the ringing of a bell; this was someone laying hammer to a wheel rim or piece of scrap iron. It clanged again and again, then after a pause, thrice more. The pattern repeated—three gongs and a pause, three gongs again, clearly some kind of signal. In all our visits to Centre, I'd never heard the sound before.

Peering across the flat, I saw two men sitting their horses on a ridge above town. They rode ramrod straight in the saddle, not with the easy slouch of most ranchers. I realized that the blacksmith's regular pattern was a warning. I shoved J. D. with my elbow.

"Federal deputies." I pointed to where the riders dropped off the ridge.

J. D. swept the pelts back and laid one hand flat above his eyes. His greatcoat was at least three decades old, but his derby, trousers, and boots were new. He wore a tailored linen shirt but the cufflinks were carved from deer teeth.

"Damn scavengers. Brother Apollo told me about these two."

Several times I had watched him climb a rope ladder to the secret room in his attic—undignified for a man starting his seventh decade. The previous summer had been the worst of all. Our neighbor Brother Olson was angry that J. D. wouldn't loan his new Morgan stallion, so he sent a telegram to Federal Deputy Marshal Danby in Eureka. He told about the hiding place and reported that J. D. had taken a new wife. J. D. hadn't, often saying that five were plenty for any man. He had warning from the telegraph clerk that the deputies were coming and had spent most of the summer in a mountain cabin.

Before ten minutes passed the deps on their horses emerged from the mouth of the canyon. J. D. and I watched as they trotted along the near edge of town, through the fields, past Apollo Store, and across the flat toward us. J. D. dumped his sheepskin behind him into the jump seat and brushed his fingers across the butt of his Spencer rifle, which he carried in a long leather boot tied to the side of the surrey. I had seen him drop a coyote from five hundred yards with the old rifle.

"If it were not such sin," he said, reverting to the lilt and roll of his native Preston, England, "I would damn every federal deputy to hell. They bear the stink of carrion birds."

For a second I thought he might actually shoot them. He was a former bodyguard to Joseph Smith and, according to rumor, had killed three men in Illinois. He often said he had no more stomach for violence, but as with most things about J. D., one could never be certain. I hoped he touched his rifle because it steadied him, not for any real intent to kill.

"A moment of pleasure isn't worth hanging."

"I know. I know. But isn't it all right to imagine?" He smiled, his first real one of the day—and we were talking about murder.

"As he thinketh in his heart, so is he."

"I'm not a deceitful man." He nodded. "My sins are readily apparent."

"That they are; your cantankerous tongue and the vanity that you are never wrong. But I admit, you have none of the hypocrite about you."

8

As the riders drew closer, J. D. stopped smiling. The larger deputy wore a slate-gray greatcoat and a flat-crowned hat of the same hue. The shorter man had fashioned himself a *serape* out of an army blanket.

"They have naught to blame on me. I'm merely traveling with my daughter."

The riders turned their horses to block the road; the green mare snorted at the smell of strange horses and riders. I glanced over my shoulder at the black gelding, dancing behind us. The smaller of the two men gripped a heavy-barreled, slim-handled pistol, unlike any I had seen before. He hefted it as if to show off. Big weapon, small man. Everything about him was sharp—a long narrow nose, pointy chin, thin elbows. The younger mare flipped her head in the air, prancing and nervous.

"Please move out of the road," I said. "You're spooking my horses. And put that pistol away. You don't need it with an un-armed woman."

"Y'all headed to Apollo Store?" The man grinned at me. He had a southern accent; I guessed eastern Texas or Louisiana. His small tongue flicked across his lips.

I looked around at the desolate flat. "How'd he guess? Must be a Pinkerton detective or a holy seer. I can't tell which." The small man's leer disappeared. His horse, a buckskin mustang, laid its ears back, wary of its own rider.

"I know you from somewhere," J. D. said to the other dep.

The man shook his head. His hair was the color of mahogany, and he had a wide mouth, dark brows, clear and good-natured eyes. He reminded me of Matthew, my childhood friend from my pre-Mormon days in Nevada. Only this man was older than Matthew would be even now, his skin weathered and his hair touched with gray.

Despite myself, I smiled.

The man looked at me and then glanced away, scratching his neck. His horse was a big brown gelding. Its ears and stance showed it to be completely relaxed, unlike the laid-back ears of the little mustang. Clearly this horse trusted its rider.

Watching the older dep, I felt a weird coldness pass through me like a shadow. It was gone before I could begin to figure what it meant.

J. D. clicked his tongue at the horses and rested his hand on my arm. "Drive around them." The ground was flat on either side of the road, and I began backing and turning the surrey. With some difficulty, the small deputy stuck his long-barreled weapon inside his belt and seized the jaw strap of the green mare's bridle.

"Take your bastard hand off my horse." I hoped the gun would go off and put a bullet through something he valued.

"Rachel!" said J. D.

The small man looked at me. "Bye'n'bye—after you learn to speak civil to authorized deputies of the law. If you warn't a woman—"

I stared at him. His body was that of a man but he had the aggressive and erratic spirit of a half-grown boy.

J. D. tried to seize the reins from me. I held them out of his reach, not willing to let even these strangers think I was not up to handling the horses.

"We're a-goin' to Hamblin. On the train. Be there a week." He gave me an addled smile, sly.

"It must be clear to you that we are federal deputies." I knew from his slow drawl that the larger man was local. "We keep our eyes peeled for law-breaking polygamists."

His voice was deep but calmer than the small man's. I was surprised, in the middle of the prairie, by a sudden desire to hear him sing.

J. D. stared at him, frowning. "You're Lottie Marchant's son."

The larger man stiffened in his saddle.

"What is it to you if I am?"

"You've turned on your own."

"I've turned from an abomination."

J. D. said something under his breath. My horse flung her head but the small dep kept hold. He turned in the saddle to glare at J. D. "Mr. Mormonite, this chile your freshest wife?"

"My daughter."

"Looks to me like they've taken to incest," he said to the large dep.

J. D. said nothing, but I could tell from his dead silence that he boiled inside. Lucky for all of us he didn't reach for his rifle. "Bring me to court. You'll only be embarrassed." J. D. peered up at the other one. "Your name's not coming back to me."

The larger dep leaned toward J. D. "Rockwood town's next on our list. We've put seven lawbreakers from Centre in prison. Now they wear striped suits and have only their fellow polygamists to tuck them in at night."

"Instead of six or eight wives keeping them warm, they got nary a one." The small dep showed his teeth in a grin, and I found my mouth opening to say that he had a perverse imagination and should keep his sharp nose out of the Mormons' business. Just in time I clamped my jaws shut. J. D. would read my words as defense of polygamy.

The small dep sneered. "A man can't get no virgins when he's in prison."

I flipped the reins again, and the green horse, confused, danced to one side. The small dep turned in the saddle, tugging at the bridle, and the mare swung her chin across the rump of his horse, which lashed out with its hind feet.

I rolled my eyes. *Bollocks*, I thought, *bloody perishing bollocks*. The swearing, even unspoken, made me feel calmer.

"Let loose, please," I forced my voice into a respectful tone, "or we'll be tangled sure."

He released his hold. I flipped the reins and the horses started forward again. The dep jerked his horse's head, pulling hard on its mouth and kicking it at the same time, forcing it to prance next to where J. D. sat. "You think you can keep secrets from us? We've got eyes can see in darkest night. We can prophesy, can know what you're after before you know you're after it."

The larger dep frowned. "Let's get on our way, Sammy." They stopped at the side of the road, still watching us.

Sammy jerked on his horse's reins, but the horse flung its head up, nearly striking the rat-like man on his nose. He slapped the horse's ears, swore, and sawed on the reins to pull the horse around, all the while spurring his mount's belly. I heard him singing in a raucous, off-tune voice: "*Joshua fit the battle of Jericho, Jericho, Jericho. Joshua fit the battle of Jericho, and the walls come a tumblin' down.*"

"Shut it!" The older dep turned his horse and leaned to say something quiet to the smaller man.

J. D.'s fingers were white on the railing of the surrey. "Damnable insolent mouths." I was grateful that the deps, now about a hundred yards away, could not hear him.

"If I shouldn't swear, neither should you."

"'Tis not swearing to describe him accurately. I'm surprised someone hasn't stopped his heathenish jabber." J. D.'s accent had come back and he struck the side rail of the seat with his fist.

"But the older one is worse in your eyes. He was once one of the Saints."

J. D. studied my face. "I have never liked waverers, traitors. He lived in Cedar Fort with his widow mother when he was a young man. She married a soldier from Johnston's army and they all cleared out. Went to live with the gentiles. Now he's come back to persecute his own people."

As I whipped the horses into a trot, J. D. said, "No need to hurry.

We don't want the horses lathered when we stop for the night. Could stove them up."

"I can't be sure that polygamy is of God. But it makes me hot as a fire that—"

"'Tis of God!"

"So you've been telling me all day." I looked him square in the eye. "I'm doubtful the Principle is for me, but if Mormons believe God wants us polygamous, the government should leave us damn well alone."

J. D. smiled in the light of the setting sun, as if he had won.

"It's not that much worse than the false belief held by all Christian men, that God wants man to be lord over woman."

"Now, Rachel. God wants you to be a queen in heaven."

"I've no such ambition. Can a queen rope a calf or shoot a gun?"

I turned back again and watched the backs of the two deps. J. D. could pick them off, but then in the place of the two deps the government would send two hundred.

"These men have been the cause of tremendous sorrow in Centre." Because he was a member of the high council and traveled from congregation to congregation, making sure the Church was in order, he knew all the gossip. "They may appear to be fools, but as that dep said, they've put a third of the men from Centre in jail for plural marriage. They have a camp somewhere up there on the skirt of Brigham's Peak." J. D. pointed to the mountain that loomed to the west of Centre, near where I had first noticed the two men on their horses. "From that vantage they peer down into every nook and cranny in town. They took the last bishop to trial in Salt Lake City, but so far the new bishop has been clever enough to avoid capture."

"How much of a lawbreaker is he?" I gave him what miners in Nevada would have called a shit-eating grin. *Sleakit.*

He glared at me. "Polygamy's God's law. Listen to scripture: If any man espouse a virgin, and desire to espouse another, and the first give her consent, then is he justified." His voice was as sonorous as if he was God himself speaking. While I drove the last quarter mile to Apollo store, he told me for the ninetieth time that in heaven single wives would be handmaids to plural wives. The Principle, by providing even superfluous women with righteous mates, would eventually eliminate whoredom and wasted lives from among the Saints. Blah, blah, blah.

"A crock of blarney."

He frowned imperiously, as if dealing with a naughty child, not the woman he pretended to think I was. "The purest truth of the gospel." He dragged the pelt over his face again.

I stuck out my tongue at him, but he didn't see.

For an instant I imagined myself able to flirt with the mahogany-haired deputy, or some other single man, maybe someone from Rockwood. Not all Mormons were polygamist, just those ambitious to be kings on earth and heaven. But if I invited a gentile man to court or even marry me, would we be one man and one woman, both sovereign?

Not bloody likely.

My alternative was entering a home where the family was already formed and I had the status of a younger aunt. In that arrangement I would probably have a more comfortable life and also more freedom. Emmeline B. Wells, my greatest hero on this wide earth, at least after J. D., preached that polygamy created a network of women in a household. It was a way of giving a woman more time for developing her mind. My favorite quote of hers was from the *Woman's Exponent*, "I believe in women, especially thinking women."

Much as I didn't like some parts of Mormonism, most of it pleased me: the idea that men *and* women are eternal intelligences, created long before we were organized as humans; that body and spirit are not enemies; that God is a being of the same species as us; that God is no tyrant and has given us agency, that death is not the end to our growth to become like him, and that Christ can redeem our sins. I had chosen these beliefs and had felt transported when I went under the baptismal water as my promise to God. If he was as good-hearted as J. D., even if his servants sometimes said and did strange things, I could give him my allegiance.

The breeze that had started up had a bitter edge to it. For sure, snow would fall that night.

I could surprise Ezekiel. "Hell, yes, I'll join your household and welcome you to my bed once a week." If he wasn't too shocked to accept, I would set myself up for life and please J. D.

All the pros and cons of marriage, whether monogamous or polygamous, seemed unimportant next to my revulsion against being naked with any man, but especially with one more than twice my age equipped with wrinkles, hair, and dangly parts. Just the thought made me want to lope away into the desert, a free wolf, not one bound to mate or pups.

The sun had nearly set by the time we drew up to Apollo Underground Store. From aboveground the main store building looked like some giant had plucked a roof off a warehouse and dropped it on the flat earth. No trees announced to visitors that there was habitation here, only a few winter-dead stalks of roses that Sister Apollo had planted along the south wall, trying to proclaim with flowers that a woman lived here. Even with the three smoking chimneys and the doorway set into the highest part of the roof, a stranger would never guess there was a whole department store buried there.

Brother Apollo, formerly a Welsh miner, had taken five years with a shovel and wheelbarrow to clear out two huge holes, one of them large enough for a wagon to drive down a ramp into the store and out the opposite side. He dug instead of building because, before the railroad, wood was scarce. The rooms, insulated by yards of dirt, were warm in the winter and cool in the summer. The shelves contained a thousand marvelous objects from the larger world—the poems of Tennyson, Sheffield silver from England, dozens of dime novels, saddles from Mexico and spices from the Orient. West of the store stood an enormous, peaked barn with its wings of corrals.

The air was so cold that the smoke from the chimneys flowed down the wood-shingled roof, across the ground, and into the winter-dead fields, where a few red cattle stood, trying to eat through the plank fences protecting the rounded haystacks set here and there. The main part of Centre spread across the opposite bank of the delta, a quarter mile away.

J. D. climbed down from the surrey. "I'll leave the team to you. Put the stolen gelding back in the pen with Brother Apollo's other horses." I made a face at his back as he opened the rough door and disappeared into the ground. For sure the horses needed care, but I didn't like being talked to as if I were some lackey.

I had to admit that he had given me freedom longer than any girl could expect. But I didn't want to be forced into the strait-waistcoat of marriage.

If Ezekiel or any other man becomes too insistent with this virgin, I thought, *I can always turn-coat and rejoin the gentiles.*

Or become a lone wanderer on God's earth. It made my spirit lift to know I had options.

CHAPTER 2

I drove the mares through the double doors of the barn. Climbing down from the surrey was difficult, with my legs stiff and cold. Meadow grass hay dropped into a manger.

"That you, Randall?" I peered up the ladder into the loft.

The whole barn smelled of hay, sweet and musty, reminding me of summer. A white horse with black speckles across its forehead walked forward and pushed its nose into the high manger. A skittish brown mare followed, rolling her eyes at me.

I led the gelding into the pen. The mare nickered and touched the black's nose, as if she was saying, "Welcome back, old friend. Where were you all this time?" I unhooked the harness from the singletree, led the younger mare out, and tied her near the tack room. Un-threading the long reins from the harness, I unbuckled the breast collar, slipped the harness backward off the horse, and hung it from a dangling hook. On the ladder from the hayloft, feet and then legs appeared—a sour face, long and thin, and reddish-brown hair, the color of fur on a fawn.

"Hey, Randall."

He wore a hemp coat, dyed blue, which looked new enough to have been a Christmas present.

"Them deps stopped you."

"They thought I was J. D.'s new wife."

Randall grinned.

"Damn dolts," I said. "I'd like to slap them silly."

"Slap them with a axe handle—the fools and liars." In the short time it took him to clamber down the ladder, he had worked himself into a fury. "Promise breakers. They were going to fix something for me." He shook his head and closed his eyes. "Sometimes they pretend to go to the train. Then they double back. Catch some poor brother unawares." When he opened his eyes, he had a silly false grin on his face.

He had gotten worse since I had seen him last. A year before, he had been digging a well when the pulley rope broke and a full bucket of dirt smacked him on the crown of his skull.

"What promises have those deps made you?"

"I had a girl, but she was stole from me."

I couldn't see his face well in the growing dark, but his emotion was clear as he whipped the sack across the mare with quick, jerky motions.

"Randall, this horse sure didn't steal your girl."

His head snapped toward me. "I'm sorry," he said to the horse, stroking her back gently with the sack. We led both mares into the pen with the other horses. He climbed the ladder and dropped more hay down.

The long, shrill whistle of the train sounded.

I grabbed J. D.'s valise and my own from the back of the surrey. When I struggled across the lane between the barn and the underground store, I saw Randall sitting in the big loft window, arms around his knees. He grinned at me and then just as suddenly frowned, scuttling out of sight. ◄

I opened the broad oak door to the stairway, and stepped inside, smelling the rich mélange from spices and grain that filled Apollo store. My eyes hadn't adjusted to the dim light, so I took both bags in one hand, cursing J. D. for making me carry his. I moved slowly down the steep, narrow stairway, my fingertips trailing across the clay-daubed log wall. I came out into the northernmost of the two large rooms—a cavernous space lit by windows set high in the southern roof. The walls here were also mud-daubed, split cedar logs; rough boards for the floor. Because of the gathering dusk someone had lit a coal oil lantern. A buckboard stood in the middle of the room; the big double doors at each end allowed a wagon to be driven inside, loaded, and driven forward out again. Brother Apollo handed up a small wooden barrel marked "NAILS" to a young blond man who I recognized as Randall's brother David. As a twelve-year-old girl, I had an impossible crush on this clear-faced angel of a man. The other man on the wagon was Randall's father, Richard Mabey Cooper, who freighted between Centre and Rockwood and was part supplier, part competitor to my ambitious prospective husband, Ezekiel.

"To quote a Latin aphorism," said Brother Apollo, leaving his work to walk toward us. He was short and portly, about the same age as J. D. Sparse strands of hair were all that kept him from being as bald as an egg, "*Comes jucundus in via pro vehiculo est.*" His face was slightly pointed and his small, portly body had always reminded me of a gopher's.

"A pleasant companion on the road is as good as a vehicle," translated David.

David's father slapped his son on the shoulder. "Brother Apollo can't say anything you can't parse out, can he?"

David, I knew, had been away at some university back east for the past year. He was slender as was appropriate for a thinker, and his blond hair looked extremely fine. Now something strained in his face made him seem older than his twenty-two years. He grappled with the heavy bag of feed with difficulty. The angel scholar. I wondered why he was home so soon from the East.

"J. D. wouldn't know that he had a pleasant companion. He just slept or preached."

"Preached what?"

19

"The perishing principle of celestial marriage."

David frowned. "A sinful principle. One which should be abandoned."

Brother Apollo walked forward and shook my hand vigorously. "Rachel, you've grown even taller since I saw you last."

"I'm glad to see you—" I hesitated. "Brother Apollo." I had always called him "Brother Apollo," but now I was nearly eighteen, fully grown. I found I couldn't make my mouth say the word "William" to him. Maybe if I practiced.

William, William, William.

"Or in the Greek," said Brother Apollo loudly, "*Charis humin kai eirene plethunthere.*"

David frowned and busied himself with the loading. "You have the advantage of me when you speak Greek."

Brother Apollo winked at me. "Grace to you, and peace be multiplied."

Brother Cooper guffawed and slapped his son again. My natural born father, even when he was bewildered drunk, had more dignity than this man. Poor David, poor Randall.

J. D. grinned. "William, you have a saying for every occasion."

Brother Apollo's family name had originally been Teifion, but upon joining with the Mormons and coming to America, he had changed his name. Few Americans could wrap their tongues around the Welsh. He chose Apollo because of his love for music and the Greek language.

He had first settled in Salt Lake City, where he tried to sell violins he had crafted from fruitwood. When his business failed, he had headed southwest to Hamblin and then Centre. He built a small dugout above the marshy edge of the delta. For the first few years he cut grass for hay and sold a few goods from one shelf in his house. The store became two shelves, then three, a second dugout, and finally the enormous underground store. When he became wealthy enough to bring in wood, he used it to wall the underground living quarters. He liked living underground because it was warm in the winter and cool in the summer.

The three older men stood at the front of the wagon, their heads together.

I couldn't hear what J. D. said, but Brother Apollo didn't speak so softly: "He's been hiding in his house ever since he was made bishop."

"I didn't know you'd be back so soon from school," I said.

David dropped to the ground next to me.

"Gone on the train," said J. D.

"... a ruse," said Brother Apollo.

David said something I didn't catch.

Brother Cooper nodded. "They double back."

"... careful ...," said J. D.

I turned to David. "What did you say? Why didn't you like it?"

But now his attention was gone. He stepped closer to the hallway, his head cocked, as if he was a dog, hearing some sound no human could.

My friend Naomi entered, and David turned toward her. He gazed as if she were the only person in the room, the only woman in the universe. They touched hands, and he glanced back at Brother Apollo, her father. If they had been alone, they would have embraced.

"Hey, Naomi." I walked forward to hug my friend. Ever since the age of twelve, Naomi had been taller than her mother and father, but as lanky as Randall. Now she was not so thin, but still kept her sharp, pretty features. "Look at you. I'm perishing jealous. I stay thin as an antelope, no matter how much I eat." I thought that Naomi had also bloomed emotionally.

"Shhh." She smiled broadly and her face became pink. "You're embarrassing me." She turned back to the wagon. "David, we need to talk about my lesson for tomorrow's class."

"I've been thinking that you should teach them the Bill of Rights. It's in the book I loaned you. I think it's good for the children to know that church and state are rightly separate."

Brother Apollo frowned at him.

"A true man of wisdom." Brother Cooper was as proud of his son as if David had finished at the university. He dumped another bag of grain on the pile and slapped his hands to knock the grain dust off them. "Salt and coffee. And that will do it."

The two lovers looked without wavering into each other's bright eyes.

"Naomi," called a woman from the back. "Don't take all evening."

Naomi grinned and took David's hand. "Now what did Mama send me for?"

"Milk." Her mother appeared in the doorway and wiped her hands so she could hug me. Mother and daughter wore nearly identical dresses, plain gingham, one blue, one red, both with a white collar and apron.

"My heavens! You're so tall!" Sister Apollo felt the material of my skirt. "Sophisticated as a Salt Lake lady in that skirt and waist." The waist was pure white and plain, with no lace or ruffles, and the skirt was a deep plum color.

"Made them myself."

"Well done. Let me put your things in your room. It'll be your usual one."

Naomi leaned to whisper something into David's ear.

Her father said, "The milk's where it's been since you were a wee babe, in the spring room." Naomi let go her lover's hand and disappeared back down the hallway, followed by her mother.

"*Incessu patuit dea.*" David raised one eyebrow at Brother Apollo.

Brother Apollo's smile faded. "Virgil. By her gait the goddess was revealed."

"Right." David laid his hand on Brother Apollo's shoulder. "You have done all this without formal schooling. Wonderful."

"Yes," crowed Brother Cooper. "But one year at Harvard places my David well beyond you."

David's face flushed and he ducked his head.

I stared at David's father, the pompous ass. I wondered how he had convinced any woman to marry him, but I knew he had wed four of them—a true mystery.

"I just wish you saw some other man's daughter as a goddess." Brother Apollo spoke so softly to David that I wouldn't have heard if I hadn't been standing close. "You don't even have a shack to offer her and you not yet an elder in the priesthood."

David turned away.

"You can have a bright future, if you work for it," said Brother Apollo. He stepped closer to the younger man. "You'll be there this evening?"

"Do I have a choice?" David's face had turned troubled in an instant.

"What's this?" said Brother Cooper.

David shook his head and pressed his lips together.

"A dress, you say, is the best gift?" J. D. said to me. In addition to returning the stolen horse, we had planned to pick up supplies— pepper, molasses, cloth for shirts for J. D.'s younger boys, and a gift for the anniversary of his marriage to his third wife, Rebecca.

"She'll like it more than something useful like a skillet or dishes." I scanned the tall shelves, which were filled with tins of tea, meat, and dried fruit. On the floor stood barrels of flour and sugar, and great sacks of grain and coffee beans. I saw coffee grinders, small and large butter churns, a pickling crock, blueware dishes and cups. I shook my head. None of these seemed right as a gift for a wife young enough to be J. D.'s daughter.

"Something practical is better. Something that won't cause dissension."

"No. Something beautiful." I felt sad for Rebecca, who wore ringlets still, though she was over thirty, as if she was making up for a missed girlhood. The staid and stoic J. D. had married her when she was just my age.

I led J. D. away down a short hallway, lined with pictures of women cut from eastern magazines. Shelves also lined the walls in this room, twenty feet high, filled with everything from fine china to the novels of Dickens, from leather shoes to bottles of patent medicine. A long glass bar extended for fifteen yards where Sister Apollo had arranged stacks of patterns, fine cloth, packets of needles and pins, as well as guns and knives.

"I'm out of my water in this."

"So am I. But even I have more sense about it than you." I lifted a fawn-colored dress with creamy lace on the sleeves, yoke, and collar—too frilly for my taste, but not for Rebecca's. I felt the cloth, held it up against myself in front of the mirror. It was large for me but Rebecca was full of body. I moved the dress to one side and frowned at my own image—thin arms, flat bosom, narrow hips—and admitted that I might never get a better offer than Ezekiel's austere proposal, which was more a business proposition or a sermon than any expression of affection. I had frightened the boys in Rockwood town so badly that they would not face me again. *Do you really want never to marry?*

I backed away from the mirror.

"This dress is right for Rebecca." My head felt like a twirling mass of cobwebs.

Together we returned to the other room, where David walked up the ramp that led out of the store, and opened the double doors, waiting while Brother Cooper drove his creaking wagon up and out.

Before the doors were quite shut again, Brother Apollo shoveled into a bucket a pile of horse manure one of the horses had left. Then he brought out his chessboard and laid it across a barrel. J. D. eagerly helped set out the pieces. "I hope that with all your worries you can concentrate on the game."

"I hope that at your advanced age your mind won't wander too far. I hate to take advantage of the elderly."

I walked down the hall and into the underground kitchen, which smelled of cedar smoke and fresh bread. Naomi stood at the table, spreading butter on steaming loaves. The room was lit by a coal oil lamp, which hung from the ceiling. A beautiful Monarch range, a sure sign of prosperity, stood against the south wall, with rows of enameled pots hanging from the walls to either side. The Apollos were as well-to-do as J. D., and I realized that physical comfort was one reason I didn't want to move out of his household. I'd had enough of poverty in Nevada in my birth father's shack.

"Smells like Christmas."

"Bread for our milk. That's all we're having."

I tried to keep my face from showing disappointment, but Sister Apollo laughed. "Your hunger will be satisfied."

"So tell me about David Cooper, fresh returned from filling his head with gentile learning."

"True learning." Naomi held her head high. "He's just made himself into a more complex man." She looked at her mother's back. "That's why I love him."

So why did he come back from college early?

"So complex he won't be made an elder in the priesthood," said Sister Apollo as she pressed butter into a mold.

"Neither you nor Father cared until Father was put in the bishopric."

"Brother Apollo is counselor to the new bishop?" It was rare for someone who would not join polygamy to be put in a position of leadership. He often said, "'Tis a fine principle, but not for me and my Gwynneth."

"Yes, he is," said Sister Apollo. Was it my imagination that a note of sadness had come into her voice?

"I'm marrying David in the spring, elder or not, Father's permission or not."

Sister Apollo turned her head toward her daughter. They glared at each other but neither spoke. I walked to the stove and lifted the lid to a coffee pot, breathing in its rich aroma.

"I was brewing it because I thought the deps were coming for dinner. None for you. We have fresh milk for you." She pointed to a large white pitcher, sitting next to the water pump.

"I *was* a Gentile. In my heart I still am." I was upset that Sister Apollo might pour out the coffee. Some people in Rockwood had also decided that drinking coffee was against the Word of Wisdom—including Mary, J. D.'s first wife. It was a bewildering sacrifice. Why did God put coffee beans on the earth if he didn't intend us to take advantage of them?

"Oh, Rachel." Sister Apollo laughed. "What if it's coffee that has stunted your development?"

She cocked her eyebrow and I knew she was teasing me.

"I'm highly developed, in certain areas." I turned back to Naomi. "J. D. told me around Christmas-time that the new bishop was courting you."

"He discovered that Susan Sharp was more—ah—agreeable to him."

Her mother seemed to choke. "It's just that you made yourself more dis-agreeable."

"I told him I'd eat potatoes and live in a shack rather than marry a man with four wives already."

"'Twas a prophecy." Sister Apollo turned out the butter, which now looked like a cluster of white grapes, onto a saucer. "If he'd just kept at his schooling until he graduated, he might get a job anywhere in the territory. As it is he may lose even this teaching job for not proclaiming the doctrines of the gospel to the students. Tonight he—"

"He's a stronger believer in the gospel than anybody in this town. You should hear him talk when we're alone."

Her eyes glistened with tears.

Sister Apollo sighed and placed both hands on the table. "Oh, Naomi, I dreamed last night that your father and I were back in Wales. We were both young and we were starting over. I was anxious about being poor again, but it was the happiest feeling I've had for months." She sighed. "I'll help you talk to your father about marrying David."

"And will you talk to my father also? J. D. wants me to marry Ezekiel Wright."

"The storekeeper in Rockwood? He's well-off."

Naomi made a face. "He's old enough to be your father."

I lifted the bail from a bottle of preserves, which was the dusky color of plums. Then I scooped the sweet into a glass dish. My saliva came sharply, almost as if I had tasted a spoonful.

"Worse than being old, he's sometimes a fool. He traded lucerne hay for wool without weighing either. He offered such a low bid for hauling flour and beef to the soldiers at Simpson Springs that, although he got the contract, he lost money on the job. He drove clear to Cache Valley to buy prize dairy cattle, and they give piddling milk. Some Swiss farmer is gloating over getting top dollar for culls."

"Well," said Naomi, "he's clearly not the man for you."

"But he's learning. J. D. is helping him be wiser. He will be a prosperous man one day."

"You should spend time in Hamblin, cast your eyes about," said Sister Apollo. Hamblin was the largest town in the region; it

27

lay 30 miles to the north. She leaned toward me across the corner of the table and suddenly I had an image of my mother doing the same about a year before. I missed her like hunger. I had gone into her bedroom one morning and found her apparently asleep. Nothing seemed wrong until I got in bed with her and discovered she was cold.

Suddenly voices sounded in the hall. I recognized the shrill whine of the small dep, Sammy: "—could eat a horse and wagon, and spit out the shoes and rims."

"I would rather go to hell," shouted Brother Apollo. "You will not eat at my table."

"They've done it again. Just when we think we have a reprieve from them." Sister Apollo stood. "Sounds like we need to go make peace before my silly husband does something he will regret."

CHAPTER 3

Sister Apollo lifted the board with the loaf of bread in one hand, the butter in the other. Naomi held the pitcher of milk. I grabbed the jam and followed mother and daughter into the hallway.

The small dep shouted, "I'm not goin' to eat another camp meal of froze hard biscuits and watery coffee."

He and Brother Apollo were nose to nose. The tall dep stood behind, looking sheepish. He caught sight of me and his face turned a pleasant, rosy red. Despite myself, I smiled at him—a man who had turned against his own people and who was supposed to be my enemy.

The small deputy's eyes shifted away from Brother Apollo's face to the food. *Sammy.* I remembered his name was Sammy.

"You had *ample* time to catch the train," accused the short Welshman.

"My horse picked up a stone. Once we got that out, the train was long gone."

"A convenient lie."

The large dep stepped forward. "What is it to you whether we missed the train or not?" His voice was deep, and resonant, as if he spoke from the bottom of a well. "I thought you were running a public store and inn—goods, lodging and meals for anyone. Just last week we paid for a meal here and you were happy to get our money. Why are you so nervous now unless you've become a lawbreaker yourself?"

"A legitimate question," said Naomi softly in my ear. "But not a safe one."

Brother Apollo backed down, his mouth opening and shutting like a fish's.

Sister Apollo's face was a study in blankness as she handed her husband the butter. *I'd hate to play poker with her.*

Sammy looked pleased. "That's got him, James. That's got him." *James Marchant.*

Sister Apollo turned on him. "Keep your peace." She shook her finger at Sammy as if he was a troublesome child. "Or *I'll* not abide you at my table." She thrust the board and bread into his hands.

Brother Apollo leaned to whisper to his wife. Standing next to Sister Apollo in the hallway, I caught the word "meeting."

"Oh. I'd forgotten." Her face turned from firm to sad in an instant.

We all entered the dining room, a rectangle about ten by fifteen feet. A plank table nearly filled the space. Naomi removed thick bowls from a cupboard and set them down, and Sammy placed the bread beside the bowls. Brother Apollo plunked down the butter. His face was still red, his mouth twisted with anger. J. D. held his hand palm down in a calming motion. The deputies stood with their hats in their hands, nervous.

"Everyone sit!" Sister Apollo commanded.

J. D. took a chair at the far end of the table. Sammy and the other dep sat closest to the door.

Brother Apollo glared at the deps and sat at the head, to the deputies' left. I took a seat on the far side of the table with Naomi and Sister Apollo.

The tall deputy, James, was directly opposite. As I slid my chair forward, my foot bumped against his.

"Sorry." He licked his thin lips, a flash of tongue.

"That's all right. You do have such long legs."

Sister Apollo glared at me, and Naomi smiled behind her hand. *You have such long legs.* The kind of thing simpering maidens said in dime novels. I decided to just keep my mouth shut.

"I will pray." Brother Apollo bowed his head. "Father in Heaven, bless this food and bless us this evening to abstain from contentious speech. Bless this man who has turned from the truth to recognize the error of his ways. We know that thou art God and art perfect, we being merely humble copies, ill formed by our own willfulness. In the name of Jesus Christ, Amen."

James's face was twisted into a profound frown.

We all broke the bread into our bowls, afterward spooning jam and pouring milk on top. I noticed that Brother Apollo's bowl was empty. He slid his chair back. "I won't be long."

James stood. "Please. If our presence here is so disturbing that you can't eat, we will leave now—" He waited until he had Brother Apollo's eye, "—and pursue our business in town."

His words were polite but something in his voice made it sound like a threat.

Brother Apollo considered and finally retook his seat. He broke a small slice of bread into his bowl and poured a little milk across. It was hardly enough to feed a cat. He frowned into his bowl. I thought his brow had been dark earlier, but now he looked as if his head might burst.

For a few moments no one spoke; all were too busy eating. The bread had a thick crust but was as soft as cake inside.

Sammy ate with his mouth close to the bowl but his eyes up, like a dog frightened some other creature would grab his food from him.

James ate slowly, clearly enjoying the taste. He had a squarish jaw and a wide clear brow. It was a comely face, easy to look at.

Brother Apollo pushed his bowl away, already finished. "Snow's coming, J. D." The room had been quiet for long enough that the sound of his voice startled me.

"Could make our travel home tomorrow difficult."

The large dep, James, laid down his spoon. "How many wives do you have by now?" He glanced at me. I smiled back and watched the red deepen and rise across his cheeks. For sure and certain he thought I was J. D.'s wife. It would make fun if I asked him whether he was married, but suddenly shy, I bent my head to my bowl.

J. D. finished chewing. "I wish to God that was none of your business, James Marchant."

"Son-of-a-bitching polygamist," said Sammy.

Sister Apollo set her spoon down with a clang. "Nobody swears at my table! So either stop your mouth or leave!"

Her look of pure anger seemed to startle Sammy, who looked at the food and then back at her face. I could see his thoughts clicking like the tumblers in a lock. Finally, he ducked his head, his mouth still twisted in a smirk. "Sorry, Ma'am, I just forgot myself."

I watched James, wondering whether he would try to arrest J. D. now or after he had eaten.

"Hearsay has no power in any *legitimate* court of law," said J. D.

"That's right. We'll have to gather evidence before we put you in jail."

"Please, gentlemen," said Brother Apollo. "Let's be civil."

"We aim to be civil tonight, but it's dammed difficult when you're breaking bread with a lustful criminal." Apparently, Sammy reminded himself that he was still hungry, because he grabbed another slice, slathered it with jam, and dropped it into the bottom of his bowl. He slopped milk across it and sucked the bread off his large spoon before I could take a breath.

I reached for another slice myself. "Please pass the milk."

"Delighted," he said, his mouth stuffed. Milk dribbled out of the corner of his mouth and across his chin.

Brother Apollo glared at the door, still refusing to eat. J. D. watched his friend's face.

"'Tis going to be a heavy snow." Brother Apollo smiled—a fake, pasted-on grin—and I could tell his body was tense as barbed wire.

I wondered why the deputies didn't want him to leave.

Sammy nodded. "We'll—" He choked on the bread still in his mouth and dropped a mouthful back into the bowl. He bent forward coughing. James pounded him on the back, and Brother Apollo stood and drifted toward the door.

James stood also. "I just have one question for you and J. D. Before we go."

Brother Apollo sat back down.

James faced J. D. "How is it that God, who is the source of all good, can ask you to break the law of this land?"

J. D. started talking before James finished. "How is it that you who were raised as a member of God's own people have abandoned them?"

"I saw through the piety of my neighbors and caught the vision of their true lasciviousness."

"Since coming to this country from Preston, England." J. D.'s voice wavered with emotion. "I have tried to obey all laws. But those which condemn us for practicing our own religion are unconstitutional."

"Unconstitutional? That's an old argument, settled by the Supreme Court."

Naomi turned and watched him with close attention, nodding her head. "The Clawson case."

Her father looked at Naomi as if a toad had just crawled out of her mouth. "The US Supreme Court is as partial as the territorial legislature." He watched James, who glared back—two street dogs with their hackles raised, a bulldog and a rangy retriever.

I wondered who would win if they grappled on top of the table.

"It's not partial to decide that freedom of religion extends to beliefs only." James tapped his spoon on the edge of his bowl. "Not to the abomination of taking more than one wife."

J. D. cleared his throat.

"That's right," said Sammy. "Beliefs only."

I smiled into my hand. He seemed such a perishing fool that he was silly instead of fearsome. James was a different matter. A man to be reckoned with.

Sammy spoke, explained as if we were school children, "That means you can believe whatever the hell you want, but when you marry too many women, that's an act, and we can throw your ass in jail."

James looked toward the ceiling and shook his head in a slight motion. "No more swearing!"

"Sorry." Sammy's face had a belligerent look.

"Freedom of religion *can't* protect those who break the law." I realized that James might hate polygamy more than Sammy because he had an intimate view of the problems it caused.

"*Circulus in probando*." Brother Apollo leaned even farther forward toward James. He clasped his hands and sent his bowl skittering across the table. I grabbed it before it hit the floor. "Does it seem just to you that we should obey a law set up precisely to prevent our religious practice? No law existed against plural marriage thirty years ago."

James leaned forward. "There's always been a law against bigamy in Utah territory."

"Bigamy is when a man lives with more than one woman deceitfully." Brother Apollo banged one hand slowly on the table, so hard that the dishes rattled. "The Principle of Plurality is entered into with full knowledge of the people involved."

J. D. made his calming motion above the table again. Naomi glared at her father as if Korihor, the anti-Christ, had been suddenly conjured up at the dinner table. I grinned, unable to remember when I had heard such invigorating dinner talk. Everyone stared at me.

"Not funny." Sammy's mouth was so full he could hardly speak.

Sister Apollo's smile was wry. "That's the difference between celestial marriage and bigamy—the first wife participates, having full knowledge?"

Brother Apollo wiped both hands down across his face. "It is sealed by the priesthood. *That's* the main difference."

James's face changed, as if he understood what Sister Apollo left unsaid. Did she know what danger she was thrusting her husband into? Or was she so upset that she didn't care?

"Whatever power it's sealed by, it is unholy." James glanced from J. D. to me, and his eyes narrowed in anger. "And I should know. As you no doubt remember, my first father was a damned polygamist."

"I am not J. D.'s wife." I smiled demurely. "I am his daughter."

"My daughter." J. D. laid his hand on the table, flat and still.

"Makes women into fornicators, adulterers, and whores." Sammy tapped his milk-wet spoon on the table at each word as if he were a judge.

J. D.'s hand slowly made a fist.

My stomach felt heavy and a shiver passed through me. It wasn't funny anymore. If something didn't change, soon there would be a brawl. If it happened, someone could die, probably not J. D.

"You have no idea what it does." Brother Apollo stood and pounded the table again. "No Gentile can comprehend the holiness of the Principle. Plural marriage can't be adultery because the woman is given to the man, belonging to him and to no one else."

James stood also, glaring down at the short, thick Welshman.

Sister Apollo gripped the bread board as if she would dump the remainder on the floor. James glanced at her, took a breath, and they all sat back down

"If it wasn't for all these eastern-made laws—" My voice sounded like the squeak of a mouse, and everyone looked at me surprised, "I could look forward to voting, when I come of age. Just like a man. The country took that away from me."

James sighed. "You would have voted your husband's mind."

I hoped J. D. could just keep his mouth shut. Only a slight misstep and the deps would arrest him.

"It's an insult to think that in a secret ballot I wouldn't cast an independent vote."

J. D. nodded. "You don't know her." He had a look on his face that I couldn't read.

James shook his head. "That's right. I don't know what you would do, just what most people would do." He slumped a little in his chair. Then he stood from the crowded table and opened the door. "I've got to check on the horses."

"I'm finished eating," said Brother Apollo, "and I have an errand in town."

James turned in the doorway. "What errand?"

"Another matter that is not your business."

"It is if you're visiting your new bishop—a known polygamist. Where is he, by the by?"

"On a long trip." Brother Apollo moved closer to the door, but James blocked his way.

"I have to ask you to stay at this table."

"You would constrain my movement, you traitorous whelp?" Brother Apollo's voice was dangerous. "I thought we inhabited a territory of the United States and that we have rights and freedoms."

"Just not tonight." Sammy took his large revolver out of his coat and laid it on the table.

"No," said Sister Apollo. "Please not this."

36

The bread turned to a lump in my mouth, and I couldn't swallow.

James shut the door behind him and we all sat, staring at Sammy, who smiled in his adolescent, cocky manner. Now I had to revise my opinion of his foolishness. With a gun in his hand, he was a dozen times more dangerous than a man who had good sense.

J. D. cleared his throat. "Can I have more bread and milk, please?" For a minute the only sound in the room was J. D.'s slow chewing.

Before long, James reentered the room and started in again before he even sat down. It was as if the gun sitting on the table had changed nothing for him. "I am not a traitor to my own conscience. For decades you Mormons have made it impossible for the law to be prosecuted as it's written. For decades you've disregarded the spirit of the law and the will of Congress, the presidents, and the people of the United States. You've had plenty of warnings." James held up one finger. "First, the Morrill Act of 1862."

Brother Apollo leaned forward across his bowl. "Which made our celestial marriages into felonies."

"Celestial marriages?" James shook his head. "Which made territorial law enforceable." He held up a second finger. "The Poland Act of 1874."

Brother Apollo pointed his finger in James's face. "Which made it impossible to form juries out of the peers of the accused."

"Which made it impossible for Mormons to *pack* their own juries." James's voice had gradually raised until he nearly shouted the word "pack." He held up three fingers. "The Edmunds Act of 1882."

Brother Apollo stood. "Which provided for men like you to invade the privacy of our bedrooms." He seemed ready to leap on James and knock him onto the table, scattering bowls and smashing cups.

"Which made cohabitation with illegal wives possible to prove." James stood halfway out of his chair, leaning forward to shake his four fingers in Brother Apollo's face. "And last of all the amendment by Representative Tucker just last week which will put some teeth in the Edmunds Act."

"Which will enable greedy and unethical men to escheat our property."

"Which will at last force the people of this territory to become law-abiding citizens."

They were nose to nose again, one with his head tipped down, one with his face tipped up.

The sound of a click stopped them and they turned as one toward Sammy, who aimed his pistol straight at Brother Apollo.

Sister Apollo spoke in a steady voice. "William, remember that you are a meditative man."

He slowly turned his head to look at his wife. His eyes widened and he suddenly lost his bluster.

"All the laws you've numbered are unjust laws," said J. D.

Sister Apollo focused on Sammy. "Please. He's no threat to you."

Sammy made an effort to be stern, but only succeeding in looking furtive. He un-cocked his pistol and moved forward to the edge of his chair. "You wouldn't know justice if it reared up and bit you on the ass." He was no scholar, unlike James who seemed to have studied out why he was putting people in jail.

James looked at his partner. "Go check on the horses, Sammy."

"Why me?"

Instead of arguing with the smaller dep, whom he clearly didn't respect, James simply stared him down.

Sammy dropped his eyes and stood. Swearing under his breath like a petulant boy, he walked out into the store.

James turned toward me. "You haven't married into polygamy have you?"

"Now how could I tell you a thing like that? If I said yes, you might pull a gun on me."

He frowned and I looked straight into his eyes.

"I just can't comprehend a god who would condone this practice."

We all sat silently for a moment. Brother Apollo looked at his watch. The room felt like water ready to boil.

Finally Sammy came in and sat down. "Snow's started up, but the light's still there."

James glared at him.

Brother Apollo stood. "I must get up to town on my errands. I ... ah ... have a delivery to make."

Sammy lifted his gun again. Sister Apollo slid her chair closer to her husband and laid her hand on his arm. "Your delivery can wait."

"Damned lascivious theocracy," said James. "I'm grateful to be shut of it. In Illinois the Mormons had a city. Every man voted the way Joe Smith told them to. Same with Brigham Young and now John Taylor. All theocrats. You are like subjects to a king. You all vote how your prophet says. It's un-American. I'm grateful every day that I see that now."

Brother Apollo's face grew red with fury. "*Uffern cols.*"

"William!" Sister Apollo put her hand to her mouth.

"Was that Latin or Greek?" I said.

"Welsh," she said. "And I will not have it said again."

I thought how wonderful it would be to have the ability to swear in four languages instead of just two.

"We will never give up. Our prophet John Taylor will never give in." Brother Apollo's face was so red that I worried about his health.

"You can't fight the power of the United States government. President Arthur is determined. The legislature in Washington is determined. Justice Zane, Attorney Dickson, and Marshal Ireland are determined. It isn't just here in Centre that polygamists are being put in jail. It's the same all over the territory. Last month three hundred Mormon leaders were put in prison. And it's just going to get worse. Mark my words: this year, 1887, is the tipping point. Very soon you'll have to decide. Either you'll give up polygamy or

Mormonism will be destroyed. Is this unnatural practice worth sacrificing everything else you've worked for?"

"That's not for you to decide for us," said J. D. "When you abandoned your faith, you lost that right."

"I know that many have fled to Mexico and Canada. Why don't you Mormons resettle there? It would solve our problems and yours, both."

"It's against the law in both those countries. They don't mind a few of us drifting across their borders, but if we all moved in, you can be certain that they'd mind. Anyhow, this land is our home now. We don't want to leave it."

"Don't you think it's ironic that you suggest we flee elsewhere for our freedom? Isn't the United States and her territories the land of the free? But no matter." Brother Apollo stood. "I am happy to have you, as Virgil put it, *sub tegmine fagi*. Beneath the canopy of the spreading beech." He raised his hands to indicate the underground store. "But now we must abandon your company."

"Spreading beech, hell," said Sammy.

"What I'm saying is I guess you'll be abandoning our table soon. It's quarter past eight."

J. D. slid his chair back. "Yes, it's about time for all of us to get to our beds."

"Our beds are two miles away and colder than a mother-in-law's kiss." Sammy turned and left the room, followed by James. Heavy footsteps thudded down the hall.

Brother Apollo's face seemed fearful. "I'm sure they're after the bishopric. We were supposed to meet at the school house a half hour ago to try to persuade David not to preach against the Principle. I've got to warn the bishop."

Brother Apollo strode out of the dining room, followed close by J. D.

Sister Apollo took off her apron and threw it on a chair. "Oh, damn him. He has lost all his good sense. They'll shoot him if he follows too close."

She followed her husband; Naomi grabbed the lantern and we hurried after.

CHAPTER 4

I ran out of the hallway into the southern room of the store. Brother Apollo lifted a shotgun from the rack and grabbed shells from a box. In the shadows, his face looked like the face of a beast.

"William, why do you need a weapon? Please leave it home."

Sister Apollo's face showed her terror, but he didn't look at her. Instead he lowered his head and rushed up the stairs. She scurried close on his heels, J. D. right behind her.

I ducked into my room, swung my coat off the chair and onto my shoulders. Brother Apollo had looked like a stranger, not gentle but wild in eye and mouth.

I stepped out into the hallway and Naomi caught my arm.

"How can we stop him?"

"I don't know."

As we crossed the store, the lantern cast strange, moving shadows, as if someone hid behind the barrels of food and hardware. When I looked closer, I couldn't see a thing. My blood pounded in my ears and I had the illusion of floating. Despite my fear, I would not be left behind.

Outside, snow whirled across the lane. It swirled like a cloud of white birds, banking and thinning. The wall of the barn was shrouded then clear as the wind shifted. The barn door already had a small drift against it. The wind whined and the snow ticked against the barn wall, where some of it stuck.

"My dearest William, you must not take your weapon. If you

shoot one of those deps, the penalty for killing is hanging. If you leave your weapon home, there can be no accident."

"Gynneth, they must not take our bishop."

"What if they do? He will be in prison for six months and return home."

He shook his head. "This is not just our problem. All over the Church our leaders are put in prison, our funds are taken from us. How will we survive this crippling persecution? No, I cannot just sit by and let him be taken."

He handed his lantern to Sister Apollo and trotted along the road that led across the fields toward Centre.

"As a people we'll survive this the same way we've survived all our persecutions," she said to his back. "But how will I survive your imprisonment or death?"

J. D. walked to the surrey in the barn and removed his rifle.

I tried to stand in his way. "J. D., do you have a plan or are you just going to run off in confusion?"

"My plan is to watch out for William."

"You are both fools," shouted Sister Apollo.

J. D. looked at her and gripped his rifle tighter. "We will be very careful."

"If you were going to be careful you wouldn't go at all."

Within ten seconds, J. D. had also disappeared behind a wall of falling snow.

Sister Apollo wrapped both arms around herself. "Foolish man. Foolish *men*." I knew she didn't mean just those two rushing off to do something heroic. She followed for a few steps, but Naomi pulled her back.

"You have no coat."

"And what can I do anyway? He has stopped listening to me." Sister Apollo sobbed once and returned to the store, followed by Naomi.

I ran after J. D., my gloveless hands already wet, chilled; the flakes melted icy on my face and throat. As I crossed the bridge over the frozen creek, the beat of warning began to sound, someone banging on iron, but faint, muffled by the snow. I couldn't see the town yet, but I remembered it was laid out in firm order, with two houses to a square, and the whole town a larger square, with the church in the middle.

By the time I caught up, J. D. and Brother Apollo had reached the first houses. The road split, the left-hand lane passing between town and the creek and the right-hand heading north into town. We took this road. Lights burned in the houses we passed and white faces appeared in the windows. The warning continued to sound directly ahead of us, painfully loud.

J. D. and Brother Apollo stepped over a log fence and crouched against the side of an adobe house, just under a lit window. Unable to step across the fence because of my skirt, which had become weighted with melting snow, I found the gate and joined them. The curtain parted and a woman looked out. When she saw J. D. and his rifle, she dropped the curtain. Soon the light went out inside. Despite the dark, I saw my own head, ghostlike, in the glass.

"That's where they are meeting." Brother Apollo pointed forward into the swirling snow. "In the church house." Light shone from the side windows, but the building itself, painted white, was difficult to distinguish in the swirling snow. The deps' horses were hitched in front. The spire pointed upward into the snow-choked darkness. The gong, gong, gong of the warning signal was so loud I put my hands over my ears.

We left the yard, moving forward along the street until we could hear shouting from inside the church. Brother Apollo trotted forward clutching his shotgun. "I'm certain that the bishop is inside. He has escaped arrest until now because he has an excellent hiding place built into his new house." He pointed toward the north end of town. "But they have a witness who has identified his five wives for the deps. He has to hide all the time and can hardly manage his business, to say nothing of the business of the Church."

J. D. ran forward and grabbed his arm. "Do you plan on just walking up to the door with a gun in your hand?"

"They'll shoot you sure." My voice shook, not just from the cold.

Brother Apollo pulled free and continued forward. "Let's go to the back of the building and come up behind them. We've got to help him."

"Help him? How?" said J. D.

Brother Apollo shook his head. His anger and fear had stolen his ability to think beyond the next step. He dashed up the road, in plain sight of the deps if they chose to look out a window or open the door. Without saying anything to me about what he was doing, J. D. cut down a side street. I followed him; he was coming at the back of the church with a block of houses shielding us.

I knew my toes and fingers and cheeks weren't frostbitten because they still hurt like hell. The wind had slowed, so the heavy snow fell silently. Except for the lights in some windows we could have been sneaking through a dead town. The warning gong continued—beat, beat, beat, pause, beat, beat, beat, pause—tolling like a funeral bell. The snow diffused the sound, so telling the direction of the source was difficult, or impossible.

We rounded the corner and crept along the lane that ran along the back of the church.

"Where is he?" J. D. hissed.

Just then Brother Apollo crept along the side of the church, the lit windows above his head. He peered through a window set in the back door. Soon we joined him. If the deps were possessed by some unpredictable impulse and decided to come out the back, they would see all three of us.

Why am I hiding from them? I wondered. I had committed no crime.

Snow fell on my coat and hair as I gripped Brother Apollo's sleeve, trying to pull him back from the door. I felt the wet flakes burn my cheeks and the backs of my hands and I let him go. The beat-beat-beat on the iron had given me a headache. A man parted the curtain of the house opposite us, and let it fall again. Soon the light was put out.

"Rachel," whispered J. D. "You shouldn't be out here. Let me feel your hands." I held them out. "Like ice. Go back to the store." He looked around. "Or better yet, go inside one of these houses and get warm."

It made me angry that he thought warmth was more important to me than the danger to him and to the town. "Not until you two do. I don't want to have to go to Salt Lake to the prison to visit you. Or to the cemetery."

"Humpff."

"He's not inside there. He must have gotten the warning in time." Brother Apollo's voice seemed too loud in the quiet of the snow.

Suddenly steps sounded inside, and the two men and I ducked around the northwest corner of the church. I heard the back door open, and I recognized Sammy's voice. "Where the blazes is he?"

Soon the door shut again. Turning my head, I saw a figure come down the lane from the north, a tall man creeping low.

"J. D.," I warned.

He turned. "Bishop Peterson."

The bishop cut diagonally across the street to join us. He touched Brother Apollo on the arm. "Brother Stewart—he is alone with those damn deps. If they put him in jail—" He spoke with a heavy Swedish accent.

J. D. held the bishop's arm. "Wait and watch. You can't help him, and he is safer without you there."

"You think they will not capture him, ya?"

"They're after you. Not him."

"How did you get away?" said Brother Apollo. "I tried to warn you earlier, but those deps wouldn't let me leave my own house."

"When I hear them come, I run out the back door into the brush."

"Why didn't you just keep running?" said J. D. "Why come back here?"

"Because Brother Stewart, he is still inside. I cannot leave him helpless."

I pressed my back against the wall of the church. The whole world was gray-black, and I shivered, my teeth chattering from cold and fear. I could no longer feel my toes or my fingers. At the same time, there was something deep in my gut that made me feel fully alive. I understood why J. D. kept chasing down criminals, despite his age and despite his eternal claim that he disliked violence.

I heard the front door of the church open. "You cain't hide him from us," shouted Sammy to the empty streets. "We will find him." The light moved as if he lifted a lantern. "He must have escaped us this way. Here are his tracks and other tracks."

We held silent behind the corner until the door shut again.

"They're leaving," said Brother Apollo.

"They'll head toward your house, Bishop, and they'll see us for sure if we stay here."

The bishop pointed across the lane where there was a fenced cottage. We all scurried in that direction.

"Here. We can see both doors from here." Brother Apollo hid behind the low fence.

"No!" said J. D. "They'll still see us."

I heard Sammy's voice and knew that any second their horses would appear as they rode toward the bishop's house.

Suddenly, a rectangle of yellow light shone on us, a door opening behind us. A white-haired woman stepped out.

"Shut the door!" J. D.'s whisper seemed loud as a shout.

The woman didn't shut the door. "Get in here, you fools." She spoke with a British accent, but not a northern one like J. D.'s. She took two quick, birdlike steps toward us. In her wide dress she looked like a thin partridge. "This fence is too short to hide you." She stood above Brother Apollo and the bishop crouched on the ground.

The men turned to look up at her, but then instead of going inside, as anyone with a lick of sense would have done, their heads swiveled back toward the church. "Go inside, Sister Griggs," the bishop said.

The bread and milk we'd had for dinner lay like lead in my gut.

"Come, come." I joined the small woman just inside the door. The room was oven-temperature. "J. D. Come inside. Brother Apollo."

"I must go to my house. Must protect my ducklings."

"And they will catch you there," said J. D.

I kept my eyes riveted on the shadow across the front of the church. We were in plain sight.

The bishop turned and smiled. "You do not know what a good hiding place I have." Then he trotted through the storm toward his house.

"Must I stand here all night with the cold rushing into my room?"

I pictured the bishop, J. D., and Brother Apollo lying on the ground, eyes staring up without blinking. "Come in here, J. D. You owe it to your wives to keep yourself safe. You owe it to me."

"They didn't arrest me at dinner, why will they now?"

"Because they're on a rampage," said the woman.

"And so far, they're empty handed," I said. "You don't know what they'll do just because they're stymied."

My heart nearly stopped in my chest as someone wearing a

bulky coat appeared out of the snow to our left and dashed along the lane. Whoever he was, he carried a rifle. He trotted northward toward the bishop's house.

The woman stepped into her yard and took Brother Apollo by the hand, leading him inside.

"But Sister Griggs," he said, "the bishop. I'm worried about the bishop." He seemed to have shrunk; he had the face of a child.

"He will be fine," said Sister Griggs. "You just sit here, Brother William."

Finally, J. D. ducked inside her door, grumbling. I followed him. When the door shut behind me, I realized I had been holding my breath. I wouldn't have thought that terror, frostbite, and excitement could blend into one state of being. I held my hands out to her stove, my cheeks stinging in the heat. Then my fingers and toes thawed enough that I felt pain in the bones, tremendous pain.

Both men went to the small front window and peered out, their shoulders touching. The wallpaper to either side of them was printed with roses, as were the other walls, a garden in her parlor.

"You're soaked." Sister Griggs was short, barely up to my shoulder, and very thin. Her eyes were as bright as a ferret's.

"I can't just do nothing," said Brother Apollo.

"But you will do just that. You won't endanger yourself." She smiled and her eyes danced. Clearly she felt as excited as I did, both of us experiencing a perverse and exquisite pleasure at the danger. She put out the lantern and she and I stood behind the men, who knelt at the window. The two deps finally appeared in the street, walking their horses northward. If we had stayed outside, they would have seen us for sure.

"I warned the bishop," said Brother Apollo, "that he'll be the next one sent to prison." He and J. D. waited until the riders disappeared into the storm. Then they stepped out the door.

I started to follow. "Missy, you'll catch pneumonia." Sister

Griggs opened a closet and handed me a heavy blanket, which I wrapped around myself. "We haven't had so much excitement since the time a bear sneaked into town and got stuck in Brother Wheeler's chicken coop."

I ran out into the snow, glancing across at the church, which was now dark. I hurried after the others. Soon I caught up to them, and we crouched to the side of a shed. The warning, the rhythmic pounding on an anvil or iron wheel, came from inside, still going, still unbearably loud. Horseshoes and old tools hung on the outside wall—the blacksmith's shop. Suddenly the sound stopped and the silence seemed to hum.

A girl came out the door of the smithy, examining us. "Hello, Brother Apollo."

"Hello, Maddy. Good job."

"I know." She turned and ran toward a house next to the smithy. Soon a light appeared inside.

"You have a child give the warning?"

"She has an adult mind in the body of a child. And besides that, she's the safest one. The deps won't dare bother her."

I stepped inside the shop, where the forge still gave off some heat. I wondered what went through the girl's head as she gave the warning against officers of the law. She was a lawbreaker as well. How did she make sense of it when grownups had trouble with the tangle?

From where I stood inside the door of the smithy, I could occasionally see far enough through the whirling snow to glimpse the bishop's house, up a slight hill opposite us. I also saw shadows of men behind a cedar tree to the left of the house—at least four of them, three men and a woman. A tall man, maybe Alma, and two thin men.

I shook my head, feeling disoriented. This kind of threat wasn't supposed to happen in Deseret, our Zion in the desert. I felt as if I was living a scene from a dime novel, or dreaming, with my sight speckled and blurred by falling snow. But if shooting started it would be all too real. That much excitement would give me no pleasure.

I could barely see the deps standing on the high porch, their horses below. A woman blocked their entrance. She held a lantern high to look at them. Sammy pushed past her and James followed. She rushed back inside and the light moved room to room, first downstairs and then on the second storey. Hearing the wail of a small child, I shook my head. Whether Mormon men were guilty of breaking a law or not, whether the women had chosen or were forced, the children were innocent. The deps should not make them afraid.

Brother Apollo trotted across the lane toward the others who hid behind the tree. Sister Apollo's voice rang in my head—"Foolish men!" I held onto J. D.'s arm and pulled him inside the smithy doorway.

Finally, the lantern proceeded downstairs. Not long after that, the deps emerged. They turned and spoke to someone behind them, and the door closed.

"Dammit to hell."

I rejoiced at Sammy's frustration. Somehow the bishop had gotten into his hidey-hole in time.

J. D. shifted his rifle to the crook of his arm, as the deps mounted their horses and rode within twenty yards of the tree where the group hid, now a woman and four men since Brother Apollo had joined them.

I pray, God, that no one shoots them.

The deps disappeared into the storm.

"They're camped on the ridge above town. I don't know exactly where." J. D. laid his hand on my shoulder. "Go back to the store before you make yourself sick. Nothing will happen now."

"If nothing will happen, come with me. I will not go home to Rockwood with you a corpse in the jump seat of the surrey."

"It will be your own death, this stubbornness." He glared at me, but said nothing more.

You damn old hypocrite. You are not the one to talk to me about stubbornness.

J. D. took my arm. "You need to get dry."

"As you do. I want to be here in the middle of this uproar just as much as you do." But my frozen hands and feet belied my determination.

He looked at me and then peered upward toward where the deps had disappeared. I could no longer see the shadows hiding next to the house.

"You misunderstand me if you think I draw pleasure from this."

Had he fooled himself? Convinced himself that the slight smile on his lips was not because of the joy of the chase? I shrugged my shoulders. "Whatever you say, J. D. Those deps probably headed to their beds." My teeth chattered so hard that I could hardly form the words.

"Let's do the same." But instead of turning toward the store, he stood in the middle of the lane and looked toward the cedar tree. "William! I think—where is he?" But Brother Apollo and the others were gone from behind the tree. "William! Damnable fool!"

"Maybe he's turned back to the store."

"I'm done with watching out for such a fool."

I nodded and followed as he strode through town and along the road through the fields. He seemed to really believe that the only reason he'd grabbed his rifle and rushed out into the storm was to prevent his friend from foolishness. Another wave of shivering passed through my body.

I'm going to die. I'm going to freeze to death unwed. I stumbled after J. D., hardly able to see him because of the falling snow.

Finally, Brother Apollo's barn loomed. Hurrying down into the dark store, I stumbled on the steps, nearly falling. In my room I stripped to my skin and climbed straight into bed. Still shivering, I felt as if I would never become warm. Sister Apollo walked in my door and thrust an object toward me, a hot brick wrapped in a rag. "Where is he?"

Naomi appeared in the door behind her.

"I don't know. The deps seemed to have gone back up the canyon, but we couldn't see through the storm. I don't know where he went."

Mother and daughter left me in the dark. I pushed the brick down against my feet. Soon they stung again, stung like the devil.

I heard voices speaking softly. Finally, doors closed and everything was quiet.

With my head under the heavy quilts, I thought about James Marchant, who had seemed sensible, but who thought he knew what was best for the Mormons, his former people. J. D. also presumed to know my mind concerning marriage better than I did, but at least he didn't try to use heavy persuasion or force on me. I was angry at the deputies for barging into the bishop's house and frightening his wives and children. People in Washington DC made laws without any consideration of what violence it did to Mormon families.

Finally, the stinging in my fingers and feet went away, and I put on dry underwear and my heavy nightgown. Back in bed, I pictured myself walking down the street after church arm-in-arm with Sophia, following Ezekiel and Abigail. My thoughts became irrational as I drifted toward sleep. Ezekiel's wives disappeared and I walked down the street with James. We were surrounded not by the Utah desert but by country as green as Ireland. But why would I go anywhere with a dep, a man who hated my people? Sammy rode an enormous black horse down a steep mountain toward me. And I sat on the peak of Brother Apollo's barn, a changeling man next to me.

First he was J. D., then Randall, Brother Apollo, the tall dep, and Matthew, who had been twelve when I last saw him in Nevada but who had grown to manhood in my dream. He balanced on the edge of the roof, as if he would soon leap into empty air. "*Sleakie,*" he called to me over his shoulder. "Come fly with me."

Later I woke, the store creaking around me. I heard J. D. pacing in his room next to mine.

When I woke again, all was still dark, and I wondered whether the first wakening had been a dream. Someone was banging on my door, a muffled thumping—not my door but another in the hallway. "J. D.," someone said, urgency in her voice. It was Sister Apollo.

I swung out of bed and opened my door. Sister Apollo held a lantern in the hallway. She spoke through the doorway to J. D. "Come quickly."

I grabbed at Sister Apollo's arm as she passed. "What? What has happened?"

"Just go back to bed. Just go back to sleep." She and J. D. hurried out into the store.

I reached back into my room for a blanket, wrapping it around myself.

When I reached the first huge room in the store, I saw Brother Apollo standing on the other side of the glass case, a candle set in front of him. He glared at the candle, shaking his head and moaning. "We are ruined."

"Brother Apollo?"

He didn't seem to hear. Light flickered across familiar objects, transforming them. The dress J. D. and I had chosen hung against one wall, looking like a spirit of a person, just rising toward heaven. A saddle hanging from its strap cast a strange moving shadow.

"What in the name of God?" J. D.'s voice came from the next room. I hurried through the short hallway, following the light.

Sister Apollo stood over something on the floor. When she

saw me, she turned, her arms spread out. "You don't want to come in here."

I pushed past and stood next to J. D.

Two men lay on the floor—the two deputies. Their faces were ashy and stark. I put a hand to my mouth; I had only seen a dead person once before—my mother—but she had died peacefully in her bed. This was different.

Sammy had lost the side of his neck and his lower left jaw. All that was left was a mass of reddish-black meat. James had a black, dollar-sized hole in his shirt and stomach, a few inches above his belt buckle, and another hole directly over his heart. The whole front of his coat was black with blood. Someone had tried to close his eyes, but a crescent of dull white showed. His lips were pale violet.

My throat felt choked with tears and I sobbed once. "I'm sorry, so sorry." I didn't know whether I was talking to James' body or to J. D., who thought crying was a weakness.

CHAPTER 5

J. D. bent over the bloody stomach of the large dep—James. Odd that a mere weight of flesh could have once worn a name. A few hours earlier, James had leaned across the table, arguing with Brother Apollo. He had been angry as spit, but still his words had been honest. I remembered him half in shadow because the lantern had been at the far end of the table.

I had flirted with him—an abomination to think about flirting with that blank face.

Sister Apollo handed me a handkerchief, and I wiped my eyes and blew my nose.

"'Tis a respectable wound." J. D.'s face was focused, alive. "Must have broken his spine. But it may not have killed him." He pointed to the wound in the chest. "This shot would have finished him off."

His eyes flicked here, there, across the body. The slightest smile was on his lips. Was he made of ice and stone? Did he take pleasure in this bloody work?

"How did they get here?"

"Have you asked your husband?" J. D. nodded toward the other room of the store. "He found them, right?"

"And called for me," she said.

"Can you bring me a second lantern?"

She handed me the lantern and left. I heard her steps as she crossed into the kitchen. Though tears were wet on my face, I didn't want J. D. to think that I was queasy. I bent to look at the jagged black flesh, determined to learn his methods. The smell of blood and meat was even stronger that close, and I stepped back.

I had seen death in the peaceful face of my mother, and it had been like sleep. The phrase, "Gone to her rest," made good sense as I stood above her body and helped Mary, her sister wife, wash and dress her. The ceremony had felt like attending a birth into a new life.

These jagged wounds and horrible faces didn't feel like sleep. So far from their homes as Sammy and James were, who would wash and dress them with love and care? These savaged bodies made me feel that earth is a hellish place. My gut tightened at the thought of someone turning a gun on a fellow human being, and I nearly vomited. The killer must have been evil, that or desperate, beyond human feeling.

J. D. shook his head and his face went sad. I wondered if he felt what I did. Maybe he thought about the skirmishes between Mormon and Gentile in Illinois, before the Prophet Joseph and his brother Hyrum were martyred and before the Saints were forced out of their homes in Nauvoo. I knew from Christine, J. D.'s second wife, that he had killed several men during those hard times, but he would never talk about it, became thin-lipped and silent when I asked.

"Takes a terrible anger to inflict such damage on a fellow man." He opened his pocket knife and probed in the chest wound, removing a bloody pellet. He held it up to the lantern between his bloody thumb and finger. "Probably a ten-gauge, and double barrel. Three shots total between the two deps. If there was only one killer, he had time to reload for his last shot." J. D. took pellets from the chest wound. "Same gauge."

Ghost shadows wheeled across the ceiling and walls of the store as Sister Apollo came out of the hallway with another lantern. My heart beat in my throat as J. D. squatted on his haunches.

"The murderer's shotgun barrel nearly touched this poor man's chest on the second shot." J. D. pointed the blade of his knife at the blackened and ragged cloth around the hole—powder burn. Then he grasped James's shoulders, and lifted the body slightly. The head flopped back and the arms hung limp. "Can you hold the light closer, please?"

Sister Apollo swung the lantern low and revealed the churned mass of red and black on James's back. J. D. looked not at the wound but at the canvas, which was printed light with blood. I set the lantern down, stepped closer, and squatted to help J. D. support the weight of the body. I was for showing him my steadiness, letting him know I was competent to help him track this killer. He was known all over Utah territory for his ability to track man or horse, read signs. I had once heard someone say, "J. D. can track a fish up a stream or a bird through the air."

As he peered down at the body his eyes crossed my face without seeing me. He let go, and the shoulder slipped through my hands as if the man were a bag of grain. He turned to the other corpse—Sammy.

"This was a difficult shot. He was far enough away that he had to aim." J. D. held his hands to complete the partial circle across Sammy's throat. "But certainly a shot of no more than ten or twelve feet." Using his knife point, he took a pellet from the wound. "If there were two or more killers, they all had ten gauges."

He rolled the body over, and the arms flipped as if the poor boy-man was a dropped puppet. A similar pattern of blood had imprinted the canvas, like roses on wallpaper. The thought that blood was like a flower made me weepy again.

Damn, I thought, *damn my woman's heart. I don't want to cry again in front of J. D.*

I breathed slowly and let my anger at the killer fill me. A

shadow leveled his gun at James, pulling the trigger. A shocked look crossed James's face as the pellets smashed into his stomach.

J. D. was intent, every muscle controlled, and I knew he would not give up until he found this killer—not only because of the adventure of tracking and chasing some prey, but because it was all he could do. A shiver went from my crown to my toes. More than anything I wanted to help him.

He turned and spoke to me as if I was his partner in this work. "I'd say the large dep was shot in the stomach first, when he and the killer were face to face. Then the smaller dep was shot in the neck as he dove for cover. Then the larger dep was shot again in the heart, to finish him off."

"Assuming that there was one killer."

"It's bad enough with one killer. If this was done by a group of men—" He shook his head.

"And to think that they broke bread with us only last evening," said Sister Apollo. Still holding the lantern, she slumped into a chair. "Now they are claiming their everlasting reward."

I wondered if she meant in heaven or hell. "It's a wonder we heard no shot." Then I felt the fool because a shot in the underground store would thunder loud enough to wake even me, and I slept still and deep as a log of wood. Sure and certain, the deps had been murdered elsewhere and carried into the store. I bent to touch the edge of the canvas and found it damp, probably from melted snow.

Footsteps sounded and Brother Apollo stood in the hallway.

"Into my store." He shook his head, as if he wasn't sure where he was. "Who brought them into my store?"

I tried to read his face, which was haggard, maybe as much from lack of sleep as from this horror.

Still squatting, J. D. glanced at him. "Who do you think?"

"I—" His hands were in constant motion, like pale, writhing

snakes; he rubbed one hand down across his cheek, put his hand to his throat. "I think I am in considerable trouble."

It broke me up to see him in such a sorry state, so unlike his jolly, sturdy self.

Still squatting on his haunches, J. D. looked up at his friend, frowning. He turned back to the bodies and grasped the small dep, Sammy, by the chin. He moved the shattered jaw up and down as if Sammy was talking. J. D. then rubbed his fingers against the dead cheek. He did the same with the other dep, James. He lifted each man's arm and let it drop.

"They've been dead more than five hours. Less than eight."

"Less than six and a half." Sister Apollo lowered the lantern. "It's half past five now. I was still awake with my door open at eleven. I can't imagine that I wouldn't have heard them being dragged in."

She glanced toward her husband, who reached for her. She didn't move to take his hand. J. D. took the lantern from Sister Apollo and strode toward the wagon ramp. I glanced at the Apollos, who stood like statues in the dark, not speaking to each other, or even sharing a look. I followed J. D., relieved to turn my eyes away from the guilt and anger between those two and the carnage on the floor.

J. D. stopped partway up the ramp and peered down at the packed clay. Because it was still dark as the inside of a cow outside, the lantern reflected in the window high overhead.

"I can see naught. We'll have to examine the entrances when there is better light."

"Naught to see. Not even you can track on these hard surfaces."

"But naught speaks as loud as any other sign. If they were dragged in here shortly after they were killed, I would expect to find a smear of blood on the ramp or the steps." He handed the lantern to me, bending low.

I thought of the canvas, barely printed with blood. I already knew they had been killed elsewhere because I had heard no shot. "You're saying they bled out long before they were ever brought in?"

"I believe that the canvas was cut from William's stock here in the store."

"So they weren't dragged in a'tall. Even now, if we dragged them across the floor or up the ramp, sure there'd be a mark of blood."

"They were carried in. Either in the killer's arms—," he pointed to an oval-shaped smudge on the ramp that might be a hoof print, "—or on horseback."

"Killed some distance away."

J. D. nodded. He returned to the south room and stopped before the racks of new guns. He tipped the end of each shotgun, smelling each barrel.

Sister Apollo frowned. "If they weren't killed here, what are you hoping to discover?"

J. D. turned toward Brother Apollo. "Where is the shotgun you carried last night?"

"I—I must have left it in Centre." Brother Apollo looked at the floor.

Sister Apollo walked to the back room, her feet thumping angrily across the board floor.

J. D. squatted before the bodies again. "Is this your canvas?"

Brother Apollo bent down. "Looks new. Must be cut from my roll." He walked back to check. "J. D., I can't tell. I think it's from this roll."

"The edge is even," said J. D., "cut with a steady hand."

Sister Apollo returned. "I've waked Naomi, so she can go for the bishop." I didn't want to miss anything, so I didn't offer to go with my friend.

"Will she be safe?" asked Brother Apollo.

His wife frowned, "I assumed that it was a Mormon who killed these men. I assumed that she'd be perfectly safe."

"Safe assumption," said J. D. "After killing, he carried the bodies into the store, cut a piece of canvas with a straight edge, and laid these two out as if for burial. He was not panicked."

"He even tried to shut their eyes," said Sister Apollo.

I asked, "What if the one who killed and the one who laid them out were not the same person?"

J. D. glanced toward me and smiled; I felt a rush of pride. "Let's have a bit of coffee," he said. "'Twill be a long and wearying day."

J. D. and I, Brother and Sister Apollo sat at the table in the dining room. The two men and I each held a blueware mug of coffee, warming our hands. I glanced at the far end of the table where the two deps had sat and broke bread with us Mormons. Sammy had been jocular and profane, James Marchant argumentative and nervous. Whatever their sins, even if James was a traitor to his people and Sammy a cruel fool, they had not deserved to die, their spirits wrenched violently from their bodies. I had been unhappy about the deps using force to impose the nation's will on polygamists, but this was the ultimate act of aggressive control—robbing someone of all of life's choices and experiences. Their dead eyes had stared at me out of horribly vacant faces. I drank deeply and felt the scalding coffee warm and wake me.

"Would it be a month now since I gave up drinking this delightful, sinful brew?" Brother Apollo's white hair was awry, and the corner of his mouth twitched. He set his coffee down. His hands shook when they were free, so he clamped his hands again around his mug.

"You've quit three times since last spring." Sister Apollo sat at the opposite end of the table, away from the lamp. She wore a somber dress and shawl and was surrounded by darkness. Her face and her clasped hands glowed white. "Naomi could've walked to Salt Lake City and back by now. I can't think what could be keeping her and the bishop."

"The territorial officials will think murder is a natural outgrowth of our other lawbreaking." J. D. stared at the table. "Centre will have forty deps to contend with."

Brother Apollo stood and leaned across the table toward J. D. "Why are they here?" He put one hand to his mouth. "Laid out on my floor. *Bene deus!*" He sat and then stood again, speaking rapidly in Welsh. Then he reverted to English. "I cannot understand why the killer brought them here. I cannot understand it."

"The bishop is a practical man," said Sister Apollo. "He'll know exactly what to do."

"We should telegraph the marshal," said J. D.

I wanted to shake them, talking past each other as they were. The room felt close and tight as my own grave. Shock stopped my mouth; I could do nothing but stare at the steady flame of the lamp. The top of the unvarnished plank table was deep brown, soft with grease. I drew a pale line in the wood with my fingernail. James's face had been earnest as he argued with Brother Apollo and J. D.

"Last night I wanted to kill them." Brother Apollo stood partway, spilling some coffee, and then sat back down again. He pushed his cup away from him. "When they disturbed the peace of my house, I wished them dead, and this morning they're stretched out in my store." I remembered his face, scarlet with anger when he had screamed in their faces.

"Just like an answer to prayer." Sister Apollo's face was drawn; she seemed to have aged a decade overnight.

"I did pray for their deaths." His face twisted into a grotesque mask. "They were already spiritually dead. *Genus est mortis male vivere.* To live an evil—"

"William, we all know what it means." Her voice rose as she

talked. "You have been saying the same quotes over and over these twenty years."

Brother Apollo stared at her, his mouth half open.

"I would like to smell the gun you carried last night."

"J. D., are you thinking that I killed them?" His hands tore at his sparse hair.

"Of course, you didn't kill them," said Sister Apollo. "You are not guilty of that sin."

"If I had killed them, I would have dumped them in the first ravine I could find. Not in my store. Someone wants me blamed for this killing. Who? Who would wish me harm?"

In his babbling, Brother Apollo had named a clue to who the murderer was, someone with a grievance against him.

"J. D. wants to be a witness to the fact that it wasn't your gun."

I glanced over, but J. D.'s face didn't change.

Brother Apollo rubbed his hands against his forehead. "I can't think." Then he stood halfway, hands down against the table. "I know where I left it."

Sister Apollo's head turned slowly toward her husband. "Where?" Her voice was cold.

"Any fool who has aught against me can inform the territorial officials. Any number of men owe me money. Many bear a grievance against me." He touched J. D. on the arm. "Can we not get these poor murdered men out of sight? My customers will begin arriving before another hour. What if I am accused? How can I defend myself when the bodies are right here in my store?"

"Calm down, William. You're not thinking clearly."

Voices sounded out in the store. Brother Apollo lifted the lantern from the table and we all followed close behind him out into the large north room where the bodies lay. The bishop, Naomi, and Randall stood above the bodies. Randall's face showed anger and confusion. He mumbled to himself, walking to look at the bodies then striding across the store to stand in the dark.

I wondered what he knew.

The bishop seemed unable to decide what he should do or say. Finally he knelt and bent to stare at the wounds. His shadow was cast forward, so he tugged at Brother Apollo's coat, pulling him around so the lantern light would shine full upon the heads of the two deps.

"They were killed with a shotgun, probably ten-gauge," said J. D., "shot elsewhere and hauled in here. As soon as we have morning light, I'll look for tracks."

"Someone has carried these deps into your store?" Bishop Peterson shook his head. "Some good brother was out of his head with anger, ya?" He lurched back to his feet.

"Horrible," said Naomi. "Whatever polygamist killed them will be judged of God." Her face twisted with anguish.

The bishop laid his hand on her shoulder. "Now, Sister, you know we all will be judged of Got."

The cords in Randall's neck stood out. "I heard shots. Three shots. Two quick ones and then one a few seconds later." Everyone turned to look at him, and he moved to the opposite end of the room, behind a barrel with a narrow hand plow sitting on top, and stood there scowling. He stamped his foot and whacked one hand against his leg.

"I also haf heard these shots." The bishop kept his face carefully blank. "Maybe an hour after these deputies leave the cemetery."

"Where did the sound come from?"

"It was an echo all around. It felt like I have cotton stuffed in my ears."

"The shots were from up in the canyon," said Randall from the corner.

"I am sure Randall speaks the truth," said the bishop.

"Did you hear the shots?" asked Sister Apollo, facing her husband.

"Brethren, please help me get these bodies out of sight. Soon I will have customers. What will it help for them to see this?" Brother Apollo indicated the corpses. "The words of Ovid seem appropriate: *Dun loquor, hora fugit.* Time is flying while I speak."

"Oh, William, what is the quote for me?"

"*Domus et placens uxor.* Horace." He touched her hand.

She smiled then, a sad smile that faded quickly. Brother Apollo turned to the bishop. "We should move them into the milk room. There is no heat there and we can have time to decide what to do."

I felt that I was all ears and eyes. Those two had secrets and their words flowed over what they wanted hidden like a riffle of water over a rock.

"These bodies cannot be hidden like dust under a rug," said J. D. "We should first telegraph the federal marshal in Salt Lake. He has jurisdiction over these deputies."

"Would he come," asked the bishop, "or would he send Deputy Marshal Danby from Eureka? He directed these deps to harm us in the first place."

"With Danby or any other federal deputy we are guilty until proven innocent," said Brother Apollo.

"One of us *is* guilty." J. D.'s mouth was firm, determined. "One of our brethren killed these men. How will it look if we delay to tell the officials? Our enemies will believe that the Church approves of the murder of those who persecute us. The man who killed them was certainly one of our good brethren pushed too far, but still our best course is to prove that we don't sanction this murderous act."

"When we had our own court, we settled such matters among ourselves, ya?"

"But these are federal deputies. How will it look if we try to settle this ourselves?"

I watched Randall, who clenched and unclenched his fists against the top of the barrel. I knew if I could get him alone and talk to him in a level voice, as if he were a horse, I could calm him enough to maybe discover what he knew. Sister Apollo took the lantern from her husband. The light flickered across their faces.

The bishop leveled his gaze on my stepfather. "Brother J. D. We shall put them out of sight, maybe in the cold room like this good Brother Apollo has said. They will not—what is the word?—decompose for several days." He nodded his head as he spoke. I felt a strong disjunction between his dire words and the singsong lilt to his voice. "Then we must speak to President Hunsaker in Hamblin. He is our leader and will know yust what to do."

J. D. stood square in front of the bishop. "I have no problem with getting them out of sight. There is no need to shock everyone coming into the store. But we must show that the Saints are law-abiding citizens."

"Except with respect to the Principle," said Naomi.

The bishop said, "Every newspaper will announce: 'Mormons Kill Deputies.'"

"If J. D. catches the murderer quickly," said Sister Apollo, "and we hand him over to Danby quickly, won't that—"

"You would abandon your brother to our enemy?" The bishop turned to face J. D. "I have say in this. Best you go to your home in Rockwood and leave the matter of this killing to us."

"You forget that I am justice of the peace."

"And a justice of the peace would be the proper one to look into this murder? You have dealings with marriages and property disputes and trouble over water rights. I think that you have no more authority over this than I do, ya? You walk a narrow path with one foot in the Church and one foot in the Gentile world. Got and Wells Fargo, which is most important to you? I have the belief that one day you will stumble."

He and J. D. glared at each other, as territorial as herd bulls.

"I beg you." Brother Apollo's voice was high and frantic. "Can we please get them out of here?" His hair stood up all over his head, scraggly as a dust mop.

"I have a good idea. I will not telegraph this morning. This matter is too difficult for that, ya? I will go on the train myself tonight. I will tell the president what has happened and together we speak to sheriff of Hamblin. He is a member of the Church. Together we can decide what is best to do. In the morning, I come home."

"Then I will telegraph."

"You will not telegraph! The key is locked in box and only Brother Franklin can open it. I will instruct him to not send message for you."

J. D. stared at the bishop. "I will wait then. It is a mistake. But if you go to the sheriff, he will telegraph the deputy marshal. This matter will keep until tomorrow. And I will try to uncover the killer."

The bishop glared at him. "I cannot stop you. But listen to me, Brother J. D. Someone who has been angered beyond his thinking may feel guilt. If we leave him alone, ya?, he may confess to me in private. Then we decide what to do. If you stir things up, he will be too frightened to come forward."

"But for now, we should get the bodies out of sight." Brother Apollo leaned down to take one corner of the canvas. He tugged at it, rolling James's body slightly toward the center of the canvas. When no one moved to help, he let the corner drop.

"Things are already stirred up. If you and Randall heard those shots, so did everyone else in town."

"Yes. But what did they hear? Shots fired by one of us or by those deputies, shooting at a Mormon and missing him? They will be guessing what happened, ya?"

"At least one of them won't be guessing. But—" J. D. held a

hand up to silence the bishop. "The fewer people who know what happened, the easier my job will be."

"So we agree what to do. We have agreement, ya?"

Brother Apollo begged, "Brethren. Please." He took up again the edge of the canvas. "We can drag them in and unsettle them as little as possible."

"Let us make this good Brother William happy." The bishop motioned for Randall to take the far corner. "Please give us a helping hand."

"In here." Brother Apollo indicated the door to the cold room. "It's the safest place." Sister Apollo held the lantern high. "Here with the milk and cheese, the bodies will stay cool." Each man lifted a corner, and they dragged the canvas down the hall. They had trouble getting the bodies through the narrow doorway and had to lift the corners until the two deps rolled together as if embracing. Inside the room the four men spread the canvas, and J. D. and the bishop rearranged the bodies. Then they all exited, and Brother Apollo shut and locked the door. He wiped sweat off his forehead with his sleeve.

"Good. Now we make careful decisions."

Back in the store, J. D. held the lantern above the floor where the bodies had lain. He bent low. Randall turned in a puppet-like motion, jerky, and left through the north room. I heard his feet pounding the stairs.

"Heavens. We need breakfast." Sister Apollo walked toward the kitchen.

"We had coffee," said J. D.

"You need more than that."

I worried that J. D. would take off after the killer without remembering to eat. "Yes. We need substantially more than that."

The bishop touched J. D.'s arm. "This whole town will think

his brother is a murderer. Every one of us will have suspicion of his neighbor."

"I pray God will guide us through this straitened pass," said Brother Apollo.

"Last night was insult to my home, ya?" He didn't seem to know what to do with his hands, so he finally stuck them in his pockets. "But they have not caught me. My Rebecca, she say that they look like beat dogs when they leave."

I remembered the relief I had felt when, crouching below the bishop's house in the snow, I had seen the deputies leave. I had thought then that Centre would not have bloodshed that night, but I had been wrong.

J. D. nodded. "The deps must have doubled back to town and caught someone with a second wife. That poor brother took a gun and shot them. One close, the other running for the side of the house." He looked up at the bank of windows in the ceiling of the underground store. "It'll be light soon. We'll wait a bit and then have a look outside."

"These deps cause much harm when alive, ya?" The bishop shook his head. "That is nothing to the harm they will cause now they are dead."

CHAPTER 6

By the time we had tucked away our breakfast, the sun had risen. When J. D. opened one side of the huge double door at the top of the ramp, light flooded the shelves of the underground store and bitter air rushed past my face. I slipped out behind him into a changed world. The desert shone brilliant as far as the eastern mountains, an unbroken sheet of white.

Smoke dribbled up from the chimneys in Centre across the delta from the store. A dark figure walked from town into the fields, solitary on the white flat. I smelled the aroma of smoldering fruitwood coming from a smokehouse behind Brother Apollo's barn, smoke and the savor of a butchered pig. Telegraph poles marched next to the railroad across the desert, diminishing in two directions. The desert was white, wide, and beautiful.

Out of the dark underground building and away from the bloodied corpses, I felt my soul lift. J. D. searched the snow around the store, obviously looking for tracks. He bent over the snow, just as he had on our first deer hunt together when I was twelve. I had been filled with a wild joy that he had trusted me to carry a rifle.

"J. D., how the devil do you think you can find tracks under the snow?"

He grunted.

The slopes of the mountain where the deps had ridden down the evening before were blinding white. Centre town was as white as heaven. How could the murderer hide himself when the world was full of such light?

"For sure and certain, we will find this killer today if we work together." I laughed and swiped a handful of snow to suck on. It was difficult not to feel like a giddy-headed child. I moved up to his elbow, trying to see what he could see in the foot of snow, which seemed blank and unbroken.

"Give it up, J. D. There are no tracks here." I moved past him. "Let's look somewhere else."

Suddenly he grabbed my wrist. His face glowered as if he was an intemperate old boar bear ready to charge. "This is not some kind of frolic. Use your eyes and don't mar any tracks." He shuffled straight south away from the buildings. "Somewhere there's blood under the snow."

I looked at the white fluff in my hand. Certainly there was no blood there. Sammy's ruined throat sprang back into my mind.

Feeling almost as if J. D. had knocked me down, I followed, stepping directly into his footsteps in the snow, which was nearly as deep as my knees. I wore high-top boots, tightly laced, but I had to lift my skirt to keep it from dragging. Not for the first time I thought it foolish that I couldn't wear trousers like a man; skirts were an encumbrance I didn't need if I was going to prove myself to J. D.

The blank field of snow surrounded the store, smooth as a quilt. How would J. D. see blood under it? About fifty yards out, J. D. started his circuit of the barnyard and buildings, head down, examining the ground for tracks. If he found even an occasional depression, the hint of a track made halfway through the storm, he had the ability to follow it clear to the place of killing, perhaps even to the killer's home. I followed just behind him but ten yards farther out. I looked at every glare and shadow, hoping to see something before J. D. did. "God," I prayed, "give me this one gift, that I can show him I am fitted for this work."

Even after fifty steps, the snow was just snow to my novice eye. It had drifted up against sagebrush and the tall evergreen stalks of greasewood—but nothing showed that someone had passed into the store. We walked along the rim of the flat. The marshy meadow at the edge of the fields spread below us.

"Not a sign. Appears that the bodies were brought inside early in the storm."

Again, nothing was as much a sign as something. I marked that principle in my memory.

Shuffling to the Centre road, we found the small footprints of Naomi leaving the store and the larger ones of the bishop and Randall coming back with her. No snow had fallen into the sharp imprints. J. D. followed the tracks along the road toward town for a hundred yards. His bearing was that of a sniffing, eager hound. I imitated, trying to see what he saw, think what he thought.

He stopped short. "There's an extra set of tracks. Brother Apollo's boot print. He came in just as the storm was finishing." He pointed to a deep hole, the print at the bottom coated with a powder of snow.

I wracked my brain for information that would help. "It started snowing about eight last night. If we can discover what time it stopped snowing, we can tell when he came back."

"Five o'clock," said J. D. "I asked him. But he wouldn't say where he'd been."

He stared at the fresh tracks, removing his hat and rubbing his fingertips in a circle on the crown of his head. Then he walked back to where we could resume our circuit of the store. Soon we stepped into our former tracks at the double doorway of the store.

"Brother Apollo was as nervous as a bitch with pups." I watched J. D.'s face for approval.

He waved his hand back and forth at his waist. "Emotions are an unreliable track. When someone is killed, people experience a powerful shock. I've seen people laugh or cry, grow silent or babble like idiots."

That Brother Apollo hid something had seemed clear to me. "I can't read tracks like you, but I can read a face."

"He found two carcasses on his floor. 'Twould put *any* man into a fright. He's worried, rightly so, that he will be suspected."

"I still think his behavior is evidence of *something*. And he was gone all night."

"You have much to learn."

And I would learn it. At least he was talking to me without anger now. If I considered my words and movement, he would have no reason to rebuke me again. Sadly, I had never been strong at thinking before I spoke or stepped.

At that instant, Brother Apollo emerged from the other door to the underground store, followed so close by the bishop that I thought they would trip over each other's feet.

I thought, *Speak of the devil and he appears.*

Brother Apollo's face was grim, his hair still not combed. The two men were so deep in conversation that they didn't see J. D. and me standing in the snow fifty yards away. The bishop had his hand on Brother Apollo's shoulder and shook his finger in Brother Apollo's face. Suddenly he saw us; he turned immediately and strode along the road to Centre.

"Guilty or not, I agree he knows more than he's saying." J. D. shuffled toward Brother Apollo. "I'll try to pry him open."

Out of one corner of his mouth, he said that emotions were not like tracks, which were sure and reliable; then out of the other he said there was something to Brother Apollo's behavior. But he would get nothing firm out of the Welshman, who was stubbornness tripled. *That's one man you won't pry. No matter how big the crowbar.*

"J. D." He turned to look at me. "I'll speak to Randall. He's had something buzzing in his addled head ever since we pulled in yesterday."

He nodded but clearly his mind was on Brother Apollo.

It entered my mind with considerable force the idea that competence equaled freedom in J. D.'s world and in my own. If I had work that I was excellent at, I wouldn't be crowded down the chute of marriage. When I chose a man, whether it be as his third wife or as another man's first, my choice would be real, not because wifehood was my only option. Emmeline B. Wells thought women should have both a career *and* an intimate family relationship. I determined that was what I would have for myself. *But for every time there is a season.* I turned toward where Randall worked in the barn.

Inside, waiting for my eyes to adjust, I breathed in the scent of grass hay mingled with the savory odor from the smoke house. Some of the tightness left my body. "I love that smell."

"Of shit?" Randall lifted a bucket and dumped grain into the horse manger.

"Of the curing meat, silly. Of the grass hay."

He grinned at me.

"Where was Brother Apollo last night?"

He tossed the bucket toward the bin where the grain was kept. "Another day or two and we'll have bacon for breakfast."

"Randall?"

"He was with *her*. Damn his fat head. After you left Centre, he stopped at the bishop's house and then went back to *her* house."

I wondered from what hiding place Randall had watched. Maybe that was the occupation of every soul in Centre—to hide and watch the deps take their brothers to prison. "Her?"

Randall stomped across the floor and climbed the ladder.

"Your girl? He married your love? Right?"

Randall stopped climbing and flung his head against the crook of one arm, hanging on the ladder. His lips were white from being pressed together.

I stepped toward him and touched his shoe.

"I promised myself I wouldn't tell who *she* is." He came back down the ladder, his face bitter. "I didn't swear not to tell who he is."

Through the doorway of the barn, I watched J. D. standing face-to-face with Brother Apollo.

"Have you worked revenge on Brother Apollo?"

"They were suppose to take him. Sammy said they'd take him on the train and throw him in prison. Instead, he spent the night with her. Again." He slammed his fist against the barn wall and nearly fell off the ladder.

Had Randall been so beside himself that he shot the deps and brought them to the underground store to lay the blame on Brother Apollo? *Not bloody likely.* Still the possibility made me ill low in my gut, worse than the influenza.

"When did Brother Apollo go to her?"

"After the shots."

"How long after?"

He climbed the ladder the rest of the way to the loft and tossed down some hay. "I've said all I will say."

I climbed up and rested my arms on the floor of the loft, which was half full of yellow-green grass hay. Randall lay on a mound. "Randall. You're not going to be able to keep anything from me. I'll worm it out of you, so just tell me now."

"I won't tell you when he went to her house, but I'll tell you something else. Brother Apollo and the bishop were below me talking just now. They didn't hear me hiding. The bishop, he told Brother Apollo to claim that the deputies robbed him."

"Robbed him? How would that help anything?"

Randall shrugged his shoulders. "I don't know. They talked so soft I could hardly understand. But I know few men are as sly as that bishop." Randall kept his face turned away from me.

I heard footsteps below. "Rachel," J. D. said, and I climbed down the ladder. He frowned and shook his head.

"What? You discovered that Brother Apollo is not good at lying?"

"I've never seen him behave so oddly. It's clear he doesn't trust me with the truth." He shrugged his shoulders. "After twenty years of friendship."

"Randall said Brother Apollo went to his second wife."

J. D. looked back at the doorway, now empty.

"I thought that might be where he was, but I wonder why William didn't tell me as much. It's not as if I'm likely to turn him in for being a polygamist when I'm one myself."

"Did he hear the shots?"

"He wouldn't say that either." J. D. walked to the foot of the ladder, looking up to where Randall paced.

"Brother Apollo didn't need to kill them here to have killed them."

"Right. But why would he then bring them into his own store?"

I thought, *You may have to face the fact, J. D., that your friend has murdered.* "To get them away from the bishop's house. Where they were actually killed."

"That thought frightens me. But I grant 'tis the simplest explanation of what happened."

"I can't hear you when you mutter so soft." Randall's voice came from above like some disembodied spirit.

Brother Apollo bustled into the barn. No humorous quotes or jibes tumbled from his mouth. "I wish you would do as the bishop advised. I thank you for your help with my stolen horse, but I wish you would go home in your surrey now and leave this to us."

I studied Brother Apollo's face, which changed from sorrow to anger and back as quick as clouds passing across the sun. J. D. often said the storekeeper was the best organizer he knew. He had made a success of a store dug out of the earth in the middle of the desert; he helped people in need but didn't ruin himself doing it. Had he killed the deps and was now figuring how to hide his sin?

"You know I can not do as you say, old friend."

"Old friend. If you really were, you would leave now."

Randall lay in the loft, his face hung down into the ladder hole. When Brother Apollo glanced at him, he jerked his head back out of sight.

Brother Apollo sighed. Then he lifted halters from the tack room wall and soon brought out two horses—the big black we had returned yesterday, probably close to seventeen hands tall but with elegant muscled legs, and the little, flighty mare, a brown Arabian-mustang cross. Then he dragged out two saddles.

"God watch you." He handed me one saddle and J. D. the other. "And God forgive me for helping you." He turned sharply and returned to the store.

"He's not a pure man," said the voice from above.

J. D. looked up into Randall's face. "You were out and about when the deps invaded the bishop's house. I saw them start toward the cemetery and then I came back here. Did you watch them longer? What else did you see? Do you know who shot them?"

"*You're* the one that is a Wells Fargo agent. *You're* the one that finds every horse or man or dog that's lost. Them that got eyes to see, let 'em see."

Or ears to hear.

The bishop and Brother Apollo's plan to say the deps had robbed the store only made sense if one or both of them *had* killed the deps and they were trying to make it appear unlike a crime. He might have loaded the bodies on the deputies' quivering horses, hauled them to his store, and laid them out for burial. Finally he might have become frightened at what he had done and wanted them gone from his store. But then where were the deps' horses? I frowned. None of it made sense.

J. D. laid the blanket on the tall horse, smoothed it and lifted the saddle into place.

"Randall." I watched his face, which was framed by the small opening into the loft. "You told me that Brother Apollo married your girl. I don't believe that you shot them, but did you load their carcasses on a horse and bring them here?"

"Course I never shot them." His face was red and the cords stood in his neck. He reached one arm down into the ladder hole, pointing at me. "Just like everybody in Centre, I heard them kilt. But I didn't do nothing else. I didn't kill them and I didn't haul them into William's store. I don't know who done that."

I thought he would fall through the opening, but suddenly his face disappeared and I heard him stomping across the floor above our heads. He danced an angry dance and swore in rushes and pauses as if he recited poetry.

J. D. looked at me across the back of his horse. "What d'you think?" His voice was soft. He touched my arm and looked me square in the face. His clear respect nearly brought tears.

Randall's stomping continued, his rhythmic swearing.

"He's for angering easily, but it passes quick. If he shot them, it was done in an instant, without thought. He would have to be carrying a shotgun that instant."

"What if the deps insulted this woman—William's second wife?"

I shook my head—it took more than anger to produce a killing mind.

"What? What's rattling around in your noggin?"

"It's a reason to kill them, but I'm thinking that nearly every Saint in town wanted them gone. Maybe more than one good brother thought those shots were an answer to prayer. So the killer could be anybody in town. It could be you. Could be the bishop."

"Me? You think *me* capable of shooting those deputies?" He laughed once loudly, a horse laugh. "But 'tis more likely *me* than the bishop. I've known him for ten years. A stable, Christian man." He laughed again, shaking his head.

"Just shows we're going to have a perishing hard time of it if we suspect every man jack who had a *reason* to kill them. When we talk to them—"

"That's why we follow hard signs. A killing will not be kept secret for long in such a small hamlet. You be patient, Rachel. Someone will bolt if we beat the brush."

I hated being told to have patience. "By bolting do you mean running away from town? What about odd behavior? Like Brother Apollo frowning and being so distracted that he *doesn't* quote ridiculous phrases in Latin? Like Randall in a fury because the deps didn't cart Brother Apollo off to prison? Or like the bishop telling Brother Apollo to confess that he shot the deps when they broke into his store to steal?" J. D. stared at me, his jaw slack. I nodded and pointed up to the loft where Randall still shouted to himself. "That's just what Randall said he overheard."

J. D. circled his fingers on his crown. "Randall's lying. The bishop and William are incapable of such deceit. They would never make up a story like that."

"You say it because they're your friends."

J. D. stepped toward me, his face angry. He had changed manner in the time it would take for me to say "father." I wanted to run away and hide from him. "What we will do is follow definite signs like those foot tracks. We will find this woman who is William's second wife and we will try to discover whether he was with her last night. We will discover where the deps were killed, if we can. We will find their horses."

I couldn't fathom his wavering nature, one second talking to me like a respected partner, the next chiding me like a child.

"You have read too many dime novels. Your speculations won't help us find the killer. Only following those tracks will—unless they've been marred this morning." He frowned at me. "It has been light more than an hour."

"That breakfast was worth a marred track." I wanted him to see I could be just as belligerent.

"You have too much pleasure in gratifying your tongue and gut." His anger had shifted to sermonizing. I had never before thought him a wavering, changeable man. But he certainly was one today. "Subdue the carnal man."

I wanted to slap him. Instead, perverse in my anger, I imagined subduing a carnal man—certainly not Ezekiel, who was as pious as a Catholic saint. I smiled and arched one eye.

"What? What is in your head?"

Not for a thousand gold dollars will I say, father dear.

"Well, you've been talking and not saddling. Do it now." J. D. checked his own saddle and then mounted, riding out into the snow.

He had no right to stir me, confuse me, and walk away.

I looked down at the sidesaddle Brother Apollo had thrust at me. After lugging it back to the tack room, I chose a regular saddle. I laid the blankets across my mare's back, and hoisted my gear up, cinching it tight. The mare was bellied out, holding her breath. I kneed her hard. She released, and I re-tightened the cinch.

Randall stood in the large upper window of the barn as I led my horse out. He was calm again. "I did commit sin. I told them deps about Brother Apollo's new wife, who should have been mine. But my sin did no good nor harm, so I don't understand how it's a sin."

J. D., who had waited for me just outside the barn door, glared up at him. "What good did you think could come from betraying Brother Apollo?"

Randall shrugged.

"Randall wanted a second chance with his girl."

"You want a chance at a woman who's already married?" J. D. shook his head. "'Tis a sin. Remember the tenth commandment."

Randall jerked back from the window.

I turned sharply and adjusted the stirrups, which hung too low for my feet. I had put on wool trousers under my dress, scratchy as spun milkweed against my thighs, but they would cover my drawers and protect my legs from cold; I unbuttoned the lower front of my skirt and straddled my horse like a man. When I had been twelve or thirteen, I had experimented with riding sidesaddle like a lady, graceful and demure; all I gained were bruises from my falls.

"Where did you get those?" J. D. pointed a crooked finger at my trousers. I flipped the two sides of my skirt forward, covering my legs.

"Bought this morning here at the store." The mare danced sideways across the lane, but by the time I walked her up to the corner of the barn and back, she had settled down. "Sister Apollo put them on your account."

J. D. towered above me on the massive black horse. "These are civilized townspeople. They will think you're a feral woman in these trousers, riding like a man, and they will be thinking about you, instead of about what happened last night. You'd best go back and change to a side saddle."

"I'd rather try to sit on a rolling barrel. I like the feeling of having a horse between my legs."

His mouth dropped open. "That is not the way for a young woman to talk or even think. You are naught but a saucy, profane goose."

Once again I had been too forward with my speech, which was all right for a man but not for a woman. No woman should talk about her own legs, especially not what lay between them. It was only in the past few months had he turned fastidious with me. Before that he'd treated me like a son. Now he wanted me to become a woman and move out of his house.

"Bollocks." A mere whisper.

"What did you say?" His nostrils flared and I saw a tuft of thick wiry hair sticking out of one. I stifled a snort of laughter. My lips quivered as I turned back toward the barn.

Undoing the cinch, I ripped the saddle off and then replaced it with the sidesaddle. "Ugly, lopsided contraption."

Randall stuck his head through the ladder hole. I glared up at him. "Don't say a dammed word."

"You shouldn't wear man's clothing. It's unnatural." He grinned, and I wanted to climb the ladder and hit him with my fist.

A couple of months earlier, I had stepped into J. D.'s study to return a book he had loaned me. Papers and books were spread on his desk. When I saw my own name written in his journal, above a sketch of a head, I sat in his chair and looked more carefully. It was a damned phrenological chart he had drawn in order to parse out my character. Underneath was his handwriting: "I am concerned that Rachel is a mannish woman. She possesses little womanly piety and not a large heart where affection can grow for a husband and children. Her head shows much in the areas of destructiveness, secretiveness, and acquisitiveness—which in a man might not produce such an unnatural shape as in a woman. She has too much of wit and firmness. But I think there is no reason for despair. I believe that just as the dark Lamanite savages can become white through their righteousness, Rachel may change the shape of her brain through behavior more proper for a woman."

Sitting in his office, I had felt as if someone had kicked me in the gut, kicked me and then stomped on my chest. I knew his drawing had been done with a biased hand—he found what he thought he would find, but that didn't make the insult any easier for me to bear.

As I cinched up the saddle, I wondered how a husband would treat me. J. D., who generally respected me, but had dealt with me sometimes as if I was an aberration. How might a less sensitive man act once I was his property?

My mind drifted to the killer, whom I had started to imagine as a man dressed in farm clothing with his face in shadow. I wondered how the killer treated his wives. Did he speak to them with careful respect? Was he kind to his children?

Randall watched from the loft as I looked at the high stirrup. I knew I would never reach it with my dress buttoned. That was another problem with the sidesaddle: a woman couldn't mount alone. I didn't want Randall or J. D. helping me, especially if they had to push me up, one hand on my rear. Neither did I want to appear clumsy before either one of those men.

I led the mare to a wooden box outside the tack room. Standing on the box, I stepped into the stirrup, grabbed the high fixed pommel, and swung myself up. I hooked my right thigh around the pommel and pushed my left thigh up against the leaping head, although I didn't think the little mare and I would be doing much jumping, unless she decided to give it up as a bad show and bucked me off. Finally I draped my skirts around my legs. The little mare danced, making me wonder how long I could stay horsed.

"Much more tolerable," said J. D. when I rejoined him.

"Perishing, hateful thing. Sure, I'm going to fall and break my hip or my shoulder."

He opened his mouth to say something but I sang to drown out his words, bellowing so loudly that the little mare jerked her head up and danced sideways:

> *Ye simple souls who stray*
> *Far from the path of peace,*

J. D. put gloved hands over his ears.

That lonely, unfrequented way
To life and happiness.

"Ah, your mother, bless her departed soul, sang so beautiful. I cannot understand why God endowed you with a raven's voice."

"I've a clarion voice. Aunt Mary said so, and she's never lied. The voice of a—loon, she said."

"Or an eagle. Mary has more charity than honesty in this matter." He smiled and I grinned back, grateful that I had succeeded in working down my anger.

Recently we had argued more and more. The bickering over marriage was only the worst. When I had been a child, it was different; he praised me whenever I made a good shot with a rifle or a tricky catch with a lariat. I wanted that again—his whole face like a sunrise when he saw me. Still, during those years he had treated me like a child, never really listening when I tried to talk about important matters, a book I had read, the doctrines I had learned in church. And he never took my advice.

What I wanted was for him to act toward me the way he acted toward his sons or his male neighbors. Even though Ezekiel was in many ways a fool, he and J. D. spoke as man to man. I suspected that J. D. might never envision me as a friend or equal; even if I discovered something that helped solve the killing, he might still condescend. I had once tried telling him how bad he hurt me sometimes, and my furious and disjointed words had just confused him. I had been fourteen and he had tried to lay his hands on my head and rebuke the demon inside me.

Suddenly tears sprang into my eyes as I hungered for the years before I became a woman when our love was not so confusing and I could do no wrong in his eyes.

CHAPTER 7

The road, white and smooth except for the lines of tracks, led down into the delta, where Lombardy poplar trees—fifty feet tall, their bare branches held tight—lined the fence rows and ditch banks. On the other rim, a mere half mile away, Centre spread across its skirt of flat land. A few pines and cedars showed green; the other trees looked like gray shadows. The sun reflected from the tall, white wall of one house on the rim, and from the white spire of the church that rose from the center of town. Most of the houses were a mixture of tan adobe and wood painted white or green. The town was as ordered as Mary's idea of heaven—a perfect square, sixteen blocks total, generally two houses to a block. Each home had room for a garden and outbuildings such as a smokehouse, chicken house, sheds for pigs and milk cow. While I had been to Apollo Store many times, I'd seldom had reason to enter the town.

J. D. hardly glanced at the ground. His eyes roved the town and the hillside. "The deputies camped up there." He pointed toward the wide canyon above town, the source of the stream that watered the fields. I scanned the mountainside, covered with cedars on the foothills, oak brush or pinion pines on the ridges, and quaking aspens in the bottom of the canyons. No place seemed flat enough for a camp.

What was he seeing that I couldn't? My salvation depended on knowing. But as much as I stared at the various shades of green and clear white, the shadow of quaking aspen trunks lower, I could distinguish nothing. It all seemed like steep hillside. Finally giving up, I looked across the town.

I imagined living under the deps' scrutiny. The townspeople knew someone was always watching from above, someone more unjust than God. Everyone, including the blameless children, would be anxious and unhappy.

We rode off the slight bench where Apollo Store sat and down into the winter-dead fields, following Brother Apollo's tracks through the tangle of others backward to their point of origin. I tried to memorize the print, which I caught a glimpse of occasionally—toe pointed more than on the shoes of most men, heels worn on the inside. Our horses thumped across a short bridge made from squared cottonwood logs. Cattle stood or lay in circles in the fields, chewing their cuds. Most of the morning feeding was over, but a few men, the slow or lazy, forked hay from stacks to feed their lowing cattle. A man in a tan canvas coat watched me and J. D., one hand flat over his eyes.

We came to a place in the snow where Brother Apollo had slipped and fallen. "He was in a perishing hurry to get back."

"Or he just slipped." J. D. frowned. "I wish you wouldn't use that word."

"What word? You mean 'perishing'?" I laughed, but it rankled that he had become critical of most everything about me.

"Yes. You use a perfectly good word as if 'tis profanity. The scripture says swear not atall. I've noticed for some time now that you have grown more careless in your speech, more like you were when you first came to Rockwood."

I felt the flare of my Irish temper and I began saying the alphabet to myself: *Ass, Bastard, Cols, Damnable.* I couldn't think of one for "E," so I skipped straight to "F."

"So I should say he was in a *damnable* hurry? J. D., you and I have both sworn a little ever since we've known each other."

J. D. opened his mouth and shut it again. "I think it's time for you to begin cultivating some feminine habits. 'Tis not becoming for a woman to swear."

"But proper for a man?"

"Nay, not proper for him neither."

Then an "E" word which would work came into my mind. "You want me to stop swearing to make myself acceptable to *Ezekiel*, but you don't hesitate to swear when the need arises."

Remarkably, instead of getting angry, he turned pensive, rubbing his fingertips in a circle on the bald spot on his pate.

A stocky man left his barn and started toward us down the lane that led from Centre to the fields. When he came closer, I saw he wore a coat sewed from a worn quilt.

"Hallo, Brother Wheeler." J. D. smiled and turned to me. "We ran our herds together in the Salt Lake Valley when we first came west."

"Decades ago. We are now venerable men." He was even older than J. D., his face burned by sun and wind. "So those spawns of Satan are dead?"

J. D. nodded.

"One of us went crazy with anger. Now someone faces hanging instead of six months in prison." He shook his head sadly. "When they push us so hard and so constant, someone was bound to lose control and do something foolish. Still, you're going to have the devil's own trouble finding the killer. Any one of us could be the one who went mad. And who will speak against one of their neighbors? The best you can do is to walk away from it."

It struck me that such madness must eventually register in a person's face or behavior.

But J. D.'s spine seemed to stiffen at the advice from his old friend. "A killer is a killer. I have never walked away from a gross injustice."

"Maybe those two didn't deserve to die, but I sure wished they had left us alone." He shrugged, his face unsettled. "Tonight will be the first night in two weeks I've slept in my own bed. This past week I was mending a harness when the alarm sounded. I hid in the root cellar, crouched behind sacks of potatoes. The next day I was helping a first-calf heifer in trouble. I got her in the barn when the alarm came. I stayed with her until the calf was born; then I crawled under hay in the loft. The deps came in the door just as I'd climbed the ladder. How much can a man take?" Like the bishop, he was a natural preacher, building in rhythms toward a crescendo. "I'm going to pray that whoever killed them will feel neither guilt nor fear."

"How will this town be pleasant ground for Mormonism if the territorial government rounds to and sends more deputies? Will a dozen be better than those two?"

"Course not," said Brother Wheeler. "I've been thinking that maybe I should head for Canada. I have a sister up there who says that they have no federal deputies."

"Brother John, did you shoot these two?"

He peered up at us. "J. D., you know I can hardly bear to kill my own chickens." He shook his head. "No, I didn't do it."

"When you heard the shots," I asked, "where were you?"

Brother Wheeler's jaw clenched and he avoided looking at me. Clearly he was unhappy that his actions were scrutinized by a woman. "I was in my sheep camp, up on the bench. I heard the shots, but I don't know and don't want to know who pulled the trigger. Now, I'm late feeding my herd. I have no more time to jabber."

He crossed a ditch on ice so thin that it cracked and bowed as he walked. But it held and he strode through the field, not looking back.

"He's not one who wears the mantle of deceit."

"He's always been forthright," said J. D.

"So we don't have an inkling whether he's lying or not."

"That we don't. That's why we have to establish the physical circumstances of the killing."

He pushed and pushed. Facts and logic are more reliable than emotion. "J. D., do you think that all emotion is womanly?"

"What? What are you talking about?"

He kicked his horse up and we trotted across the last fields and up a rise into town. To our left I saw the school where David and Naomi taught. J. D. dismounted, bending over the tracks, which were crossed over by a muddle of other walkers, men and women about their morning chores.

Even after I couldn't discern any hint of Brother Apollo's boot print, J. D. didn't hesitate as he followed the tracks through the middle of town. Four women stood on the corner of a lot, heads bent together. When J. D. and I appeared, the group broke up, each woman going her separate way home. Nearly every window we had passed had a face in it—all women; the men must be either down in the fields, or hiding, or in prison. My body felt unreal, as if I existed in a fairy tale, passing through a silent town, the people frozen. I imagined the echo of the shots, deadened by snowfall, rolling through town. After that sound nothing would ever be the same. I saw many tracks going house to house—women likely gossiping about history and implications, specifically what would happen to the town if it became known that a citizen had killed agents of the federal government. J. D. followed the sign of the one track through the tangle, finding a curve of instep or sole printed into the snow, never losing it, even though as we followed the tracks backward, they became more covered with snow.

I realized that he was single-minded about most everything, and that this quality might be both strength and weakness. I felt surpassingly smart thinking this.

In one yard, a woman used a wedge and sledgehammer to split short stumps of wood for her fire. A schoolboy and girl retrieved the pieces and stacked them in a wheelbarrow. We passed the school where children played outside. David Cooper stood on the porch and rang a bell. All the children ran inside. On the east end of the school building, two men unloaded cans of milk from a wagon.

I glanced up past the church toward the cottage where we'd hidden. Sister Griggs, standing in her doorway, waved and walked down the lane toward us.

"Those deps are dead, J. D. Rockwood. I heard the shots. This is the most excitement we've had in Centre since Mahonri Cooper's second wife hit him in the head with an axe."

J. D. rode past without a glance.

What was it in this woman that made him forget all human courtesy? Whatever it was, I wanted to know.

"Good morning."

Her crinkled face was intelligent and I couldn't take my eyes away. "Good morning, child. I wish you good hunting."

"Oh, I still have your blanket. I left it at Apollo Store."

"Don't you worry. I'll fetch it sometime."

When I caught up, J. D. said, "Meddlesome old woman. Ten years gone, a couple of town boys stole from William Apollo, sneaking down into his store at night. The bishop locked them in a back room in the old storehouse. She strolled over one night and unlocked the door, set them free. They fled to Salt Lake and I had to follow them there and capture them again. She said she didn't want their futures ruined by a minor indiscretion. I couldn't persuade her that stealing someone's property was more than a minor indiscretion."

I glanced back at the woman who had stood up to J. D. Such a tiny, innocent-looking person. She smiled at me, somehow managing to look like the cat that drank the milk.

I grinned back and nodded my head with respect.

Soon we came to the northern edge of town and the blacksmith shop I had seen the night before. Its walls were wooden, painted over with black tar and hung with horseshoes and old tack. A girl perched on the ridgepole. She was very small but her face was that of a ten- or eleven-year-old. In front of the building, a second girl, a couple of years older than the first, lifted and inspected the hoof of a bay horse. I realized she was the one we had seen last night during the storm. She had been coming out of the smithy.

A small man in a suit sat on a bench against the sunlit wall. Both he and the larger girl watched me and J. D.; she held the hammer suspended. Across from the smithy stood Bishop Peterson's elaborate house set on a slight rise. The yellow adobe brick glowed in the sun.

J. D. nodded to the man and the girl and we left them behind. I felt their eyes burning into my back as we followed the tracks up the lane to the left. At the last house in the northwest block, J. D. followed the tracks straight to a lone cabin next to the barn.

The cabin had a small yard, fenced by willow sticks woven onto cedar posts. A white face flashed in one window; then the curtain fell back into place. I imagined living alone on the edge of town in a cabin, probably built when town was first settled. I would wait nights for my husband, an older man, to sneak away from his first wife. It would be such a straitened existence. J. D.'s house was a community, not that every member of the household was joyful, but that everyone knew she belonged. Mary, the matriarch, forbade any kind of ostracism.

Brother Apollo's tracks emerged from the doorway—the only tracks in the yard.

"He sought shelter from the storm." I found myself unable to keep bitterness out of my voice.

"'Tis surely his legitimate wife. Gwyneth should have been consulted, but even so, he is married to both women before God."

I blew air through my teeth. My liver seemed to boil.

J. D. dismounted and dropped his reins, striding into the yard. As soon as he left his horse, the black started back toward town, head to one side so that he wouldn't step on the reins. I dismounted and grasped the wayward horse's bridle.

"J. D., you'll need to tie this one." I flipped the reins around a gatepost.

He glanced back, a small, forced smile on his lips. I couldn't tell whether he was upset that I lectured him or that he smiled because I was also one who would not stand unless tied. I gave him a wolf-grin right back.

A young woman with a plain face and stout body opened the door. She leaned against the doorframe, holding one hand across her flat stomach.

"Hi." I smiled at her.

"I don't know either of you." She bit her lip; her face was pale. She was so young, perishing innocent. "But you do seem familiar."

J. D. strode forward and she shrank back into her house. "I'm J. D. Rockwood, and this is my stepdaughter, Rachel O'Brien."

The woman nodded. She had tied her blonde hair up in a knot. I imagined that at eighteen, Sister Apollo had looked much like this woman.

"I'm Sarah. Sarah—ah—Stewart."

J. D. frowned, staring at the doorpost. "The bishop is worried—ah—needlessly I think—that—I mean needless in the sense that everyone already suspects." I had never seen him so befuddled. He took a breath and proceeded more directly. "Those two deps were shot to death. Shotgun. Real bloody."

"Thank God," said Sarah.

"Now that you're posted up on that. I—we're looking into the killings. We hope to discover who it was murdered them."

I glared at him. If Sarah knew anything, J. D. had just sealed her lips by naming the killer as a murderer. He was known all over this part of Utah territory as a good man to find any lawbreaker, but that was when the job required tracking. He was clearly no good at getting delicate information from young women.

"I thought them was shots I heard early on in the storm. But I thought it might be somebody killin' skunks or something." A thin smile crept onto her lips.

"You heard the shots?"

Sarah glanced at him and frowned. "Yes." Her voice and manner were tentative.

"During the snowstorm?"

"Yes."

"Did they wake you from sleep?"

"Yes."

"Then they may have been shot on this side of town. Not in the canyon."

"No, they weren't loud. Very soft."

"Was your husband with you last night?" I asked.

"I have no—" She frowned down at her hands and shut the door.

J. D. turned toward his horse. "This is what persecution does to us. Teaches us to mistrust our neighbors and to lie." Then he spoke much more loudly. "Polygamists go to prison for a mere six months but a killer will face hanging. Sarah can hardly understand the danger her husband is in."

The door opened and Sarah looked down at the tracks. "You can see as well as I can. Do I need to say it?"

"We are concerned about timing," said J. D.

"I heard the alarm and later the shots."

"Alarm first and shots afterward. How much later?"

"I don't know, maybe an hour."

"And when did Brother Apollo come?"

"He came here before—after the alarm but before the shots." She burst into tears and turned inside her house.

"You see that talking to people bears such unreliable fruit? Give me a muddled track any day. 'Tis much clearer than people's words."

I wanted him to know I'd paid attention to the woman's words. "She has tremendous reason to lie."

We rode past a house where a woman hung laundry on a line. The longest trousers hung nearly to the snow.

"It's clear William hasn't told Gwyneth about this girl. This is not the way it should happen. The only way a plural marriage can work is if the husband and his first wife go into it together, clearheadedly."

"How can anything about polygamy be clear headed?"

"Aye. With this tremendous persecution."

I hit my fist against the horn of the damnable saddle. "I think marrying into polygamy is like sitting buck nekkid on a red ant bed."

J. D. stared at me. His mouth started to turn up in a smile, but he fought it back until he had perfect control of his face. "'Tis a dark time and we can't see far ahead. I am sure those two are in hell. May God's judgment fall in like manner on every deputy in the territory."

"J. D."

Finally he looked at me. "What?"

"You could have avoided frightening her."

"How?"

I watched his face and knew he was already working himself into a huff over my criticism. I should back off, the only smart thing to do.

"By smiling when we talked. Letting her know we aren't a threat."

"But we are a threat. A smile would be a lie."

"Well, we've frightened her into her own lie—that he was with her when the shots were fired."

"He was with her and didn't leave until this morning early. The tracks show that. We just don't know for sure when he first arrived. This is just as I have said all morning: we can trust the physical evidence but not what people say."

"I agree. It's going to be the same no matter who we talk to. If everybody wanted them dead, then everybody will suspect that one of their good neighbors did it. Everyone will lie to protect their neighbors, whether they know who the killer is or not. It's a tangled mess." I took a breath. "But the way people's faces register their distortions is as much evidence as a marred track."

J. D. looked at me as if seeing me for the first time that day. "Persuasive." He was so surprised at my vehemence, I guess, that he forgot to rebuke me for my profanity.

The bay horse still stood outside the smithy. The older girl looked up at us as we dismounted. Then she bent to lift the horse's left hind foot, holding it frog up between her thighs. She took her pincers from the bucket at her feet and snipped the edge of the wide hoof, trimming it back. Then she took out a curved knife, sliced away the spars, and smoothed the bottom of the hoof with a rasp. Every motion was precise, a pleasure to watch. I heard the whir of a forge, the ping of hammer on metal, and finally, the hiss of hot metal in water. A coal-smudged man, half a foot taller than J. D., walked out of the smithy with a horseshoe held in tongs. He had a thin and lanky body but muscular arms. He compared the shoe to the trimmed hoof and nodded. He dropped the shoe in the snow, where it hissed and sank out of sight. The girl took a pinch of nails and thrust them between her lips. She took the shoe in a gloved hand and laid it on the hoof, hammered in the first nail.

J. D. and I followed the lanky man through the double doorway, wide enough for a wagon. The inside was dark except for the red glow of coals. The lanky man turned the crank of the forge, three quick, powerful strokes. He was so covered with black soot that he seemed ageless.

"How is the world using you, Brother J. D.?"

"Poorly."

"You must be doing something right then if you're suffering—that's what this world is made for." He took another horseshoe and held it in the flame. "What trouble you aimin' to stir up here?"

When my eyes adjusted, I saw another man inside, standing to one side of the forge, his hands held above the fire. He was the man who had earlier been sitting outside. "J. D." he said, nodding. His face was thin, his chin sharp.

"I never intend to stir up trouble. Rachel, this dirty man is Alma Wright and the clean one is Brother Heber Stewart, newly in the high council with me."

"Six months in the high council. I guess that's still newly."

"Sarah is your—"

"Daughter." He frowned at J. D.

The blacksmith nodded at me without turning away from his work. His beard seemed to be sandy colored under all the black, and thick down his neck. I remembered J. D. telling me about him once, a widower with two daughters—surely the girls outside.

"J. D. You may not stir up the trouble, but you're never far behind it. You sniff out problems quicker than any soul I know."

In a moment, the next horseshoe was red-hot, and Alma struck the edge, curving the tip more sharply inward. He held it high, examining it.

"My business is pretty much untangling trouble started by someone else."

Alma snorted, showing his white teeth.

The girl who had earlier balanced on the ridgepole now sat in a half-attic built into the eave of the small building. She wore a bright blue dress made from homespun cloth. Because she sat on the edge of the platform, her legs hung down below the edge of her dress. Seeing her tiny ankles and wizened calves, I wondered whether she could walk. She stitched an intricate pattern of beads into the back of a doe-skin glove. Her eyes were bright and intent, flicking toward whoever spoke. "Them deps were rightly killed."

Her father peered up at her. "Psssst. Molly, shame on you. No man is rightly killed."

"I heard the shots. I knowed what they meant."

"Are you a seer then? I can only suspect. Anyway, you hit the hay long afore the shots."

"God struck them down for persecutin' the Saints."

"Does God use a ten-gauge shotgun?" asked J. D.

Alma held his body still and then he struck the horseshoe again, banging it so hard with his hammer that the gong nearly deafened me. "Shotgun?" He glanced over his shoulder at Brother Stewart, then toward the back of his shop. I saw a double barrel sticking above a box behind a wagon wheel. Brother Stewart frowned, clearly displeased.

"What time did you hear those shots?" I asked.

"I—" Alma hesitated. "I didn't look at a clock. It was probably afore midnight."

The horseshoeing girl leaned against the doorframe. She looked to be about twelve years old. "Ready for the next one."

"I'll have it in two claps, Maddy."

"I'm sorry they are dead," said Brother Stewart. "They were always after me, asking me which of the young women in town I had bedded with, making me ashamed. Still they didn't deserve to die." He shook his head.

"They seemed to know a body's hiding place afore he got into it," said Alma. "Brother Sharp was in his father-in-law's attic. They knew right where he was. That scrawny dep shot through the ceiling and nearly kilt him. Brother Nielsen was in a sheep camp with his Lucille, in the backyard of his first wife's house. They didn't even look around, just walked straight to the camp. It was as if they could peer down from their perch up there and see through walls. Even after dark they knew right where to look for an unfortunate brother and his wife."

"They spent all their time in Centre? Seems too small to keep them busy."

Brother Alma paused in his work. "No. They were in Hamblin half the time."

"When we'd see them head east to the train, we felt like having a celebration. But then they'd double back without any warning, and someone else would be in prison. That's how it happened with Bishop Sharp. We'd relaxed because they was gone, but they had just pretended to leave on the train. When it's discovered that they were killed, and they send a dozen deps to take the place of those two, we'll have even less peace of mind. I'm tired of it all."

"Brethren." J. D. stepped forward. "Have you considered that someone has been informing on you, that he told the deps exactly where to look?"

Brother Alma looked up from the glowing horseshoe. "Of course, people have talked that way. Nearly driven us crazy—ever' man suspecting his brother of denying their faith. We've never been able to find out who it could be."

"Worse than the deps is this mistrust," said Brother Stewart. "And the fear."

"People have even suspected me, on account of me being wifeless."

"My papa just don't want to advance in the Church," called Molly from the rafters. "That's why he won't marry again after our mam died."

"Well, Molly, who's to say I don't have a secret wife like everybody else?"

"I am. I'm to say it."

"No woman in town wants to be husband to a sooty, greasy man. That's my misfortune." Alma stroked his chin. "Or is it my

99

fortune? I'm beset by too many women already." He looked up at the rafters. Only his eyes showed his smile.

"You should take a bath more often. Then you could get us another mother."

He examined the horseshoe and then whanged it with the hammer again. "Good thing my daughters are so clever or I would be impoverished."

"You are impoverished," said Maddy. Molly giggled above us.

"Too damn clever. Every one of them too damn clever. Five are raised and married. Soon's I get these last two gone, I'll be a free man."

Molly pointed her finger at him. "Papa, you'll go to hell sure you keep swearing. I won't even be able to bend down from heaven and give you suck from a wrung-out cloth."

"Are your daughters too clever to go to school?" asked J. D.

"They go half a day. That's enough for anybody."

"People say that Sister Griggs must be the spy," said Brother Stewart. "Or maybe Randall Cooper. He always talked to them deps when they came in to Apollo Store."

"They've even said that Maddy informed against us because I sent her up on the ridge to keep an eye on them. She's saved the bacon of several men in town and that's how they show their gratitude, blame a motherless child and her wifeless father for trying to help their neighbors."

J. D. sighed.

"Who employs you, J. D. Rockwood?" asked Alma.

"Nobody employs me for this."

"Gentiles always employ you," said Molly above our heads. "Territorial dep gentiles. You could be an informer."

I craned my head to look at her.

"You must parrot what your father speaks," said J. D. "But I'm no informer." He turned to Alma. "I'm sure you're clever enough to see we need to distance ourselves from this killing before Deputy Marshal Danby misses his deps and brings a pack of men to ask the same questions I'm asking nicely."

Alma held the shoe, red hot, up to the light from the doorway. "That may make sense to someone from outside Centre. But do you think I'd want to give up one of my brothers to the law? Not many here see the federal government as any kind of standard for justice."

"So who owns a ten-gauge shotgun?" J. D. stared at the gun Alma had back in the corner. I leaned in the doorway where I could watch Maddy at work.

"I do, as you well know." Alma kept his eyes on the shoe he was heating in the forge.

J. D. walked back to sniff the barrel. He frowned and sniffed again.

"To my knowledge it was last shot two days ago."

"Would it smell this fresh after two days?" J. D. held the gun out to Alma. "I'd say it was shot more recently."

Alma bent to sniff the barrel, still holding his blackened tongs. "You're right. But I didn't shoot them bastard deputies."

"So who else has a ten-gauge?"

"Besides me and Brother Thomas? Bishop does. Brother Apollo. Brother Samuel Franklin. Brother Cooper. Don't know of anybody else." He looked up through the rafters at his daughter sitting in the heat, peering out her window toward the pathway to town. "But anybody could have used mine. It's here for everbody to use and everbody does so. In fact—" Then he frowned and shook his head. "Could have been anybody." He stepped past me, measured the shoe against the horse's hoof and dropped the hot curve of metal in the snow, where it hissed.

J. D. stepped out as well. "We need to take a look at their camp."

Maddy looked toward her father, who nodded. "Couple of

miles up 'bove town. High up on this flat space like a bib under the ridge. The gunshots came from up there."

J. D. turned and scanned the low hills above Centre.

"There." Maddy swept her hat off and pointed. "See that triangle mountain and that patch of cedars in the shape of a mitten? Their camp is just down and to the left of the thumb of cedars."

"She rode up and watched them nearly ever' day," said Alma from inside. "They didn't even know she was there. Bishop Sharp and now Bishop Peterson paid her to do it."

"I can't see the camp, but I know where it is now." J. D. mounted and started for the canyon. Maddy walked over and gave me a leg up and I smiled my thanks. They all watched as I kicked my horse to catch up. Alma stood with his tongs in the doorway. He shook his head and said something to Maddy.

I wondered what information they weren't sharing; they had been about as forthcoming as a pack of coyotes.

J. D. and I rode side by side. "Do you think that gun was the weapon used to kill the deps?"

"I don't know much of anything. It was shot recently, in the past day."

"Which makes it highly probable—"

"Makes it a bewildering concern. How could the killer use Alma's shotgun and him not know it?" He shook his head. "Could be that everyone but us knows who the killer is."

I said softly, "The Principle is training in lying."

"What? Couldn't hear you."

"They've had to lie to survive."

"Yes. Damn those deps. Damn a government that refuses to give us our Constitutional freedoms. They're going to destroy the Constitution, and God will give them war and famine, and we'll be the only ones with wheat. You watch, in the next ten years the crisis will come, and we'll be able to shuck these deputies and the corrupt judges and the whole gentile nation off our backs. This persecution won't last forever."

"And *after* that day, there'll be no more lying."

J. D. glared at me. It was a look he would never have used on one of his neighbors in Rockwood. Why would he never brook any kind of criticism from me? *Because I am a woman and young, not that he has grown to dislike me.* I repeated the words three times. Even though I knew better, I felt in my gut that he had lost his love of me. Being a woman and being young were part of my nature. When he criticized those aspects of me, he criticized me.

I waited for him to turn round so I could give him his evil gaze back with interest, but he didn't look at me again.

We passed several houses as I breathed and calmed myself. Once again, I told myself that the only way I could impress him now was by helping him solve this crime. I forced myself to consider what I knew.

I knew that most of the people who seemed to be lying were innocent, just lying to protect one of their brothers. That obligation to the others in their community confounded our investigation, making everyone seem guilty. Riding behind J. D., trying to keep balanced as we rode up the gully at the top of town, I tried to imagine the face of the killer. Whoever he was, I believed he deserved no sanctuary. I knew that whatever conniving manipulation and petty force existed in Rockwood or any other desert town, nothing was worse than the tyranny of murder, which might rend Centre into fragments.

I steered my horse back toward the school and bishop's storehouse. I was curious about Naomi and David and wanted to see them teaching. J. D. followed, looking warily toward Sister Griggs's house.

"What?"

"That damnable old woman. I want to avoid her if possible."

I laughed out loud and he glared at me. My every motion seemed to rasp him.

"'Twill be impossible to be discreet about anything with her watching and meddling."

"She has sharp eyes and sharper ears."

"To plague me with." He shook his head sorrowfully."

As we passed the church lot, we saw two men unloading cedar posts from a wagon and stacking them against the west end of the bishop's storehouse. A woman left with a wheelbarrow that had in it a sack of flour, a leg of wrapped meat—small enough to be mutton—and a few other bundles.

"Time is of the essence," J. D. called. "We need to examine the deps' camp."

Disregarding him, I turned my horse aside and rode into the schoolyard, dismounted and peered through the corner of one of the eastern windows. The children sat in rows, listening to the schoolmaster, David Cooper, who stood at the front of the room. Naomi bent over the desk of a student. Then she straightened and smiled at David. They watched each other over the heads of the students, their two faces bright. I smiled. The children, watching David and Naomi's dance of love, probably learned much more than what their books could ever teach them. I sighed; despite the fact that marrying into polygamy made social and economic sense, I was attracted to Naomi's situation—a handsome, intelligent man loved her alone of all the women in the world.

I glanced at J. D., who rode straight past the school. He peered angrily back toward Sister Griggs's house. I laughed again, kicking my horse so I could catch him.

I thought we were headed up the mountain, but J. D. stopped at a ramshackle wooden house in the southwest corner of town. I sat my horse, watching as he dismounted and knocked on the door.

The big-boned woman who answered wore a worn dress and apron; her hair was blond turning to gray. She was as big and fierce of face as Abigail, Ezekiel's first wife.

"What do you want?"

"A word with your husband."

"Am I my husband's keeper?"

J. D. rolled back on his heels and considered the formidable woman. Before he could gather his wits to answer her, she shut the door in his face.

We rode into the yard to where a tall girl leaned against the smokehouse. She looked to be about eleven or twelve, and she had Randall's face and her father's flaming hair.

"We'd like to talk to your father."

The girl stared at him.

"We're not deputies." I dismounted and smiled as sweetly as I knew how.

"I know that." The girl took a meat hook from its nail on the wall and opened the door to the smokehouse. Hooking it into the floor of the small building, she lifted a trap door.

Brother Cooper's face, round and white as a moon, appeared in the darkness below. "Judith. You have betrayed me."

"Papa," an older girl called from the back porch. "It's not the deps. They're dead. You don't have to hide."

"It's impossible he harmed those deps." His wife stood in the side door of the house. "He hid when he saw you coming because he's a nervous man."

Brother Cooper climbed out of his hiding place. He looked at J. D. "Of course, she's right, I'm a nervous but peaceful man. They poisoned my oldest sons against me, but even though I was angry for that, I couldn't harm a fly." He stumbled out into the bright sunlight, blinking.

J. D. stood square in front of him. "Where were you when the deps were killed?"

He looked at the sky, at the haystack, at the ground. "I—"

The woman strode to the edge of the porch. "He was with me. All night long. It was my night and I promise you he didn't leave."

"Except when he was at Apollo store."

"Early in the evening. After that, he was with me."

"Where is your shotgun? Can I take a sniff at it?"

The woman beckoned to her daughter. "Judith. Run and get it."

The girl walked into the house and soon returned with the heavy gun.

J. D. lifted the weapon and broke it open. He smelled the barrels and handed the gun back to the girl. "Thank you." She smelled the barrel herself, and I reached my hand to take the gun. The barrel smelled like metal, and the faintest hint of burn. I couldn't tell anything from it.

I frowned and shook my head. J. D., the old skunk, smiled. He turned and walked to his horse, mounting and riding into the lane to wait for me. There was no fence close for me to use to clamber on, so I hoisted my skirts up and stepped into the high stirrup, swinging myself up and smoothing my dress down again over my trousers. Once settled, I looked across and found Brother Cooper watching me, a small smile on his lips. It was an insulting smile, secret, almost demanding. I gave him my most *sleakit* face. He grinned and turned away.

He has three wives already. Why does he need to stare up my skirts?

Ducking his head, he followed his first wife inside the house. A repulsive man.

I kicked my horse and caught up to J. D. "What did you discover?"

"It's been used sometime recently, but probably not last night."

"How can you tell?"

"You just have to smell one that's recently been shot, then you can tell."

"Who next? Who do we talk to next?"

"No one. We find where in the canyon they were shot."

I glanced up at the mountain. Every inch of ground was masked by a foot and a half of snow. "I think it's silly to ride up there when the deps are no longer there. We should talk to every man in Centre. The killer may get frightened and let something slip."

J. D. paid me less mind than he did his horse. He just headed toward the mouth of the canyon. *Damn.* "Sorry, J. D. I forgot I'm just a child."

Finally he turned in his saddle and stared at me, clearly perplexed.

"J. D. Oh, J. D." Sister Griggs waved and hobbled toward us.

"Fiddlesticks."

"'Tis a word that's saving place for profanity." I affected his Liverpool accent. He glared at me, then shrugged his shoulders, turning his horse toward the old woman.

Sister Griggs was dressed in an ankle-length wool coat, bright red. "Young man." I watched J. D.'s face, trying to hide my own grin. He hadn't been a young man for nearly five decades. "I've decided to do what I can do to help you." She smiled up at him.

His face remained impassive.

"We can sit in my parlor where it is warm and I'll tell you what I know."

J. D. still sat his horse.

I swung down from mine and stood next to his knee. "She, for one, has no reason to lie to us."

"Except her own natural perversity."

"J. D."

He remained seated on his horse. "Thank you for your offer, but we have to ride up to the deputies' camp before much longer."

She turned on her heel and walked back toward her house. "What evidence there may be will keep."

J. D. swore steadily under his breath, but he dismounted and joined me. We followed her inside and sat in her soft chairs. I watched her closely. She had refused to talk until she had his full attention. If I tried a trick like hers, he'd just ride away.

J. D. gave her a forced smile. "What did you observe?"

"Well, I was just getting ready for bed when the alarm started. I looked out my window as the deputies entered the church. I saw the bishop run out the back door and into the brush. David Cooper came out but didn't run. Then not long after that you came and I wisely invited you to get off the street and come into my house. After you left I heard the shouting at the bishop's house. Then not long after that the deputies rode past again toward the canyon. I prepared myself for bed, but I couldn't sleep so I got up and made myself a cup of tea. I had just started sipping it when the shots sounded out. I believe this was about an hour after the deputies left town."

J. D. wiped one hand down his face. "Do you think that when they left town they rode straight for their camp?"

"I couldn't see clearly through the storm, so I don't know. But the shots came from some distance up the canyon."

J. D. stood and waited. When she said nothing else, he stood again. He nodded, opened the door and escaped.

"Thank you."

Sister Griggs returned my smile. "You're quite welcome."

Outside, J. D. waited for me. I hoisted my skirts and mounted my horse.

"That silly woman has nothing to do but sit up all night and watch her neighbors." He turned his horse south and we rode along the lane between town and the cemetery, a few stone monuments set into the ground under a cluster of cedar trees.

"It wasn't a normal night. Most excitement since the second Sister Cooper went after her husband with an axe and the bear got trapped inside Brother Whoever-it-was's chicken coop."

"She who mocks shall mourn. Your turn will come."

I snorted.

"When I get so old I can do nothing but watch out for other people's business," J. D. said, "shoot me."

"Isn't that what a detective does, push his nose into other people's business?"

He didn't respond. I looked across at him and his face was as sad and serious as I'd ever seen it. "You're bothered that your mind will go weak?"

"I don't mind dying. I just don't want to get old." What he said surprised me, because I hadn't thought anything would bother him.

"You *are* old."

He smiled at me. "And you're just a child."

"So we're even. Both of us are unsuited for this enterprise."

His hand was up, circling his bald thinking spot. "If we can prove that they were killed on the mountain, we can clear Brother Apollo." He smiled, clearly relieved. "He couldn't have been both up there shooting them and in Sarah's house at the same time."

"Sarah didn't have the manner of one telling the truth. He may not have been with her until later."

"What is the *manner* of telling the truth when everything is so mixed and mingled? I've said it before: I wish we had a clear track to follow to the killer and not all this confusion."

As we passed the Cooper's house, the curtains twitched and I wondered who was watching us. I heard someone call and turned in the saddle. The bishop walked briskly up the lane to catch us.

"Brother J. D." He grasped the big black's rein near the bridle. When the horse jerked its head, he let go. "I know you think you must talk to every man in town because you think we cannot take care of ourselves to solve this problem." His face was haggard. "It's not for sure a murder has happened. I have a new thought about all this. Maybe Brother Apollo shoot those deps when they break into his store, ya? Right after I eat I will speak to him again."

"I wonder why he said nothing this morning." J. D. dismounted and stood face-to-face with the bishop.

"You have frightened that poor brother." The bishop shook his finger in J. D.'s face. "Everyone is frightened, ya? This is the reason I have asked you to leave us. I think once you are gone away, whoever have killed the deps, Brother Apollo or maybe somebody else, then this poor soul who raised his hand in anger will have the courage to come forward. You must take to the marshal any man you discover, but I do not. The killer knows this, so long as you are around he will not have the courage to come forward."

"Well, bishop, I believe you are bound as much as I am to turn a murderer over to the proper authority. And we both can use discretion."

He shrugged and sighed. "I don't understand why you are so stubborn about tracking down this killer. You will not get paid to do it."

J. D. stared at the bishop, clearly surprised. "Because he should be caught and brought to justice."

I nodded. *We are the same, J. D. and I.*

"This is not even your jurisdiction as Justice of the Peace. Please, J. D., have the responsibility to just go home."

J. D. shook his head. "Where were you when you heard the shots?"

The bishop shrugged.

"Time is the key."

"Where were you when you heard the shots?" I asked.

The bishop scratched behind one ear. "Can you think what the newspapers in Salt Lake City will write about this? Every thieving official in Salt Lake will celebrate." Suddenly he smiled. "I want you to come for food at my house." He reached to squeeze me on the arm. "J. D., this young woman looks famished. She is only skin and bones."

J. D. looked at the sun and then at the mountain. "We don't have time."

"I know you are on the hunt all day, but the deps' camp can wait. That is where you are heading, ya? You must eat with me first."

I turned my horse, following the bishop as he walked back through town. We had passed along the same lanes so many times that our horses would soon wear ruts in the road.

J. D. wasn't following. I turned and asked him, "Do you have some food in that saddlebag?"

"We had breakfast just an hour ago."

"Three hours if it was a minute."

Finally, he directed his horse to ride after me and the bishop. At the bishop's house, I slipped straight off my horse, flipping my reins around a post in the front yard.

A young woman with white-blonde hair and a pale complexion came out onto the porch; she reached to ring a bell that hung there, but then she saw us. "Oh, I was about to call you for dinner. It's time." She was very young, an older daughter or a new wife. Her skin was as smooth and clear as a child's. She walked toward him, her motions languid, her eyes on J. D. and me.

"We will have company, Susan." He put his arm around the young woman. "J. D., this is my newest wife."

"I'll set two more places." Her voice was soft, ingratiating. One woman in Rockwood used a similar tone—Brother Hansen's third wife, also a very beautiful woman. The bishop's new wife walked from under his arm and held the door for us as we entered. Her manner was so proper that J. D. and I might have been on the doorstep of a mansion in London or Salt Lake, instead of in a small village in the middle of the Utah desert. This was probably the young woman the bishop married when Naomi would have none of his proposal.

J. D. swung himself down from his horse.

I couldn't imagine Naomi so demure, downcast eyes, perfect manners—an ornament in the bishop's house. Then I shook my head; I didn't know anything about this young woman except appearance. She might have an independent spirit masked by her perfect grace.

Just inside the door, a set of stairs rose to the rooms on the second floor. The bishop led us back through a short hallway to the dining room, which was full of the clamor of children. A piano stood at one end of the room; at the other end was an enormous china cupboard. Opposite the entryway was a coal heater.

A tall woman, regal as a queen, sat at the head of the long table. Halfway down, a large woman with a childlike expression held a baby on her lap. Not much farther down sat a tiny woman with a nose as hooked as a parrot's beak. Between them sat twelve children.

Susan retrieved two plates and the bishop commanded two children to leave the table to make room. They complained until Susan laid a cloth across the piano bench and set it near the heater.

"Warm as summer, but don't get yourselves a sunburn."

The children giggled and held their hands out to the warmth.

After the bishop raised his voice in an interminable prayer, I forked the beans into my mouth. They had been cooked with a shank of pork and tasted like manna from heaven. For a few minutes I shoveled them in; then raising my face, I saw that everyone else, including J. D., was watching me eat. I sat up and ate more demurely, trying to imitate the angel-woman, Susan.

"There is a young woman who appreciates her food," said the woman with the pointy nose.

"That she does." J. D. pointed with his fork. "She will eat any poor husband out of house and home."

"I will think better about this killing if I have sustenance."

The corners of J. D.'s mouth twitched, and I thought for a second that he was going to say something about the quality of my thinking—that my thoughts were merely speculations.

"Young woman," said the bishop, "you have not yet married?"

"She's considering joining with my neighbor Ezekiel in marriage."

"A woman who accepts sister wives will go to the highest level of the Celestial Kingdom. In Father's house are many mansions.

Are you willing to lodge in heaven's cellar when you could reside in the most glorious rooms?"

I swallowed the food I'd been chewing. "Heaven's cellar might be cool in the summer and warm in the winter."

Susan smiled and then covered her mouth with her hand.

The oldest wife smiled at me in a condescending manner. "You look like a fine young woman, raised in the proper manner. I'm sure you'll do what is right."

I opened my mouth, but J. D. glared at me, and I clapped it shut again.

After dinner, the three elder wives took the children out of the dining room. Through the window I saw them run toward the school. Susan started clearing the table, and I rose to help.

"No," said the bishop, "you are a guest." After everyone had left, he and J. D. had moved to sit at the corner of the table where they could talk easily.

"I still think we can outsmart them sons of—" The bishop ducked his head and color fled up his face. "Sorry. I have forgotten myself." He looked at Susan.

I sat next to him and J. D. and the bishop glared at me.

J. D. leaned forward. "What if we can find the killer before the train this evening? Then we could take him to the sheriff in Hamblin and this thing would be over before it starts."

"How will you do this?"

I leaned forward to make sure he saw me. "By talking to people to find out what they saw."

"I'm trying to mark in my head where everyone was last night."

"When the shot sounded, I was just getting into bed."

Susan carried the nearly empty bowl of beans into the kitchen. *With which wife?*

"After the deps went to the cemetery and J. D. and I went to Apollo Store, Brother Apollo didn't come home."

"J. D., what is the use of all these questions."

I leaned forward again. "So where is *your* hiding place?"

Susan dropped a plate, which hit the side of a chair and rolled across the floor, somehow without breaking.

I continued. "The deps looked all through this house. It must be a good design."

"A secret room in this house?" She retrieved the plate. "You must have read too many novels."

The bishop turned to J. D. "I have hardly told my own children this."

"I'd trust her with my life."

Watching me, the bishop considered.

"Show her the rooms. Maybe I trust her with my own life, too."

I followed Susan into the kitchen. She took a key from a drawer and unlocked what looked like a cupboard, but which had no shelves inside. Two ropes ran along the edge of the space. Susan pulled one rope and the cupboard lowered slightly. "Whenever we need fruit, potatoes, or apples from the cellar, we send this platform down. There is also a stairway to the cellar and someone else must go downstairs and load this dumbwaiter, but at least we don't have to lug the food up and down the stairs." She smiled at me. "Climb in."

I wondered if she would let me drop or lower me to the cellar to trap me there. Finally I shrugged my shoulders and clambered in, finding it large enough that I could sit or kneel comfortably. I felt the cupboard move upward and all light was gone. I panicked for a second, then called out, "Dark as the inside of a horse."

But then the cupboard stopped moving and I saw a line of light, like that at the lower edge of a shut door. I reached out my hand and fell forward out of the cupboard into an ill-lit room, which held a plain table, a bed, and a few chairs. The ceilings were low on the sides, but slanted sharply upward; the room was inside the roof of the house. A small stove stood in one corner. Narrow, horizontal windows, tucked up in the eaves, let in some light. I peered out on the town and, in the distance, Brother Apollo's barn. I shifted my gaze to the school, where children played and Naomi and David talked as they sat on the front step. Walking to the opposite side of the room, I saw the expanse of Rush Lake Valley and the line of the railroad extending north toward Salt Lake City, which lay beyond the mountains.

I walked back to the dumbwaiter and examined the ropes, but when I reached to touch them, they moved. When they stopped, I heard Susan call up the shaft, "Pull hard on the left rope." I bent into the shaft and pulled downward on the rope, hand over hand; the dumbwaiter moved up slowly. Soon, Susan's face and shoulders appeared inside the open shaft.

I laughed. "Perishing heavens, this is ingenious."

"Brother Alma invented it." Susan stepped out into the room. "He has the pulley counter-weighted so that it's easy to pull up a load."

I sat in the chair. The bishop had built this clever room into his new house, proof that he thought the war over plural marriage would last a damned long time.

"I have hidden here when those two deps have come to the house. The children don't even know it's here or they'd give it away."

"They'd want to play up here."

Then we heard the bishop's voice calling up the shaft. "Susan, you must send J. D.'s daughter down."

I climbed into the dumbwaiter and felt it fall slowly. The doors opened and I stepped back into the kitchen.

J. D. and the bishop both wore angry faces, clearly still entrenched in their argument. The bishop quickly led us to the front door.

"You must know what happened to the deps' horses." J. D.

stepped out into the bright sunlight. "You know everything that happens in town."

"I wish you all the luck in the world." The bishop shut the door.

J. D. and I mounted our horses. I gave J. D. a wry smile. "What kind of luck do you think he was wishing on us?"

"He's certainly not himself. It takes something tremendous to ruffle his feathers."

"I think he could have killed the deps. They did invade his house last night."

J. D. was silent, frowning down at me. "That's nonsense. He's just driven crazy with this problem. Can you imagine how difficult being bishop here would be?"

I thought that J. D.'s weakness in this matter was his habit of trusting those he knew. He forgot that one of the good brothers in town *had* killed the deps. I reminded myself that I didn't have to trust anyone. "I'm your conscience. I keep you thinking about what you don't want to consider."

"Some women don't say everything that comes into their heads."

"I'm like Alma's daughters. Somebody has to speak up to you patriarchs."

He didn't respond, just rode toward the canyon.

Talking straight to him didn't work anymore, neither could I just back down. I wondered if we'd ever be friends again.

CHAPTER 9

The sun hung low to the south, pale and weak, but the air was warmer than it had been for weeks. The horses followed a white pathway that went up along the creek, and soon the houses of town were out of sight behind us. I felt purest pleasure flow through me as we entered the canyon. For sure, I felt relief at leaving behind the dour-faced people in town who were too frightened to say the truth. But mostly I was thrilled to be on any hunt, whether for animal or man, with J. D.

Brigham Peak rose high above us, a massive white beacon. The gulch we rode up was nearly a hundred yards wide; a thin snake of willow shoots marked the iced-over creek. "I should be glad if it had snowed *before* the killing," said J. D. "Then we could track the murderer."

"He's a praying man, for sure. This snowfall was the gift of heaven for him."

Talk and talk, don't argue, don't contradict, I said to myself.

"Gift of the devil. 'Twill be a piece of luck to find blood. An echoing shot can scatter sound so that nobody knows its distance. They could have been shot at any point along this canyon and nothing to mark the place." He took out his pocket watch and frowned down at it. "'Tis frustrating that nobody is clear about the time."

"Nobody but Sister Griggs."

He just grunted without looking up from his watch. His mouth twisted as if he had bitten something unsavory.

As we rode higher, the sides of the gulch rose as well, soon turning into steep canyon walls. Above us spread the patch of cedars, now appearing less like a mitten than the head of a whale. I looked back over my shoulder at Centre. I could see only a wedge of the delta where the fields lay. A haze of smoke rose from behind the ridge. A single wagon crept toward Apollo Store. Beyond shone a white, undulating desert.

The broad plain behind and the white mountain ahead appeared too pristine to be the location of a gruesome murder. But, as J. D. had said, blood lay somewhere under the snow. One man's stomach and heart had been blown into tiny bits. The other man's neck had been hacked away by the force of the pellets. For sure and certain, tremendous anger was the true force behind such a savage act. A hardened man might kill and suffer no personal change, but any normally peaceable man from Centre would find the very fabric of his soul rent by the extreme act.

Despite my pleasure at being away from town and up on the mountain, I still thought that J. D. and I would have better luck down below, talking to each family, watching for a face more haggard and guilty than the others, evidence that someone was unstable inside. Or we could listen for a slip of a tongue, showing that someone knew more than he should.

The little mare, striding up a slight incline, slipped but quickly regained her footing. I clutched at the brace around which I hooked my knee. "Bollocks! This saddle is a perishing nuisance."

"You'll get used to it."

Like hell I will.

"It's not becoming for you to ride any other way."

This was *not* what he seemed to think when I was eleven and he gave me my own horse and saddle, a real saddle, not this device for torturing females.

My heart still beating rapidly, I kept my eyes forward and low

119

so I would have some warning of unsteady ground. My face felt hot as hell from the sun rebounding off the snow, and I heard a trickle of water from the near bank of the ravine where the sun struck with force. I saw no sign of a path the deps might have used to come and go between camp and town.

After twenty minutes of riding, J. D. forced his horse up the right bank and the big black took the slope in a bucking motion. I remained below, watching his progress up the steep canyon wall and wishing again for a real saddle.

I pictured myself slipping off the back of my horse and sliding on down the canyon on my butt.

Will J. D. think that *is ladylike?*

"The way is clear here." He motioned forward with his arm. "But I think 'twould be better if you continue a little farther before trying to climb."

I followed the bottom of the main channel as he rode the high side of the ravine. I watched the snowed-over pathway closely and soon saw it rise along the edge of a hollow. The little mare tried to turn back, obviously peeved she had to make the steep climb. "You and me are both of one bloody mind." I dismounted, unbuttoned my skirt, and remounted, flipping my leg over to ride like a man and spreading my skirt across the horse's rump. Then, clinging to the upper knee bar of the double-horned saddle, I urged the mare up the side of the ravine. She took it like a soldier and soon we came out on the hillside.

J. D. was ahead of me, snaking back and forth up a steep, sagebrushy slope. I examined the hillside for tracks under the snow but could see only those made by J. D.'s mount. A patch of cedars, apparently the one close to the camp, spread above us. J. D. crested and disappeared. Then he appeared again and whooped.

"I've found their tent." I followed his tracks up and came out on a skirt of ground, perhaps a hundred feet across. Against the back edge of the flat stood the deps' pale canvas tent. Snow had slid down the sides, making a long grave-like mound against each wall. To my right, a spyglass stood on a tripod. It crossed my mind that they must be wealthy to be able to afford one.

However wealthy they were, now they're just dead.

To the left of the flat stood two cedars; a rope had been stretched between, presumably for hitching horses.

"Where are their horses, J. D.?"

"The same has been bothering me. I saw no sign of them anywhere in town."

I had been asking about them, but I hadn't looked. J. D. was right: I had a lot to learn.

J. D. removed his hat and rubbed his pate. "The killer must have kept them. Maybe he will be discovered because of his greed. Killing brings a passel of other sins after it."

A bag, tied-off, hung from a high branch of a cedar tree that stood a few paces to the right of the tent. I saw a black circle rimmed by rocks with a second tripod rigged above, this one of green willow canes—the deps' cooking pit. I noticed that there was no snow inside the ring of rocks, even though all around was deep white.

J. D. dismounted and stood looking at his pocket watch. "We've taken an hour from the cemetery." He walked to the fire pit and squatted at its edge. "If Sister Griggs is right, they had time to get here before being shot. Barely enough time."

I pointed to the blackened pit. "They must have built a fire after getting here. No fire would have burned steady through that fall of snow." Against the trunk of the tree was a tangled stack of wood, the top pieces sleeved with white.

J. D. re-pocketed the watch, and walked forward to the fire pit. He nodded. "But if they built the fire and were shot right after, why did the fire last through the storm? I suppose they could have put a big log on."

I considered. "Even if someone rushed after them in anger, they may have had a few minutes to build a fire big enough to last."

"Maybe the killer stood and watched them bleed. Warming himself at the fire. He may have built it up."

I watched J. D. chew the edge of one lip. He was finally listening to me as if I had a brain. "If someone killed in a burst of anger," I said, "wouldn't he most likely rush straight back down the mountain instead of building up a fire so he could stand in a blizzard?"

"This calmness, standing over a fire while his victims bleed, matches how carefully the deps were laid out in Apollo Store. He was not a panicked killer." J. D. walked to the tent and poked his head inside. He backed out quickly. "What an unholy stench. That bedding hasn't been washed since Noah's flood." His horse had turned and was heading toward the path home, when I grabbed the reins.

"If you were kinder to him, he'd stand for you."

He glared at me. "He wouldn't stand for the prophet himself." He led the animal toward the hitching rope, where there was another mound of snow. I watched him reach down and lift the edge of a tarp, uncovering two hackamores and a shabby set of saddlebags. He scanned the ground and then tied his horse to the rope.

I kicked my left foot out of the stirrup and slid off my mount. I thought again about the perishing beastly sidesaddle; for sure and certain, it was a man invented it due to his delicacy over seeing a woman with her legs spread around a horse. No female would subject one of her sisters to such an abominably uncomfortable saddle.

The dangling reins, I had discovered that morning, were enough to hold the small mare to one spot. I walked to the spyglass. Centre lay in full view below, spread out like a map in a book. I brushed the snow off the top of the instrument and then tried to peer through the end. I could see nothing but a narrow crescent of light.

By the time I had found a way to see a whole circle of town, my breath had fogged the lens. I took out my handkerchief and polished the eyepiece. Finally, holding my breath, I looked through the glass in a proper manner. Susan, the bishop's young wife, emerged from her house and walked down toward the main part of town. She paused to speak to a woman carrying a basket. Another woman spoke to Sister Griggs, who leaned over her gate. I saw a different horse, a pinto, in front of Alma's smithy. Maddy, still not in school, squatted under the horse. Children played in the schoolyard; David Cooper, looking like a thin giant, stood inside a ring of children. It was odd to see but hear nothing.

I called out to J. D. "If I had two months to watch through this spy glass, I'd wait until some stranger rode across the flat and Maddy sounded the alarm. Every man in town would run to his hiding place, and I'd mark them all down. Later, I could clean them out. To the poor people down there, it would seem that I could see through walls. Maybe there's no informant."

"You could be right, but I think not. They were only here a day before the first arrest."

I turned the glass toward Apollo Store and in the fields I saw one rider leading another saddled horse south. He rode a big brown; the lead horse was a small buckskin. The man was thin and wore a long blue coat. "J. D. why would Randall take two horses off south?"

The shock that took over his face was worth more than a hundred gold dollars. He strode forward, removed his hat, and bent over the spyglass. "So they have turned up. I thought they might." He looked at me. "Is Randall the killer or is he removing the horses for the killer?"

"Or is this more of the bishop's subterfuge? We need to leave this camp and go down to ask him."

Perversely, J. D. simply returned to the cedar tree. He removed his knife and reached high to cut down the bag. "Coffee, flour, salt. Some jerky and beans. We might as well take it down to the Bishop's Storehouse to give to a needy widow." He carried the bag to his horse, and looped the bag over the saddle horn. "Now we'll look for blood." He walked to the cedar tree and cut a branch for a snow broom.

"But J. D., he's getting away with the horses."

"He'll come back. What can we discover by running after him? It would take us two hours to catch up to him, longer if he tries to run away."

"Oh." I still thought J. D. was just being stubborn as a doddering mule. I scanned the skirt of flat ground, forty feet wide and a hundred feet long. "I think this is perishing useless."

"Patience, Rachel. If we reconstruct the killing, we will know something about the mind of the killer. You'll see I'm right. The location of the blood may tell us what kind of man he is."

"Seems we could find a more direct route to knowing than moving all this snow."

"So we use our noggins." J. D. tapped his head as if he were talking to a baby. "From whence came the shot?" I wanted to tell him off for being so pompous and condescending, but instead I turned to look at the point where the pathway came up over the edge of the flat. J. D. walked to the rim and stepped down below the edge. "From here? So where were the deputies?"

I walked to the fire pit. "Here, you think?"

"I agree. They were probably trying to get a fire going when they were shot."

I frowned, picturing the deps huddled around a fire in a blizzard. I would have gone straight to bed, where I'd be dry and warm. "After getting it going, they'd still be cold." Either they were stupid or they had done something else.

J. D. pointed with his arm as if it were a gun. "If the deps were near their fire, I would rise over the rim and shoot them across the flat."

"But you said the shots were from closer than that." I remembered the hole in the stomach of one man, the large hole in the neck of the other. "You said the farthest shot was from about twelve feet away."

He stepped the distance from the rim to the fire pit. "More than nine yards. Two or three times as far as I estimated." He walked back to the fire pit and rubbed his crown. "We'll have to fire Alma's gun from several different distances to make sure, but I'd guess that at almost thirty feet the spread of pellets would make a larger wound."

"Another thing. A man who was a good shot wouldn't hit someone in the gut. Not from twenty feet. Certainly not from twelve feet."

"Even a capable shot might miss when firing on a man; 'tis more soul wrenching than firing on a deer or coyote. And he was in haste. He may have been so full of anger that he busted up from under the rim and ran across the flat to shoot them while he was running. That would make sense of the pattern of wounds. Both men are standing at the fire, the large one—"

"James."

"—turns at the noise and is shot in the stomach, the small one—"

"Sammy."

"—dives to one side, taking the pellets from the second shot in the neck." He watched me and waited, smiling as if he were a schoolmaster. Made me want to slap him.

"No. Sammy would have fired back with that long-barreled pistol." I walked to the rim and ran partway across. "Bam. The first shot." I shuffled through the snow ten more steps. "Bam. Sammy would have had at least five seconds to return fire."

"Maybe not as long when there was less snow. What if both

deputies were looking down at the fire and the killer crossed the flat before they heard him? He gets within ten feet, they hear him and turn. He shoots once, and the little deputy is diving to one side, and the killer steps forward and blasts him."

"Seems like they'd be more wary than that. Seems like they'd both be diving and maybe shooting soon as they heard any faint sound."

"Likely the little deputy was a contemptible shot as well." J. D. watched me, waiting, and I realized he was waiting for me to see something that he already saw.

Damn his condescending hide!

"The people in town heard only three shots. Neither dep shot. J. D., you're talking to me like I'm an infant. I don't have any pleasure when you treat me this way." His eyes widened in surprise. Then he pursed his mouth before going on with his speech. "The killer had to shoot from the only other hiding place." He turned toward the tree near the fire pit. "He could have sneaked up very close to the deps behind this tree."

"He steps out and the deps look straight into the double-barreled shot gun."

"He shoots one sitting across the fire. The other dives to one side after the shot."

"So the blood would have been here." I stood near the fire opposite the tree. "And maybe here." I stood a little farther away.

"I agree completely." He bent and began sweeping the snow with the branch he'd cut.

I glanced at the tent, the place where the deps had lived for several months. Lifting the flap open, I smelled rank and unwashed male, a quadruple dose of it. I wondered how much they earned for each man they brought in. I would need a pile of money or a wad of hatred before I'd sleep in that stinking tent.

"Intolerably heavy snow. Do you think you can find it in your heart to give me some aid?" He had cleared a crescent of snow from the edge of the fire pit.

"Looks like you need a better tool. We should have brought a shovel."

J. D. knelt and scooped the snow with his gloved hands. I lifted the flap again and, holding my breath, ducked inside. I knelt on the bedding, which was stiff with grime. No wonder they had stood outside to build a fire in the wet and cold. I jerked the heap of blankets out onto the snow. Two mice scurried in a circle inside, finally slipping under the tent wall. Propped back in a corner was another set of saddlebags, wet from where the tent canvas had acted as a wick to pull water in from the bank of snow. I dumped both pockets out on the hard-packed ground inside the tent: old jerky, rifle shells, a Bible, a letter addressed in a feminine hand, a small bag of gold coins, a shaving razor and bar of soap, mouse-eaten candles, extra shirts, and one pair of long underwear. Thinking that the dep was dead and couldn't use his gold, I slid the envelope and the bag into the pocket of my dress. I shoved the dep's belongings back into the saddlebag. Then I thought about how miserable an act it was to steal from a dead man.

Damn! I'm too much a saint to be a good sinner and too much a sinner to be a good saint.

I took the bag of gold out of my pocket and replaced it in the saddlebags. I rummaged through a duffle, which contained much of the same kinds of personal belongings. In the bottom of the bag was a piece of paper.

J. D. shouted. Holding the scrap of paper, I crawled out through the opening of the tent. He stood a couple of yards from the fire pit, pointing straight down at a patch of darkened snow and, underneath, a patch of black and icy ground, several feet across. Widening his circle slightly, he uncovered another patch, overlapping the first. "This is probably where the large deputy was shot, the one with the double wound." He shook his gloves, which were dark from wet snow.

I considered the distance between the tree and the doubled patch of blood. "The tree is still too far away for the hiding place, isn't it?"

He scratched his head in a circle on the crown. "Maybe I mistook the distance. All I had to go on was the spread of the shot."

I had never seen J. D. doubt his own judgment. I looked down at the paper, on which someone had penciled a grid of sixteen squares—a rough map of Centre. On the top right square was a large "X." To the side was written, "The chicken coop has an attic." The only other mark on the paper was the name "Joshua," written in the lower left corner, outside all the squares. I walked to the spyglass and aimed it toward the upper left of Centre. Behind the house on the northwest corner stood a small building; black and russet chickens foraged in the yard.

"Look at this, J. D." I handed him the note.

He looked down at the map and then walked to the spyglass, peering down on the town. "Brother Sainsbury lived there. He's one of the seven who are in prison."

"Proof certain that there is an informant."

"Or that the deputies made a map to remind themselves where someone hid when the alarm sounded. They might have sent one deputy down while the other watched."

"I thought they were always together. And doesn't this 'Joshua' look like a signature? Neither of the deps were named Joshua."

"I don't know anyone in Centre named Joshua."

"Someone new? A child perhaps?" I was sure I had heard the name but couldn't remember when.

"If someone from Centre made this map, he has apostatized. Damned his own soul for all eternity."

Then I remembered the letter and retrieved it from my pocket.

The return address was in Ohio. I slid the letter out of the envelope and spread it open.

Dear James,

I received your last after I had sent mine, so forgive what I said. I just imagined you with all those Mormonite girls whose morals are no better than they should be. I have thirty scholars. Some who can't read at all, some are ready for real learning. Several I am encouraging to go to college either here or back east. I pray every night for your safety and I admire your courage. You daily walk into the mouth of the viper for the cause of Christ. Some in my school have no desire to learn. They know they will be behind a plow all their lives and they can see no use in what I am trying to teach them.

We have a playhouse now. Last week I watched a traveling show with a magician, a man who performed Hamlet's speech, and a lady who wore a diamond tiara and sang beautifully. I wished you could have been here with me. But soon enough that will happen. I know you are doing this for us. With the money you've been earning and what I've saved, we can build our own house. We won't have to make do like most people just married.

I love you and think about you constantly. I want your arms around me again.
Love,
Cynthia

I folded the letter and returned it to the envelope. I had felt nervous reading something not intended for my eyes, but I also felt confused. James, hated by the Mormons of Centre, had been a good and worthy man in the eyes of this woman in Ohio. Now he was decomposing in Brother Apollo's cold underground storeroom. I felt myself getting weepy again and thrust the letter back into my pocket. Someone should write this woman, Cynthia. Otherwise she'd wonder for months, maybe years, what had happened to him.

J. D. walked back from the spyglass and stood in the middle of the flat, his hands on his hips. "Let's try this direction." He pointed toward the tent. "Maybe the second dep was shot diving out of the tent." J. D. had resorted to kicking the snow with his boots.

"This will take perishing forever." I bent over the pile of wood and lifted a log, heavy with clumps of wet snow—too unwieldy. I cast about on the flat for something else, and finally found a board leaning against the pile of wood, apparently carried up to burn. Using the board like a shovel, I helped J. D. scoop snow.

J. D. and I soon cleared a wide swath of ground toward the tent. When sweat dripped down my sides, I removed my coat and hat. The path we had already cleared reminded me of those I had made as a child playing fox and geese. I thought again about the three shots, one in the gut, one in the heart, one in the neck. I shook my head, telling myself that knowing where they stood when they were shot wouldn't help identify who pulled the trigger. Still, I kept my mouth shut and resumed work, pushing the snow away.

Not far from the tent door, we discovered more discolored snow and underneath, a great sheet of black, blood-soaked ground. J. D. stepped off the distance between the second pool of blood and the edge of the tree.

"Five steps. Fifteen feet instead of ten. See what we've learned about the killer?"

I walked to the black circle of ashes. "What?"

"We've confirmed that the killer was not impulsive. Just what we thought! An impulsive, angry man—Brother Cooper, for example—would have burst up over the rim and run across the flat. This man stopped, saw the situation, and took time to sneak up around behind the tree. I told you the blood would give a picture of his mind. He is someone like Brother Alma, able to hold and make use of his anger."

"So this man stepped from behind that tree, shot the dep by the fire, and shot the other as he came out of the tent, then reloaded and finished the first one off at close range."

"That's how I read the sign." I pointed down at the blood spot close to the tent. "But this blood is toward the fire. Hearing the shot, why didn't the man in the tent run away from the sound? He was moving toward the fire when he was killed. How many men would run at a man aiming a shotgun at him?"

"That idiot small dep might have."

"But he was shot in the neck diving to one side."

His hand circled on his bald spot. "I don't know."

"And something else still bothers me. The deps rode up here about two hours after the snow started. Every stick of wood must have been at least partly wet because of the snow. Remember? It was almost like beastly rain."

"Wouldn't have been so warm up here," J.D. said. "But still a heavy snow."

"Anyway, because the weather has been dry so long, they didn't think to cover their wood pile with a tarp. Even if they could split some wood to get dry kindling to build a fire, why do it? Why not just climb into bed inside the tent? As smelly as it is in there, it would still be better than standing in a blizzard and trying to start a fire with wet wood."

I squatted at the edge of the fire pit. At the outer edge I saw a small object under the snow, which I uncovered with my fingers—a shotgun shell. I laid the shell in the palm of my hand and presented it to J. D.

"So he shot from near the fire." J. D. held the shell in the palm of his hand. "Damned perplexing."

I dug through the snow and found another, also near the firepit.

"I still believe the killer shot the first dep in the gut, then shot the second in the neck. Then seeing that the first wasn't dead, he reloaded to shoot again." J. D. stood back from the fire pit, looking over the whole scene, his hat off, circling his fingers on his crown. "Anything else in the tent?"

"A letter from his fiancée." I removed it from my pocket and thrust it toward J. D. He scanned the sheet and handed it back to me. Clearly he thought it was not important evidence. Whether it was or not, it was something essential to James. I put it in the pocket of my coat.

"I guess even deps are loved by somebody." He strode toward his horse. Mounting, he looked out across the valley. "Mormonism thrives in this desert soil. Our system 'tis a very liberal government. Like the desert, it gives the people plenty of room to grow. The United States is not so liberal. This killing will fill the valley with federal deputies. I don't know if I'll ever have my dream—a time of quiet and plenty with my family all around me." I thought he would say something about me marrying Ezekiel so that I would be part of the family around him, but he turned back toward the tent. "I want to get this man who allowed his own self-ish temper to endanger the stability of this town. He has opened us to even more threat from the territorial government."

J. D. is the strangest mix of sentiment and mind, obedience to law and disobedience, I thought.

"Joshua fit the battle of Jericho. Sammy had sung that song when we first met him." Knowing that, what did I know? That the deps had been helped by an informant, one with knowledge of men's hiding places, knowledge possessed by every child in town?

The name Joshua might be significant. I'll ask Naomi or Sister Griggs who he might be.

CHAPTER 10

As I rode off the flat, I saw movement below on the flank of the mountain. Two people led their horses across a meadow and into some pines. I thought, just for an instant, that somehow, impossibly, Deputy Marshal Danby, who was in charge of all the deps in this area of Utah Territory, had already sent new men. Then I remembered that the bishop wasn't going to town to report the killings until that evening. There was no way on earth or in hell that Danby could know so soon.

"J. D." I pointed at the pines. "Two riders just rode into those trees."

He only grunted, but instead of following our tracks back toward town, he rode the gelding down the spine of the ridge toward the meadow and grove of pines. It proved to be easier traveling that way; the snow on top was lighter, the bulk of it blown into the canyon. The first problem came when gnarled fingers of oak brush blocked most ways off the end of the ridge. J. D. didn't hesitate; he just forced his horse through the brush and down the hill. I followed and the little mare took the slope like a warrior, spreading her forelegs and snorting.

"Snort all you want." I snorted along with her.

J. D. rested one hand on his rifle as we threaded our way through the pines just above the meadow. At the edge of the trees the two horses stood, loaded with green boughs. I reined in my horse and watched for the riders.

Suddenly a woman came out of the trees—Naomi, laughing. She threw a snowball at David. He lifted his hand to catch it and snow sprayed across his face. He made a ball of the small piece left in his hand and threw it back at her.

My mare whinnied and the two lovers froze, looking toward the pines, which still masked me and J. D. I kicked my horse forward.

"Naomi, I can't believe you didn't notice us until just now."

"We were busy—ah—gathering pine boughs." She grinned like a child caught in mischief.

"Gathering kisses."

She smiled and turned even redder. "Nothing wrong with kisses."

David moved closer and laid his arm across her shoulders. He pointed at the pine boughs. "They make the classroom smell like a forest."

"Does it help the children learn faster?" asked J. D.

"No."

"But 'twould make it more enjoyable, I suppose."

"David places some on his mother's grave. Evergreen." Naomi looked up at the mountain. "Did you find their camp?"

"Yes."

"Uncovering clues. The two detectives." David gave a wry smile.

I smiled back. "Famous lawman J. D. Rockwood tracks down and captures the evil killer with his quick-drawing sidekick, Rachel O'Brien."

J. D. said nothing, watching the two with his hawk eyes.

"Tell them what you saw." Naomi looked up into David's face.

"No, I don't think I should." He frowned and shrugged his shoulders.

"*I* will then." She walked toward J. D. and me. "David was at the church before the commotion happened."

"Yes. William said they were trying to speak with you about your habit of leaving God out of your lessons."

"This was afterward." David joined Naomi. "The alarm sounded and everyone scattered. A little later I heard shouting over by the bishop's house."

Well, you didn't require much persuading to tell your story.

"I ran toward the sound and found Susan, I mean Sister Peterson, you know, the bishop's new wife, hiding behind a cedar tree. She said that when the deps came in the front door, she went out the back. She didn't have time to run far, and the bishop barely got into his secret place before the deps burst in. While she was whispering all this to me, Brother Alma Wright came up to us as well as Brother Stewart. And finally Brother Apollo."

"I saw you."

When I spoke, he turned to me, working his lips, pensive. "Yes, we moved as close as we dared. Then I left. I could see no benefit from staying because I thought that there would almost certainly be violence and I wanted nothing to do with it."

"What made you think there would be violence?" J. D. cocked one leg across the cantle of his saddle.

"The way the men talked. Alma and, later, after the deps went to the cemetery, Brother Apollo. Sorry, Naomi, I must tell him everything. They talked about ending the trouble with the deputies right there. I did not approve, so I crept home like a coward. I was hiding in my bedroom when the shots rang out."

"What could you have done?"

"I could have done something."

"So did they have shotguns or rifles?"

I moved my horse closer. "You heard the shots from your bedroom?"

"One rifle." David spoke to J. D. and ignored me. "My father's. And a shotgun, Brother Apollo's. Alma talked about going after his."

"Brother Apollo or either of those two could have gone up the canyon after the deps," I said.

"Rachel, let him talk."

"They did go up the canyon. The whole bishopric."

I ignored J. D.'s warning. "You saw them from your bedroom? Which way does the window face?"

"I didn't see them. Maddy told me about them going up the canyon. She is a brilliant student, but her father often keeps her out of school. She confides in me. I was worried because the bishop, Brother Stewart, and Brother Apollo followed the deps into the canyon. Maddy's father went up too, but she said that his purpose was to try to persuade them to come back. She believes he was successful, but she was so worried about it that she told me. I'm worried about it as well but for different reasons. I believe that the bishop is capable of blaming Brother Alma or someone else for the murder. If only I hadn't gone home, I might have prevented this tragedy." He looked like he was going to weep.

I nearly laughed, he was so pious and self-righteous.

Naomi must have felt something similar. "David, stop it! You can't be responsible for everyone in town."

David turned away.

"Thanks. That's a clearer picture than we've had from anyone." J. D. lifted the reins and turned his horse away from the couple.

I thought there was much more that we could learn from David, but J. D. was clearly finished. I turned my horse to follow.

David walked forward and laid his hand against the cantle of my saddle. His arm brushed my leg and he drew back, clasping his hands as if praying. "Naomi told me you are considering marrying into the Principle. Please examine your feelings. If you feel reluctant, it must be that God doesn't want you to go forward with this kind of marriage."

"David and I don't believe in plural marriage for us."

"I don't believe in it for anybody," David said. "I don't believe it's God's will."

"Such heresy." I smiled.

"You think what I'm saying is a joke?"

I shook my head. "No. No joke. I smile so I don't weep because of the tangle that polygamy is."

"We haven't dared tell Papa our beliefs because he'd just have one more reason to forbid our marriage." Naomi put her arm around David's waist. "He hasn't always been so dogmatic, but since he took Sarah as a wife and was called to the bishopric, he's different. He wants me to have nothing to do with a man whose soul is damned by not believing in the Principle."

David gave Naomi a slow smile. "You would take a damned soul for a husband?"

"A person will not be damned for believing that polygamy is not inspired of God."

"A damned husband in the hand is worth two pious ones in the bush," I said. "Especially if every pious man has two or three other wives with him in the bush."

"You are very light minded, Rachel." Naomi took his arm. "David feels so strongly about working against polygamy that he left school before graduating." Then she let go his arm and grasped the edge of my skirt. "Living here is like being trapped in a net. David's job depends on the good will of every parent. He can never publicly say what he believes. Don't you tell even J. D."

David is the informant for sure and certain.

He frowned bitterly. "Can you imagine how it is to have a father who sneaks off to lie with other women?"

I looked toward the edge of the meadow where J. D. sat his horse, impatient for me to follow. Whatever his faults, he never sneaked about anything. His marital habits were clear to all his wives and to most of his children: he went to each wife in turn, except for my mother, who had wanted him more rarely.

"As if lying and adultery are moral," said Naomi. "A week ago, we were out walking late at night because we have no place to go to be together alone. We're always either with the children or working."

"Or in the pines."

"Open your ears instead of your mouth. That night, we saw my father walking toward us through the fields. I thought at first he was after me, somehow following my tracks in the frozen dirt. David wanted to leave me, so it would appear as if I had been walking by myself. But then Papa passed right by us, not twenty yards away. Just staring at the ground. We heard him mumbling to himself. 'Sin. It's a sin to obey and a sin to disobey.'"

"He's divided himself into two contradictory people," said David, "and he wants Naomi to do the same."

Brother Apollo's voice rang in my head, defending the Principle to the deputies.

Naomi gave a choked laugh. "Our fear that night was unnecessary because he was sneaking to his new wife's bed, not worrying about me." She couldn't go on because of her emotions. "I will not again feel guilty for holding David's hand or kissing him without my *papa's* permission."

David frowned. "Do you think he killed them?"

"No. He was at Sarah's. She said so."

"Sarah would lie for him," said Naomi.

J. D. had started toward Centre again. I kicked my horse. "I'll see you at the store tonight."

David kept pace with my horse. "You don't have to become a plural wife. You don't have to bind yourself to a ridiculous and evil marriage."

David's words sounded like those of the dead deputy, James. "Did you inform on your own brethren?"

He stopped short. "What makes you think I would do that?" His face closed like a vice.

I shook my head and trotted after J. D. He was the informer, I still believed, but he wasn't ready to be open about it.

David called after me: "The scripture says, 'Choose ye this day whom ye shall serve, God or mammon.'"

God or mammon. David seemed to think that betraying his brethren was serving God. But what he said certainly applied to me. It would be easy to marry Ezekiel in order to secure a prosperous future. I would be marrying not a solitary man, struggling to begin his life, but a man already established. Marriage in the Principle was not an adventure, not a romantic hazard, not the economic uncertainty Naomi faced.

Of course, Ezekiel would be only one-third mine. He would come to me and try to engender children on me, but not every night. Many nights I would sleep alone in my own bed, just as I had my whole life since coming to J. D.'s home. I would have my own space and the community of women I had already observed in J. D.'s household. I doubted it would be as congenial, because the sister wives were Sophia and Abigail—not generous, loving women like J. D.'s Mary and the gentle Rebecca. Of course, J. D. was still patriarch, but in some ways he was shut out of his family of women. A man like Ezekiel would be even less a lord; he possessed neither J. D.'s intellect nor his aggressive will.

I would also sacrifice the kind of marriage most girls dreamed about—a man and a woman alone in each other's arms. Naomi would think me deranged to even consider rejecting that dream. Perhaps I was. It was clear that neither Naomi nor I believed polygamy was divine.

I caught up to J. D. "So how many wives does Brigham Young possess in heaven?"

J. D. looked at me strangely. "Dozens of women have asked to be sealed to him. They will be his in heaven."

"I wish we lived on a different planet. One even farther from

Kolob." I knew J. D. believed Kolob was the sun of the planet on which God resided. "A planet where there is no polygamy."

"What's gotten into you?"

I shook my head. I didn't know myself. When I read Emmeline B. Wells and when I considered J. D.'s household, polygamy seemed a benevolent system, where everyone's rights and needs were met. A woman could be alone when she wanted to be and could have sisters and a husband to share. But most of the time polygamy seemed a seedbed of injustice, manipulation, and coercion.

"The clearest picture we have is that the bishopric walked up the canyon and killed the deps. If there were two shotguns firing, the patches of blood make sense. If there were two shooters the deps could be in the same place at the fire and the shotguns could be at two different distances."

His face looked as if he had aged ten years in a few seconds. "No. No. 'Twas a lone man."

"Now, who's using emotional evidence? You can't bear to think that it was a conspiracy of the bishopric. But it might have been. Maybe Alma *and* Brother Stewart *and* Brother Apollo fired on them. They all have ten gauges. Maybe the bishop stood right behind them, urging them on." My horse slacked its pace and I kicked it up again. "How can the Principle be good if it drives sensible men to murder?"

J. D. faced me. "'Tis a mistake to blame the foibles of mankind on God. The Principle did not commit this murder. The bishopric neither. I know it could not have been those good men. One forlorn, mistaken, angered man dropped the reins of his own soul."

I opened my mouth and shut it again before the wrong words came out, or the right ones at the wrong time.

He pointed his hand at me. "You are quick to judge the servants of God."

"You judge me now—as if you've placed me in a box, a child's coffin. You know I trust authority that is reasonable."

"Are you the final judge of what is reasonable?"

For me, I am. I knew if I pushed him further, he'd lose his temper.

In sullen silence, I followed him through the cemetery. My stomach hurt from hunger, which didn't help my temper. I resented J. D. lecturing me about what was a righteous judgment and what was not. And I was furious at David for talking about the integrity of choice but refusing to admit he was the informant.

I looked across the stones and wooden crosses of the cemetery. Because it was on slightly higher ground, it was another vantage point from which the deps could have kept their eyes on the activities of people in town. One grave had dry pine branches arranged around the stone—probably the resting place of David's mother.

"You don't have to bind yourself to a ridiculous and evil marriage." David's words rang in my head. He was such an idealist, a cowardly idealist, that he couldn't understand my decision wasn't simple.

My mother's monogamous first marriage had been filled with pain. My father, an Irish miner, was sweet when sober but had given me and my two siblings nothing but starvation and rags. Whenever he had found a thin vein of silver in his claim just outside of Osceola, Nevada, he drank it away. Finally, my mother tired of dragging him home by his heels. She left him, traveling east with her children to Utah Territory, where she had heard that Mormon patriarchs took compassion on orphans and widows. She showed up on the doorstep of J. D. Rockwood—the wealthiest man in the first Mormon town on her eastward path. He took in our bedraggled half-family, fed and clothed us, and Mary taught us the gospel. The baptismal water was hardly dry on my mother's back when J. D. made her his fifth wife. He sent me to school through the eighth grade, and gave me access to his library, even giving me money for books of my own. Best of all, he taught me cattle ranching, tracking, and hunting, just as if I was a son.

My brain felt like a boiling cauldron of confusion. I didn't have the mental strength to deal with polygamy and the confused killing and David's piety and Ezekiel's offer and J. D.'s new strangeness toward me. My self, the core of my being, seemed nothing more than crumbling sand since I had become a woman.

Sometimes when J. D. looked at me and I felt the distance between us, I wanted to do something drastic. Once, when I was fourteen, I hacked my hair shoulder length with a knife and bound my slight breasts with strips from a pillowcase. I thought it would make me like I was before, when he loved me. My mother found me and unwound the strip. She held me as I wailed, "I want to cut them off." She didn't say anything, even though I'm sure she was bewildered by her strange, hysterical child.

J. D. was a man among men, a father among fathers. He had four hundred head of cattle, three thousand sheep, and thirty horses; he was high in the councils of the Church and acted as justice of the peace for the southern end of Rush Lake Valley. At his table I ate beef instead of mutton, spread thick white butter on my biscuits instead of eating them dry, and spooned snowy sugar into my tea. J. D.'s children wore store-bought shoes; their shirts and waists were sewed from factory-woven cloth.

I decided that happiness depended more on human character than on society's trappings. I also decided that affluence was important to me. Proof was that I kept reminding myself of the prosperity I enjoyed in J. D.'s home.

Who would find joy in life, Naomi or I? Who would suffer bitter poverty?

CHAPTER 11

J. D. and I tied our horses in front of the bishop's house. He raised his fist to knock, but the door opened before his blow could fall. Susan stood in the doorway. She squinted at us in the bright light.

"Please come in." Her smile was still sweet as an angel's.

"Is the bishop home?" J. D. stepped inside.

"He left more than an hour ago. I don't know where he went." Her voice had an edge of anger. Then she took control of her face more firmly, smiling again.

"We'll be back."

We remounted our horses and rode to the front of the church, where J. D. reined in his horse. "He's not listening to his own best thoughts."

"You're going to rub yourself bald." J. D. jerked his hand down from circling his pate. "What do we do now?" I knew what *I* wanted to do—shake the bishop. I doubted he killed them, but he certainly was trying to keep us from pursuing the killer. After I shook him, I'd talk to every man-jack in Centre, look him in the eye. Even David's closing off had been clear evidence. Mormon farmers, innocent in nature, could not avoid giving some sign of real guilt. A violent act would be like a cancer inside the killer or killers. I also knew that if I tried to dictate what we should do, J. D. would balk.

"I was thinking that there's one man in town who is certainly capable of killing without anger, of building up a fire while the deps bled out, and of laying them out for burial. I knew him in Illinois. Brother Stephen Franklin. We were—" J. D. frowned.

"Good, J. D. I'm all for this plan." I discovered that my smile was *sleakit*.

"I'm grateful that you approve." He fairly growled at me. "Why are you being so strange with me, Rachel? You used to have good sense."

I used to have good sense? I'm the one being strange? I shook my head, thinking that maybe we both had lost our minds.

J. D. turned his horse. "We knew each other in a military capacity. He is one man in Centre who could kill without compunction. He is from the south of Liverpool along the border with Wales. His ancestors spent their lives in skirmishes with the Welsh."

After J. D. was converted in Liverpool, he had joined the Saints in Nauvoo. Rebecca, his second wife, had told me that he had fought in the bloody battles in Illinois. I had once asked him how many gentiles he had killed, and he sent me to bed without food, the worst punishment I could imagine.

As we passed through town, every person—man, woman, or child—stared at us, turning their heads like owls so we were always in sight.

"I can't think of a reason that the informant's identity would come out now," said J. D., "but if he's discovered, he might be in danger. If the man who killed the deps is someone like Brother Franklin, he might become angry enough at the informant to kill again." We knocked on a door at the south end of town. The house stood just above the delta of the stream that came from the canyon. A girl, apparently one of Brother Franklin's daughters, opened and without answering our query, pointed behind the house. As we walked around the corner, I noticed a cluster of ducks hanging from the rafters on the back porch. As we walked down the slope toward his barn to the south of his yard, we saw Brother Franklin working on a Jackson fork, a waist-high contraption with four-foot teeth, sharpened. I had operated a Jackson fork on J. D.'s spread to move hay into the loft of our barn, so I stepped forward to examine it. The tripping mechanism, which allowed the fork to drop its load of hay, was missing.

"The damn bolt is stubborn as a Welsh mule." He used a hammer and a huge nail to try to knock the old bolt loose.

"Brother Franklin are you thinking of harvesting snow?"

"No, child. It's been broken since late last fall, the last load of the season. The horse was tired and wanted to go in, a young horse that I was just training. He got the bit in his mouth and tried to jerk away from me. The rope broke and the fork stabbed into the ground within two feet of my son." Brother Franklin put the old tripping mechanism in place, secured by a new bolt. "I got rid of that horse."

Probably with a gun.

"I see that you've been hunting," said J. D. "Appears you've killed all the ducks on the whole marsh."

"No, the good Lord keeps sending more for me to harvest."

"You must be a good shot."

He paused in his work to glance at me. "With one shot I killed them."

"Bol—" Looking at his face I could not finish. Instead I said. "There are nine or ten birds there."

"Let me show you." He walked to a shed and opened one of the two wide doors. Inside, he removed a canvas from a two-wheeled cart, on which a narrow-barreled cannon was mounted. "Four-gauge shotgun. A toy, I admit. Almost useless here on the desert. I traded fifty pounds of flour for it from a Gentile on his way to the gold fields. He used it to harvest birds on Lake Ontario. I don't understand why he dragged it west. With this I can kill a whole flock of birds with one shot." He covered the gun again, and we walked back out to the barn.

He took the hammer and with a solid blow knocked the old pin out. He put oil on the pin, set the new tripping mechanism in place, and knocked the pin back in.

"Help me." He tied the end of the rope to a pulley on top of the fork, handed the coil to J. D., and climbed to the loft. When he appeared in the window high in the barn, J. D. threw the coiled end up to him. He threaded the end through the upper pulley. Soon the snake of rope dangled toward J. D. and me. I caught the end of the rope, and J. D. took it from me and threaded it through the lower pulley. Then he threw the rope back up to Brother Franklin, who put it through a second wheel of the top pulley. After Brother Franklin tossed the rope back down, J. D. pulled it with me until the Jackson fork rose. I tied the rope to a fence post, and the fork dangled ten feet off the ground. Brother Franklin pulled the smaller rope, and the fork swung straight down.

I looked up at the tines. "Perfect."

"Stephen, we have come—"

"I know why you've come. You wonder if I killed them. Only the good Lord knows how much I wanted them dead. The Book of Mormon says that God commanded the prophet Nephi to kill that evil priest Laban because the children of God needed to be preserved. The goal of every deputy is to destroy us as a people. A hundred times I prayed, 'Let me know, Lord. Should I kill them tonight?' I'll probably be judged evil at the bar of God for having murder in my heart. But I never received permission.

"It would have been so easy. I would have convinced any one of the polygamist men in town to let me take their place in their hidey-hole with my four-gauge. You would've had to scrape their bodies off the ground and walls to bury them. Like everyone else in this town, I was that angry after they invaded the bishop's house. I know I will suffer stripes at the bar of God because of my anger and hatred." He squatted in the window of the barn. "And there is something else you haven't thought about. If I had killed them, this would be a perfect time to put you out of the way."

I looked up at the fork dangling above my head. I was surprised that I felt no fear, but I did step to the side as he lowered it slowly.

He turned, and we heard his footsteps cross to the stairs. Soon he emerged from the barn.

I looked him in the eye. "Why would you want them dead if you're not a polygamist?"

"Polygamy is not for me, but in this country every man has the right to choose."

Every woman, too.

"Those two were destroying this town. No community can survive with half the men gone. I didn't kill them, and they deserved to die. If you still think I'm lying, talk to my wife, Amanda. She never lies. I'm not so pure."

J. D. and I both shook his hand. Then we remounted, leaving his yard.

"Not a man to have as your enemy," said J. D.

"No. For sure and certain, he is a dangerous man."

"Luckily his natural instincts are tempered by the fact that he is a Christian." J. D. sat his horse, studying the town that spread slightly above us. "After those deputies sent seven men to prison, only the cleverest men are left in town."

"Cleverest—or the best liars."

"He's not lying."

"You can't know that for sure. But," I held my hand up as if to block his words, "we don't have anything else to go on except what people say to us. Sometime one of them will slip and say something we can use."

"We also have facts to go on."

"Wonderful facts, revelatory facts: one or more people shot the deps at their camp. The shots came from closer than the edge of the rim. So either the shooter or shooters rushed across the flat as they shot or he or they hid behind the cedar tree near the fire. Then one or more people hauled them to Apollo Store during the storm. Their fire burned on to nearly the end of the storm. Brother Alma's gun has been used recently. Randall probably took the deps' horses and saddles away to the south. These are the facts that will solve the case?"

"I must see the bishop." J. D. turned his horse back toward the northern edge of town. He dismounted, tied his horse to the bar, and planted his butt on the middle porch step. Susan, who soon opened the door, looked down at his back with clear displeasure. I glanced at an upstairs window where I'd seen movement; the matriarch looked down on us. When I smiled at her, the curtain covered the window. Susan shut the door.

I waited with J. D., even though he was just a glowering lump, until the waiting seemed useless. Then, without saying naught to him, I stood and walked toward Sister Griggs's house.

She was trying to scrape the snow off her doorstep with a short, narrow stove shovel.

I held out my hand for the shovel. "Let me do that. You really need a proper tool."

"I would have finished before now but the snow was frozen too hard this morning." She turned to me. "I'm so glad you didn't leave me out of the excitement. Have you come to the conclusion that I pulled the trigger?" She grinned, her tiny face alive with the pleasure of her joke.

"You're about the only one who hasn't said you wanted them dead, so it must have been you." I touched her on the shoulder, but she pulled back from that contact. "Naomi says you know everything that happens in town."

"Except this time. This has me baffled." She lifted her shovel and turned toward her house. "I want you to tell me all you've learned today, but first I have a question for you." She turned back toward me and asked sternly, "Do you obey the Word of Wisdom?"

"So far as is humanly possible."

"Good. I was going to make some tea, but I won't now. I'm glad you're holding to your principles."

"What I mean is how far is humanly possible?"

"Well then, sweetie, we'll go inside and stimulate the carnal."

The whole house was warm. The small heating stove glowed red, and the room was so hot that I felt suffocated. The north wall, the one opposite the front door, had a single photograph hung on it. The man wore a black suit, too tight for him; the woman's dress was covered with white eyelet.

"That's me. Me and my husband Benjamin. Gone fifteen years."

Sister Griggs had once been tall and dark-haired. Now she was small and stoop shouldered. Her face was as translucent as a ghost—a being already halfway through the veil—Mary would have said.

"Best fifteen years of my life." She said it with a perfectly blank face. "I keep the picture to remind myself how happy I am to be shut of him."

I tried to laugh in a dainty manner but just snorted. "You should have become a polygamist; then you wouldn't have had to bear him alone."

"Then I would have had to bear him *and* his other wives. I'm too independent."

I heard the whistle of a kettle and Sister Griggs hobbled back to the kitchen. She soon returned, carrying a tray on which she had set a small pot and two cups, two small cookies. I smelled the wonderful aroma of tea.

"You should be ashamed of yourself, leading a young woman

like me astray." I held my cup while Sister Griggs filled it, and then I took one cookie from the tray. It was so tiny that it was a single mouthful.

"You've obviously already been led astray, young woman. Tea is against the Word of Wisdom for everybody but the English converts. I believe God has different expectations for each of us. After all, the scripture says, 'In my father's house are many mansions.' In some of them the pinched-faced Pharisees sit and watch each other to prevent sin. In others they have tea, biscuits, and a whacking good time."

I snorted again, nearly spilling my cup.

"Careful, girl. How can I explain a brown stain on my rug when the bishopric come to visit?" She settled herself, peering at me over the rim of my cup. "Now, tell me everything."

I described our visit to Sarah's cabin, our talks with Alma and Maddy and Brother Cooper, and our trip to the deps' camp. I told her my doubt that either Brother Franklin or Brother Cooper knew anything about the killing. "The killer was not a man who became wild or careless with anger." I told her about the bodies laid carefully out, the straight edge of the canvas, the killer's patience in sneaking up behind the tree instead of rushing across the flat.

"So the killer acted with more care than haste." I told her about the talk with David and Naomi and what he'd said about the bishop and the others rushing up the canyon. "So either the killer was cool and collected or there are three killers." I sipped my tea.

"You should be careful about listening to David. He is so bitter against polygamy that his words don't always come out straight. I wish I'd put my big coat on and stood in the cemetery watching who went up the canyon and who came out. Then we'd know whether David is telling the truth." She shook her head. "There is a wall between believers and non-believers concerning the Principle and both sides are daily adding stones to make it higher. Now it's so tall they can hardly shout at each other over it. On one side you have those who mistrust polygamy, on the other the murderer and those who wished the deputies were dead. Such hatred and division make it hard to get at the truth."

"J. D. says that polygamy is not the true cause of this murder."

"Maybe. Still I think the Principle was the seed bed." Sister Griggs took another sip of tea. "In a monogamous town, this killing would never have happened. When a father goes to a woman other than their mother, it destroys the confidence of the children and upsets his first wife. It destroys the natural balance between man and woman. When I sit up late at night, I see a few men going from the house of their first wife to another. The Principle is a state of unbalanced confusion. The natural state for man and woman is monogamy. Cleave unto one woman and none else. God reprimanded Solomon, didn't he, for having many wives?"

I swallowed and shifted uncomfortably in my seat.

Sister Griggs sighed and sipped her tea. "But you didn't come here to listen to a lecture on natural morality."

"I always have time for listening to good sense." I saw a crumb of a cookie on the tray. I licked my finger and brought the crumb to my mouth.

Sister Griggs smiled. "I can see that you are a bright child. Does your father see your true worth?"

I froze, feeling as if she had opened my chest and looked straight at my insides.

"J. D. is an unusual man," she continued. "But he also is blind to women. I don't think David Cooper is blind to women. He has a woman's heart." She leaned forward. "I was thinking that he and Randall have come by his hatred of polygamy naturally. Do you know their history?"

I shook my head.

"They are sons of Brother Cooper's first wife. When he took a new wife, a domineering woman, and then married their household maid for a third wife, their mother seemed to lose hope. Luckily, she died before seeing him take still two more, two young sisters whom he married in one ceremony. Five families is too many when Brother Cooper hasn't the ability to support one. He neglected David and Randall's mother, and they both blame him for her death, because she was undernourished when she died in childbirth. So David hates the Principle."

I remembered the grave and its shroud of drying pine.

Sister Griggs took another sip then licked a drop of tea off the edge of the cup with her catlike tongue. "But the story goes back even farther than that. David's mother's mother was a newly married woman in Blackpool, England, when she joined the Church. Her husband, a Brother Stringham, joined shortly after. They traveled together to Nauvoo. When the exodus came, he was down with pneumonia. He urged her to go west and stake out some property. He told her that all the good places would be taken by the time he could get better and go. So she took their capital. Something like $1,500. David's mother was born on the trek west. When mother and child came to Salt Lake, Alfred Wheeler, who was at that time important in the Church, took her under his wing. Started urging her to invest in some fine property he had. And it was good property, only three blocks from where the temple foundation was laid. She bought it from him, and then he persuaded her to marry him, convinced her that her husband would be a minnow in the kingdom of heaven, while he, Brother Wheeler, was a whale."

I snickered.

"Or some such nonsense. Finally she consented, and he put the farm she'd bought from him back in his name. He moved her off her property and set her up in his house with his second and third wives. The first wife got the house on the farm. Then the original husband, Brother Stringham, who had by then recovered from pneumonia, came west. He found his wife taken and his money gone. Swore he was going to kill Brother Wheeler. Brigham Young told Brother Wheeler to give back the wife. He gave up the woman but not the property. Brigham said that to prevent all their lives turning bitter he would call Brother and Sister Stringham on a mission to Centre in the desert.

"The wife told David Cooper, her grandson, this story, and he told it to me. Then add to that story the misery his own mother received from polygamy, having younger, more attractive wives move in on her, and you have a maternal tradition of anger concerning polygamy. So the inscription on his mother's grave may seem pious, but it has a private meaning."

"What inscription?"

"'Choose ye this day whom ye will serve.' He believes the Saints of the Church have a choice about polygamy. He's told me many times, 'We don't have to follow our leaders to hell.'"

"He used the same scripture just now when he told me to avoid marrying into polygamy."

Sister Griggs raised one eyebrow.

"He reverences the Church," I said, "but hates the Principle."

"Yes, just like you and me. Or I assume like you." She looked at me and waited, but I kept my face passive. "Or you'll make up your own mind, independent of silly old women." She shook her head. "But David, he's not at peace with himself."

"I don't *hate* polygamy. I'm just examining it critically." I told her about J. D.'s desire for me to marry Ezekiel and about my own indecision.

She watched me from her ferret-bright eyes, her mouth a flat line. "Enough talk about your eternal future. What about the crime?"

I grinned. "We know that the deputies were killed at their camp. No tracks showed, so they were killed early in the storm."

"The same time the bishopric was in the canyon. Did anyone see them come down?"

"Maddy might have. She's the one told David they went up."

"While you're asking that, ask Brother Stewart why he was returning Alma's shotgun early this morning when he went to have his horse shod."

I stared. "He did *what*?"

"Returned Alma's shotgun."

"You've been saving this, you evil woman. You could have told me about the shotgun this morning, but you didn't."

"I wondered if Brother Alma or Brother Stewart would come forward with it. I wanted to give them a chance." She smiled, a more *sleakit* smile than I had managed during the whole of my short life.

"What else are you holding back?"

"The bishop has returned from his journey into the south desert."

I turned and stared out the side window and saw a rider just entering town. "You are incorrigible."

She grinned and lifted her cup to me. I set mine down, rushed out the door, and trotted down the lane, arriving on the bishop's porch just as he came out of the barn. He was dressed in his work clothes with knee-high boots covered with particles of dirt. He nodded toward me and J. D. "Please forgive me. All day long I been shoveling the cow shit away from the manger down in my fields." I looked at his boots, which had only dirt on them.

J. D. stepped directly in front of him. "You have not been forthright with me. You and some others in the bishopric followed the deputies up the canyon after they left the cemetery. Were you at their camp when they were shot?"

The bishop frowned. "Who—?" He looked straight at J. D. Finally, he let his gaze drift elsewhere and he shrugged his shoulders. "After those unfortunate federal deputies have left my house, Brother Apollo, Brother Stewart, and Brother Alma, they come to me. When I see they have guns, I am grateful they never used them. I thought we escape serious trouble, but we do not. As you may guess, they were all crazy with anger. 'We must kill them,' Brother Alma said. 'We must put end to danger and insult.' He said we should run behind them deps and shoot them off their horses right then." He shook his head. "Of course, I try to talk them out of such a murderous plan. But they wouldn't listen, ya?

Brother Alma said he must get his shotgun. He run to the smithy like a crazy man and came back empty-handed. Then he grabbed Brother Stewart's gun from him, and Brother Apollo and him follow those deputies. Brother Stewart and I run after our brethren, calling for them to come back. Finally, we catch up and stop them. I describe what maybe would happen if the two deputies are dead. I told them it would ruin the town. We might be forced to abandon the principles of our religion. The four of us come back down. We each go to our homes. Soon after that I hear the shots. And so what I warn them will happen. Unless we find the miracle, this town will be ruined, ya? We will be so overrun with deputies that no one can obey Got."

J. D. shook his head. "How long were you talking in the canyon?"

"Maybe fifteen minutes, maybe half an hour."

"And all four of you came back down?"

"Yes. I want them all to come in my house with me. I want to watch them till I sure they don't change their minds and go after the deputies. But—"

J. D. stepped forward until he was nose to nose with the bishop. "You said you wanted Brother Apollo and the others to come in your house. They didn't?" Neither man looked away.

"No, J. D. They do not. We talk at the foot of the hill below my house. And then we agree that best thing is to go home to bed. I do that very thing. I saw Brother Apollo go—" The bishop frowned. "Well, he wasn't going toward the canyon, that I know for sure. Brother Alma and Brother Stewart both go toward their wives." He turned his back. "I still believe they are innocent. But perhaps that belief is wrong. Maybe I should have watched longer. I now believe that one of them went up and killed them deputies. Those two were hot with anger. Brother Stewart was not so angry. I'm most worried about Brother Alma. He is capable of this killing, ya?"

If Sister Griggs is right about when the shots occurred, and the bishop is telling the truth, then Brother Apollo didn't have time to talk and run and argue and return to town and run back up to shoot the deps. I shook my head, not believing that the tangle of evidence would ever give us a clear picture.

"You told them you wanted the deputies dead," said J. D. "Maybe one of them took your words as instruction."

"I think of this. That is why—"

I lifted my hand toward the bishop. "Why was Brother Stewart returning Alma's gun early this morning."

The bishop stared at me, then his face turned bright red—from anger or embarrassment I couldn't tell because he held his features immobile. "We might just as easy ask why he bring it back in daylight, in open manner, ya?"

"Who told you this?" J. D. asked me.

"Sister Griggs."

"She will make guilt where no guilt is, ya?"

J.D. stared hard at him. "You heard the shots. Why did you immediately believe that the deputies were dead?"

The bishop looked at his hands. "I know what you are saying to me. You think I knew them deputies were dead because I have something to do with the killing. This is not true. When I hear the shots, I know that either one of my brothers is dead or is a killer. Neither should make me happy. I stood at my window and watch the mouth of the canyon, but no one come down."

He thrust his hands into his pockets. "Perhaps you will say I should have watch longer because then I would know who come down the canyon with the deputies' bodies. But I didn't want to know, so I went to bed quicker than I should have. Maybe I was a coward."

"Why didn't you tell me all this before?"

"I want you to leave our town. You have no official responsibility, but people think you do." He laid his hand on J. D.'s shoulder.

"This is war, not just a crime done by some criminal. Those deps should die, ya? The federal government has provoked us beyond what we can endure. Some say we should abandon Utah Territory and move again—to Mexico or Canada. But this is my home. I wonder if we have grown big enough to fight the United States." He chuckled. "Think of that. We might make our own new nation. The southern rebels lost, but we are far away and in our own land. I believe we did all right when Johnston's army come decades ago and try to subdue us. I not here in America then, but I hear what happen."

"'Tis an illusion to think we could stand against the whole United States Army."

J. D. had told me stories about riding with Captain Lot Smith. In 1857, just before the outbreak of the Civil War, General Albert Sidney Johnston was sent to bring Utah Territory into line. The Utah militia had made the lives of the soldiers miserable—stealing their livestock by night, burning their supply trains, laying dozens of campfires on the cliffs above the marching army. They danced around the fires one by one, shouting out songs, making a couple of dozen men appear to be a multitudinous foe.

"I still think with Got on our side, maybe we fight the gentiles. They that be with us are more than those that be against us. Maybe we drive them away, never have them to rule over us." The bishop smiled grimly, and turned away from J. D. "But my will is not my leaders', ya? I do not blame you for trying to discover this killer. But my people of Centre Ward are frightened. I must pull them together, to heal this town. For this reason I have called a fast. We begin tonight and continue until tomorrow afternoon when we have testimony meeting. Will you join with us in a fast?"

"Of course, but I will not stop looking for the killer."

The bishop shrugged his shoulders. "And I will not stop

pursuing what I think is right to do. But now I need to change my clothing and meet the train.

"What was Randall doing, leading two horses south?"

The bishop turned quick toward me, looking like an angry bear. "Young sister, you will have to ask him."

"Bishop, you know as well as he does what he was doing."

"Sister, will you fast with us?"

Thoughts of stew and fresh bread and lying bishops tangled in my head. Finally I nodded. *Dammit to hell*, I said in my heart. I had starved all day and now I'd given my word to not eat for another day. *Fool. Triple fool!* I called myself.

From the bishop's house we rode south along the lane. "We need Brother Stewart's version. We need to talk and talk until we find a flaw in someone's story."

J. D. nodded grimly.

Sister Griggs stood on the porch of the church. "J. D., Rachel, there's something else I want to tell you."

J. D. rode on but I stopped. "What other secrets have you kept from us?"

Sister Griggs watched J. D.'s back. "I'll wait."

"J. D., she wants to tell you also."

J. D. rubbed his face hard with his palms. Finally, he turned his horse and rode back. His hand had been perfectly even, handling his horse. I admired that no matter how frustrated he was he never took it out on a horse.

But he has lost his temper with me. Am I less than a horse in his eyes?

I had to admit that even his occasional thunder burst of anger was clear and straightforward. He was not like the deps and not like the bishop who both used deceit to get what they wanted. Both thought they knew best and would never back down as they forced others to obey.

He reined in his horse next to the white picket fence and glared down at Sister Griggs. "Do you know who killed those deps?"

Sister Griggs frowned back. "Young man, if I knew that, do you really think I'd hesitate for a minute to tell you?"

"You said you wanted to tell us something else."

"I'm curious as to why Brother Cooper drove a wagon back to Apollo Store before he started off on his shipping route and why the bishop and Brother Apollo rode with him."

"What?" said J. D. Then he shook his head and turned his horse away.

"Any more? Or are you going to parcel out bits of information until the Millennium?"

Sister Griggs looked sharply at me. "That's all."

I turned my horse and trotted to catch J. D. "Well?"

"I can't fathom what the bishop's up to. I worry that he's guilty of this terrible sin." His face was haggard, so I didn't pressure him further.

We rode past Sarah Stewart's cabin and up to a wooden house, which, like the bishop's, was large as a barn. The house had once been painted white. From the front fence, made from cedar posts and poles, we could see Brother Stewart in back hammering on a chicken coop. Two small children played with the chickens.

J. D. and I dismounted, tying our horses to the pole fence. As we entered the yard, Brother Stewart said to one of the children, "Hand me a nail." A very small child in a smock handed him up a square, rusted nail. It had probably been used several times before. "You will have no luck here, J. D. I'm not your man."

J. D. opened his mouth, but Brother Stewart rushed on.

"Last night I took up my rifle and—"

I leaned forward. "You said rifle not shotgun."

"A Winchester repeating rifle." He held and hit another nail. "As I was saying, I took up my rifle and ran to the church, ready to kill a fellow human. After I returned, I was awake all night thinking and praying about what I'd done. What if I had seen a deputy and killed him? I would be guilty of murder instead of some other poor brother. So this morning I made up my mind to stop obeying the Principle."

"But you have three wives," said J. D.

"I've told them I will help them financially but no longer be their husband. I'll set them up a way of employing themselves and—" He hit the nail so hard that the board broke. "Eliza has a loom. I'm going to send her to Hamblin to live with her sister. Samantha lives down the street and has fifty hens and ten sows. My first wife lives here and we have almost nothing. The twelfth Article of Faith says that we believe in obeying the law of the land and I aim to obey that law. We've fallen from the truth when we have laws which contradict each other."

"I'm sorry for your wives. They will lose a good husband."

Brother Stewart looked up at him. "Be sorry for those be-nighted souls who feel like they'd rather wither in prison than give up an Old Testament practice." He smiled. "But you didn't come to hear me preach heresy. You came looking for their killers. Last week I could have done it. Those two asinine deputies wouldn't leave me alone. Now I've almost made my peace with myself. You see, my hatred is proof to me that polygamy is no longer of God. What else but evil could stir up such contention between factions of God's children?"

He looked down at the small boy. "Nail." The boy, serious about the importance of his job, handed his father another bent nail. Brother Stewart tried to hammer it in, but it just bent double. The girl ran after the chickens, scattering them across the yard. "You're going to stop them laying."

"We came to ask," I said, "about Brother Alma's shotgun that you returned this morning."

"Did you go up the canyon with Bishop Peterson?" J. D.'s voice was angry. "Did you carry Alma's gun up with you as you went after the deps?"

Brother Stewart's fingers turned white on the hammer.

I leaned toward my father. "J. D., watch him." I imagined him swinging the hammer down on J. D.'s skull.

Then I looked up at Brother Stewart's face. His eyes were wide, maybe with fear. His lips trembled. "I followed up the canyon with the bishop, with Alma and Brother Apollo. But by then I'd cooled off, frightened at my own anger. I was so relieved when we all came back down. But one of us doubled back up, I guess."

I shook my head. The bishop had said the same—that he was relieved when they turned back, but that someone must have gone back up. *Perishing impossible.* Bishop was at home when the shots sounded, Brother Apollo was at Sarah's, Brother Stewart said he didn't go back up the canyon. That left Alma.

"What about the shotgun?"

"I found the gun leaning against my front door this morning. When I opened the door, it fell inside, pointing right toward me. I thought it would go off when it hit the floor, but it wasn't loaded."

He turned his back to J. D.

"Daddy," said the child, holding up a nail. "Daddy." Finally Brother Stewart turned his face to us, his eyes red. "I am not your man."

Both J. D. and I mounted and rode away.

"A man of sensitivity and conviction."

"The wrong convictions. The devil's way is broad and God's is narrow."

I stared at J. D. "Did you listen to him? Did you hear anything he said?"

"Yes, I did. And I—I think he could have chosen another way than casting off his wives."

I breathed and breathed without saying anything. Anything that came out of my churning brain would only send J. D. into anger as well.

"I also think that this talking to people is useless. We are not getting closer to the killer, we're only uncovering their private sorrows. Useless, useless."

I stared at his back. We had just learned essential information about the nature of life in Centre, in this community. We had laid our finger on its warp and weave. Why did he consider that useless?

I wondered if it frightened him, the unraveling of his sure universe. But he had passed through Nauvoo when everything collapsed, when the perfect town and social system designed by Joseph Smith had become a battleground and the Saints were forced to flee across the Mississippi River. He had starved with the others in Winter Quarters, where children and the weak died. Why did he back down when someone showed the evil that polygamy could be when the participants were bad? I could hardly wrap my mind around his stubbornness and contradictions.

We found Brother Alma working in the smithy, heating a wagon wheel and hitting it with a heavy hammer. "You'll have to talk to the bishop. I will tell you no story."

"Alma," said J. D., but Alma beat so rapidly on the wheel that I covered my ears from the ringing.

"Go. Leave me be!"

J. D. slumped in his saddle as we left the smithy and rode for what seemed like the hundredth time along the main street in town. We dropped down into the fields, cutting across toward Apollo Store. I had never seen him so unhappy. We passed through a cluster of cattle that nibbled at the tops of some tall weeds that poked up through the snow. The sun was resting on the western mountain, and I thought again that I hadn't eaten all day. We heard the long whistle of the train.

"Hopefully the bishop got there in time."

"Hopefully he has repented of his deviousness."

When we came to the store, Brother Apollo's cow bellowed repeatedly, as if she hadn't yet been milked. We took our horses to the barn, unsaddled them, and removed their bridles. J. D. turned them into a pen while I scooped oats with a bucket and poured the grain into the feed troughs.

Sister Apollo sat in the dining room, staring at the top of the table.

J. D. sat across from her. "Where is William? I have several more questions to ask him about what he did with the bishop last night. And I want to know what he and Brother Cooper have been doing today."

Sister Apollo's voice was flat. "He's gone to the train."

"The train? He's going with the bishop?"

"You should ask *him* what he's doing. "Once I was in his confidence."

J. D. put one hand over hers.

She removed her hand from under his. "J. D., I don't know any more what's right and what's wrong."

He bent toward her, talking softly and earnestly. "He's not doing righteously in this decision to invent a robbery. He's acting dishonorably and foolishly."

Crossing to the kitchen, I saw that the butter churn stood untended. I lifted the handle and found it moved easily: the butter was unfinished. I looked at the bread box. I seemed to smell the bread through the wood, and I had second thoughts about fasting with the people of Centre.

I need all my mental and physical capacity.

I removed a loaf of bread, walked to the table, and sliced it there. Then, wanting butter and milk, I left the dining room and walked out into the store, where I lit a lantern. Moving into the cold room, I collected a square of butter and a crock of milk. Standing with the milk in my hand, I realized what the bishop and Brother Apollo might have been trying to accomplish with their trip to the south.

"Stupid. I'm so damn thickheaded."

Holding the lantern high, I saw the bare floor but no bloody bodies.

I rushed back into the dining room. "J. D.! The deps are missing." I shook my head. "I mean, the corpses are gone."

"What?" J. D. followed me back into the cold room.

He looked inside and then slammed the door, striding back to the dining room. He put his hands flat on the table and leaned toward Sister Apollo. "Did William and the bishop move the corpses again?"

"They asked me not to tell you." She sat hunched over, staring at the table. "The bishopric has designed a subterfuge."

"A further subterfuge?" J. D.'s voice shook with anger. "Beyond the lie that the deps held up this store?"

"J. D., let her speak."

He sat down and clasped his hands, resting them on the table as if he were praying.

"We have a difficulty here. He made me promise not to tell you where he and the bishop took the bodies. I will tell you that earlier today Randall took two horses over the mountain."

"We saw him from the deps' camp," I told her.

"So what's he going to do with them?"

"I believe that he's taking them to Skull Valley where he will set them free. I believe he is going to go close enough to the Gosiute encampment that the deps' horses will find their way into the Gosiute herds."

"Are they going to lay the bodies out on the open? Will they say that the Gosiutes killed them with a ten-gauge shotgun?"

"No. They took picks and shovels."

"They buried them in frozen ground?" I said.

J. D.'s shoulders slumped. "Only the top foot is frozen. Once they broke through that it would be easier to dig." He walked out into the store and I heard him climb the stairs.

I looked toward the kitchen, where I had left the sliced bread. I put it away in the bread box and followed J. D., muttering. "I get the message, Lord. I will fast with them." By the time I was up the stairs, J. D. was already a fourth of the way to Centre. I couldn't imagine what he planned to do.

I walked back down into the darkening store. I lit the lantern so I could examine Brother Apollo's stock of shotgun shells. They were identical to the ones I found at the deps' camp. But that discovery, like most of the others J. D. and I had made, proved little, especially not that Brother Apollo had murdered. The killer or killers were obviously from town and would have had no other place to purchase shells than at Apollo Store.

A half an hour later J. D. returned. I had pulled a chair up next to the potbellied stove in the south room of the store and settled down with a book. He leaned against the glass case and wiped one hand down across his face. "The bishop is a good man, but he's so intent on covering the past that he can't see the future."

"You still talk as if he is innocent of any specific knowledge of the killing." I shook my head. "How can you think that these are the actions of an innocent man?"

"Who can say?" J. D. moved away from the counter. "Maybe he's innocent and this is the wisest course. I did talk to Brother Cooper. He told me that he and the bishop helped Brother Apollo load the bodies in the wagon. Then they buried them and their saddles somewhere between here and Rockwood. With the horses gone, who from the outside will question the story that the deps robbed Apollo store and fled? Brother Cooper seemed confident that they were doing the best thing." He stood and began pacing the floor. "I also talked to Alma briefly. He said he knew it looked suspicious, Brother Stewart returning the gun this morning, but he asked me the same question the bishop asked you and me. 'If Brother Stewart was the killer, why would he be so open about returning the weapon?'"

He turned and walked back into the living quarters.

Lying in bed that night, I thought about the three blotches of blood under the snow. I pictured someone, possibly the bishop, stepping from behind the tree, his shotgun blasting. In the morning the whole town would gather in the church; the building would be tense with their anger and fear. If J. D. and I discovered the identity of the killer before then and stood, naming him, would we simply be giving the town a scapegoat upon which they could heap their guilt? As I slept my dreams were of giant loaves of bread, big as a house. I tunneled inside a loaf, eating my fill.

CHAPTER 13

The next morning I woke in my square box of a room, nothing inside but a bed, a chair, and a wardrobe. At first I could not place myself, but then I remembered I was in Apollo Store, ten feet underground. It could have been my own coffin but more spacious. And most coffins were not furnished. Only a faint light came through the narrow window high on the side of the wall, so I knew it was still early.

I rolled out of bed and pulled on my dress. The bishop would return on the morning train, which Naomi said came through at about eight. Had he been forthright with the sheriff?

Not bloody likely.

I bent to lace my boots and left without brushing my hair.

J. D. sat in the dining room. He had spread brown wrapping paper across the table and had drawn a map that included Centre and the mountain. He had penciled lines between Apollo Store, Sarah's house, the bishop's, the cemetery, and the deputies' camp. He had written times and names along the lines, his tiny print as regular as a colony of ants marching across the paper.

I watched him for a while but he was too intent to do more than glance at me and say, "It can't be any of them."

J. D. is too damned stiff-necked to admit his friends looked him in the face and lied.

It was triple useless to keep trying to deduce who the killer was from the physical evidence, because the evidence could apply to almost anyone in town. "Stop wasting our time on confusing sketches. Talk to people. They are in such uncertain states that their faces will show their very souls."

"Dammit, Rachel, help me or leave me be." He looked at me with red-faced anger. Maybe that was progress, a way of making him see me, but it didn't feel like it. I felt that I was walking on ice that would crack at any moment.

I stomped into the kitchen, willing to break my fast if I could get anyone to backslide with me, but to my sorrow, there was no scent of breakfast. Sister Apollo bustled about the store, sweeping—as taciturn as J. D., who was as close-mouthed, turned-in, and grumpy as a damn hibernating bear.

I tried to read—a book of poems by Elizabeth Barrett Browning—but my stomach ached so much that the words seemed to shift on the page. Finally, I went up and sat in the loft of the barn, watching for the train, wondering where Randall was, and whether he'd been successful at getting the deputies' horses to stay in Skull Valley. Unlike the previous day, when the sky was blue and sunlit, the morning had dawned overcast. The next storm was coming faster than anyone had thought. Shivering as I sat, I finally decided to head back into the store. Just then I heard the long howl of the train whistle.

I ran down to tell J. D., who said, "Just a minute," then remained working on his map as if he could force a revelation out of it.

"Give it up, J. D." He glared at me, just as angry as before. "Let me help you. I can't help you if you won't listen to anything I have to say."

He looked up from his maps and his was a stranger's face. "I've had forty and more years experience with this kind of business and you've had a few weeks. Also it requires logic and careful calculation more fit to a man than a woman. Our brains are different."

"You just as well stab me in the heart as say that."

"'Tis true and I must say it. You must become more like a woman."

"Why did you train me as a boy to hunt and shoot and follow tracks? It's my inexperience that I don't do those as well as you, not because I'm a woman."

He shook his head. "I taught you those things because you were so eager to learn them. I fear I've made a mistake."

I turned on my heel, walked back up the stairs to the barn, and stood again in the loft. My hands and legs were shaking. I was so furious that I could hardly keep myself from jumping from the loft window, just to distract myself from the pain. I hit the barn wall once, as hard as I could, and it brought tears to my eyes. One breath, a second, a third—ten.

I felt that a mortal disease lay in my bones. I was damn hungry, an ache in my gut shared with everyone in Centre who was fasting, but that was not the real source of my unhappiness. J. D. seemed like a fool to me, poring over his maps and his time schedules. How could I be angry with the best man on God's earth? I don't know how to describe what it felt like: conscious sin, wrongness, that my own flesh was traitorous. At the same time I knew in my bones that I was right and he was wrong, not just about how best to solve the crime, but about me. He thought that my womanhood meant that God limited me, made me suitable for nothing but following and bearing children, being a helpmate.

You will not beat me this way, J. D. I will prove myself to you.

And I couldn't do it by running away. I turned to climb down the ladder, when I saw the bishop and Brother Apollo, both on foot, cut straight across the flat toward Centre, instead of following the road which curved to Apollo Store.

I rushed to catch both horses. I had our saddles on and cinched tight before J. D. finally tore himself away from his useless cartography. He stood in the barn doorway.

"I was very sharp with you." Then he saw I had both horses ready. "Where are you going?"

"We're going. The bishop and Brother Apollo. They're already in Centre. They gave us a wide berth."

J.D. nodded. "Either they're all lying or I'm wrong in all my conclusions from the basic physical evidence."

My body flooded with relief. He was talking to me again, despite my fury and stubbornness, and despite his own. "Everyone in town is lying?"

"The bishopric. They all say that they were together from the time they followed the deputies up the canyon to the time they gave up and came back down. Say that took them a minimum of half an hour. The shots came an hour after the deps left the cemetery to ride back to their camp. It took us an hour to ride up there, and we were moving as fast as we could. So they were shot close to the time they arrived."

"We had the snow to contend with."

"But it didn't slow us that much after we left the canyon floor. It's impossible. By the time the bishopric went up and came back down, there wasn't enough time left for one of them to sneak back up and kill the deputies."

"So someone else went up." A smile came to my face.

"What are you grinning about? Dammit, Rachel, take what I'm saying seriously."

I couldn't tell him how good it felt to be talking again, working like left and right feet. "Go on, J. D. What were you going to say?"

"The bishopric were in the canyon. They would have seen anybody else going up."

"Unless the person rode up the ridge, the way we came down. Or someone could have gone ahead of the bishopric."

Then he shut down, beyond listening. His mouth drawn into a profound frown, he swung onto his horse and trotted toward

Centre. The slump of his usually proud shoulders showed me what a disappointment it was to discover that his friends of decades were dishonorable. We crossed town without speaking and walked our horses up the incline to the bishop's house. J. D. banged on the door, ready to confront whoever opened. Finally Susan answered, immediately frowning. She stood with the door against her shoulder, holding it partway shut.

"Where is he?" J. D.'s voice shook with anger.

Susan smiled back at him, her blue eyes wide, innocent, unwavering, and cold. I glanced toward the mountain, where smoke rose from just below the mitten of trees. The column boiled up, charcoal black at the base, lightening to white as it spread against the peak.

"Look. He's burning the deps' things."

J. D. jerked around and stared at the smoke.

Susan smiled slightly. "He's burning what will burn and he will bury the rest." She tipped her face up toward J. D.'s. "You tried to stop him, but he's too smart for you."

Then J. D. turned from the door, to me. "'Tis a shame, but your suspicion may be proved right. Would an innocent man work so to cover his tracks?"

"You're baiting me." Susan was quicker of mind than Sarah Stewart, the last woman J. D. had tried this trick on.

J. D. whirled to face her. "Your husband is acting like a guilty man."

"He couldn't have killed the deps. I *know* he couldn't have."

"I said naught about harm to the deps. Why are these the first words to your mouth?"

Susan looked again at the mountain and the smoke. Her smooth face clouded. "I'm in the middle of baking, so I can't talk to you now." She turned to go inside but then stopped. "You have no power to harm him." Her voice broke; clearly she was not sure.

"Come in. I need to check the bread." We followed her through a swinging door into the kitchen.

Unlike the hallway, which had been chilly, the kitchen was filled with oven-warmed air and the aroma of baking bread. Saliva sprang painfully into my mouth. I noticed again that the kitchen was enormous, wide as the whole house. The double Monarch range was nearly as large as the entire kitchen in my childhood shack in Nevada. Rows of blue-ware pots hung on the wall.

Susan gloved herself in quilted mittens, and opening the oven door, removed the bread. She deftly turned out each loaf onto the wooden table then stacked the bread pans, each inside the other, on the corner of the huge oak table. "Twelve loaves every day. I'm the bread baker for the household."

The loaves were brown and lovely. I nearly ripped the newest one out of her hand. I could break it in half and bury my face in it, just like in my dream. "*Effernin colls.*"

"Rachel! What did you say?"

"Just quoting Brother Apollo. I forgot that I committed myself in my heart to this—this perishing fast." I watched Susan dip her fingers into a crock of butter and swipe the top of the loaves. The sweet fat made the crust glisten. Then instead of licking her fingers clean, she wiped them on a cloth. Her will was as inflexible as an angel's; she was an unnatural woman.

If I knock her off her chair and grab a loaf, J. D. will stop to help her up and I can eat half the loaf before anyone can catch me.

"How can you cook when you're hungry?"

"With discipline I don't feel the hunger." She put her hand in the small of her back then stretched and sat. "But I admit that I'm still tired from night before last. I don't recover easily from a sleepless night."

"Sleepless?" J. D. focused on her.

"Because of the deps. Every member of this household knows

173

what to do when the deps come. One of them forced his way in the front door, and I left by the back. I didn't see the other dep until I was already outside. There he was—sitting his horse in back of the house. I nearly bumped into him. The storm was swirling around, but all he did was lift his hat and smile at me. He was the larger of the two deps."

"Then you—" J. D. leaned toward her.

"—ran across to the tree and hid behind it, just like I already told you." She rested her fingertips on the edge of the table. "Brother Alma Wright and Brother Stewart were there, behind the building. Then Brother Apollo came last. He and Alma argued. 'Of course we don't want to shoot them,' Brother Apollo said. 'If we do nothing and they find nothing, then everyone can go back to bed. We just want to be ready if something goes awry.'"

"David Cooper?"

"Oh, yes, I forgot, he was there for just a little while."

I opened my mouth, but J. D. moved quickly to lay his hand on my arm. "Every man had a gun?"

"Just Brother Cooper. Oh, and Brother Apollo. After the deps came out of the house and rode up to the cemetery, the brethren started talking about going after the deps. Brother Alma went to get his shotgun but came back quickly and said that it was gone."

"Gone?"

"Yes."

J. D. glanced at me then turned back to Susan. Her story, so far, matched David's.

"Did you notice whether the guns were shotguns?"

She frowned. "I guess I don't see why it's important."

"The deps were killed with a shotgun," I said.

"I don't really know how to tell them apart."

"Then?"

"Then Brother Cooper left—walked in the direction of his home.

Alma asked to borrow his gun. Then the bishop came out and sent me inside. That's all."

I found that my eyes kept drifting back to the sweet, steaming bread. "David said that the whole bishopric went up the canyon—them and Alma."

"And the bishop confirmed it."

"Yes. They went up the canyon, but that was after David left, so how did he know?"

"He said Maddy told him."

Susan turned her head slowly. "David Cooper is a wavering apostate. His soul was lost at that eastern school he went to." She frowned. "I'm concerned that he will lead the children astray." Replacing the butter in the icebox, she stood a moment with her hand on the door. "The bishop said he went up with the other men to talk them out of going. He was frightened one of them would kill the deps. Luckily, he succeeded in bringing them back with him. He told me they had all gone home to bed."

"The bishop and the others went up the canyon, and then the deps were shot."

"I—" Susan paused, frowning. "The shots came much later. The bishop was with me then." Her eyes widened and her face turned soft and blank. I couldn't tell whether she was lying or hiding something.

"With you? What do you mean, *with* you?" J. D.'s hand was up, circling his crown.

"I mean just what I said." She stood and turned her back to us.

"I don't—"

I stared at J. D. I wondered how he could be so smart about some things and so dense about others. "She's saying what Sarah wouldn't."

"I want to have a child. I am *nothing* in this household until I have a child. A male child."

175

"Oh." J. D. turned away and looked at the pans hung on the wall. "Please forgive my indelicacy."

But I knew Susan was lying about the bishop bedding her. I took a breath.

"You're saying that after the uproar, the bishop was calm enough to—"

"Rachel!" J. D.'s eyes were wide. "Is there nothing you won't speak about?"

Susan spread her hands before her as if to stop my words. "Yes. Please, don't say more. I said he was here in this house when the shots were fired." She walked toward me. "He was here with *me*. Right in this house. He went up the canyon briefly, and when he came back he said that he had succeeded in preventing any violence. 'I just hope they all went home to bed,' he told me. He watched the canyon from the window for a while. He was with me when we heard the shots. I don't know what the others did. They may have gone back up the canyon by a route he couldn't see. I don't know. I only know about him."

Tears streamed down her face. "When the shots came, he ran to the window and opened it. The wind blew snow inside on my quilt. He said, 'Oh, no, we're ruined. Ruined.' Then he left, running outside without his coat. Soon he came back."

J. D. lifted one hand as if he would pat Susan on the arm to comfort her. She backed away from him.

"How long had he been with you when the shots were fired?" I asked.

She was no longer in control, and the words gushed out. "I don't know. Five minutes or so from when he first came in. Ten minutes, maybe. You are wrong to accuse him. The bishop is a good man. Better than me or you or anybody. Your questions are those that only an apostate would ask." She walked to the swinging door, holding it open for us. "So, you see, none of us got much sleep. Now please leave our home."

We waited on the bishop's porch for about an hour. I could smell the cooling bread through the barrier of two walls, or maybe I just imagined the aroma. Finally, I saw the bishop and Brother Apollo ride down from the canyon and pass through the cemetery. At the front gate of the bishop's house, Brother Apollo continued on toward his store. He didn't even glance at us. The bishop rode to his barn.

J. D. walked forward to meet him; I followed. When the bishop dismounted, J. D. caught his arm and turned him around. "You must talk to me."

"Those deputies are gone. We have no obligation to say where."

J. D. wiped both hands down across his face.

"Nobody will lay blame on us—unless you think to answer questions which the gentile authorities won't think to ask. The safety of this town is in your hands, ya?"

"This is a stupid, dangerous act. It will not produce good fruit."

"Brother Apollo, he has sent a telegraph to the marshal about the robbery. He has said the deputies wanted liquor but he choose not to sell. They become angry with him and just take the liquor. When they become drunk, they rob him of his gold and his script."

J. D. shook his head. "Ah, if only I had ridden and told the authorities myself. This plan will cause tremendous trouble." He paced back and forth in front of the bishop's house. His hands jerked and his eyes were white and wild. "They will track the horses."

"So? Randall took only the two horses. He probably got close to the Gosiute camp about midnight last night, and that is where he will set the horses free. He was to sleep a while, then start back before dawn this morning. It may seem that the Gosiutes have killed these two men for their horses."

"How can you think that no one will see Randall's return tracks?"

"He will come back a different way. And in the early morning, the ground is frozen or maybe the snow is scant on the other side of the mountain. It usually is. It may take someone better at tracking than you to follow him."

"Bishop," I said. "Where—"

J. D. stopped me with a wave of one hand. "Not now, Rachel."

"Where were the horses!?"

"I said, not now, Rachel," J. D. thundered.

I turned toward the bishop's barn and stared at the red wall which had dark iron chains and tools hanging on it.

Damn him for speaking to me like that; damn him for treating me like a child. A blow to my temple with his fist would have felt better. The true pain came from the fact that he was transformed in my eyes into a person with an irrational temper and supreme blindness. It felt as if the man I once knew had died.

J. D. strode back and forth. "If new deps come tonight or tomorrow, they will see the tracks and follow them until they see sign of Randall dismounting and returning. You think they won't have an expert tracker with them? You didn't think this through carefully."

The bishop shrugged. "I pray for more snow. My prayers will be answered, ya?"

J. D. turned away. "I can't believe you've done this."

"I take full responsibility if this plan fails. It is wrong to hold the truth inside and not speak it. It is even more wrong to lie. But with a choice between lying and allowing Centre to be destroyed, I will lie. You understand? I will tell a hundred lies to protect this people."

"Then you destroy them in a different way. You destroy them morally."

"You say this is so, but I do not believe it. My lie cannot hurt the people of Centre. They have done nothing, ya?"

"They are complicit in your lie. Everyone in town heard those shots. You give them no credit for intelligence."

"I do not know this word 'compli—'"

"They lie with you by their silence. You force them to lie. Because they heard the shots too."

I turned back, angry enough that I would not let him intimidate me. "Bishop, you sent Randall off with the bodies of the deps draped over their own horses. Where did you find the deps' horses?"

J. D. glared at me. Then his mouth opened and the anger drained from his face. "Oh."

"One was in my own stalls. When I go out yesterday morning, he was in my barn. The other one was in Brother Cooper's barn."

J. D. grabbed the bishop's shoulder. "And you didn't tell me?"

"I know what you think about me saying that I just find them. I know you say, what—that I was complicit—ya?" The bishop shrugged from under J. D.'s hand.

J. D. raised his arms above his head and dropped them to his side. "I need to talk to your councilors and Brother Stewart and Brother Cooper all together. Here in the church in fifteen minutes. You get your councilors. Rachel and I will bring the others."

The bishop blocked J. D.'s way. "So you find this killer. What then? What will you do then?"

"I will uncover this infection to the air so it can be healed." He turned to walk toward town.

The bishop clutched at his arm. "You make a bad mistake. You will harm many innocent men."

"'Tis a strange definition of 'innocent' you live by."

He strode off and I followed him perforce.

CHAPTER 14

The five Centre men, J. D., and I met in the chapel, sitting on the first bench, not far from the sacrament table.

"Must she be in our councils?" The bishop didn't look my way.

J. D. turned toward me. I didn't move. There was silence in the room for a moment while I waited for J. D. to say how invaluable I was.

He did not say it.

"So tell me what is your plan? What can you hope to prove by this meeting?"

"I hope to flush truth out of this tangled brush."

"Are you suggesting that one of us has lied?" said Brother Cooper.

"Are you suggesting you haven't?"

Brother Apollo rose in place. "Ironically, by bringing this truth into light you will transform it. *Obscura vera involvens.* The truth is that a good man panicked. If you open his name to the public, you make him a murderer." He sat.

J. D. shook his head. "It may be that only one of you is lying, but all of you were in the canyon just before the deps were killed. None of you volunteered that information until you were forced. I have come to believe that all of you are lying, because your stories are so similar and because you have gone to such lengths to hide evidence, even to the extent of burying the deputies."

They all spoke at once. "It isn't me." "I'm not lying." "I was with my wife when the shots sounded." "I go home after we talk."

"I was with my wife," said Brother Apollo, his face and ears red. "This will be the end of our friendship, you naming me a liar."

"And you all suppose that you have just proved your innocence?" I asked. "Do you think that a federal court will credit anything your wives say about your whereabouts?"

They all looked at me as if surprised I could speak. *I may be old and gray before I get used to the fact that men don't listen to women,* I thought.

I had thought J. D. was different, but he glared at me, exasperated, his face harder than the others. I had committed the unforgivable—contradicting a man to his face.

Brother Cooper spoke: "Brother Stewart and I were angry, but the bishop and Brother Apollo were the ones who said the survival of the town depended on getting ourselves shut of those two devils."

"Listen, here are the facts." J. D. leaned forward and emphasized each word with his hands. "The shots sounded an hour after the deps left town."

Brother Stewart shook his head. "Not that long."

"Sister Griggs said it was an hour." I knew they wanted me to remain silent, but I couldn't help saying what I knew.

"The four of you went up quite a ways into the canyon." J. D.'s voice was harsh. "You were angry, walking fast. It took you what— fifteen minutes?"

"Probably twenty," said the bishop.

J. D. continued, "Say fifteen at the very least. After you calmed down, you came back together, probably using less time because you were going downhill. Say ten minutes, and you talked for another five or ten at the cemetery. Thirty minutes minimum, probably longer. That's half of the time between the time the deps left the cemetery and the time they were shot. None of you could have walked or run or ridden back up the canyon." He shook his head. "So you are lying."

"Or Sister Griggs mistake the time," said the bishop.

"Or someone else who was not with us killed them," said Brother Stewart.

All heads turned toward Brother Cooper, who stood and shouted in Brother Stewart's face: "I left you because we had all agreed that violence was not to our advantage. Now you accuse me of the murder?"

"I said nothing about you. Why are you so defensive?"

The bishop stood as well, glaring at J. D. "This is what you do—urge us to mistrust and accuse each odder. Well, I do not trust *you*. Your questions divide us so we are not of one—"

"I wish whoever done it would confess," said Alma, his eyes on Brother Cooper. "I think he's a damn hero, except for he won't admit what he done."

"We still have the same problem. Let's suppose that someone, Brother Franklin or anyone, tried to go up the canyon. How is it you didn't see him? Did he rush past you while you were arguing? Was he a spirit? Brethren, does it seem likely?"

"Nothing seems likely," said Brother Stewart. "It's not likely that they were killed."

"Tertullian. *Certum est quia impossibile est.* It is true *because* it is impossible."

"Brother Apollo, how you help with all these words? How do you help?"

Brother Apollo folded his arms in front of him and glared at the bishop. In all my years of coming to the store, I had never seen him respond with anger to any situation, until the past couple of days.

J. D. looked at each man in turn. "I've considered whether someone went up ahead of you, while you were still arguing at the bishop's house, but why would someone do that? The deps were threatening the bishop, not anybody else."

"There wasn't much time," said Brother Apollo. "We left five minutes after the deps did."

"Maybe someone was angry *because* the deps threatened the bishop," I said. "He could have followed right behind them."

J. D. looked at me, his mouth working. He looked as if all the contradictions were too much for him. Then he held his hand out as if he was going to clap it across my mouth. He might as well have slapped me and been done with it.

"Let me finish one line of thought." His voice was louder than it needed to be. He turned back to the bishopric. "I've thought that someone might have ridden up the ridge, up through the pines, across the shale in the snow, fought his way through the oak brush. That way you wouldn't have seen him." He spread his hands wide.

Alma shook his head. "No."

I got up and walked back and forth along the aisle next to the wall. In another second, I would have exploded with anger at J. D. I had once thought he was almost a god, but he was as bewildered as the other men. And his inability to solve this problem had led to frustration that he heedlessly let spill onto me. He wanted me to become a silent child again.

"He would be much slower than an hour," said the bishop. "And you say the shots came in an hour after the deps left town."

"Well," said Alma, "a person on foot could keep up with someone wading through the snow down below, if he was real fast. My Maddy did it the night the deps were shot. You saw her come out of the smithy after sounding the alarm. When the deps left the bishop's house, she followed them to the cemetery. She was watching them there." Alma furrowed his brow. "Then she followed them up to their camp. She was above them on the ridge. The snow wasn't deep up there, and she has a pathway that a horse can't follow."

We needed to talk to Maddy, discover what she'd seen, but J. D. was not the one for that job.

"Someone must have slipped past her in the dark," said Brother Stewart.

Brother Alma shook his head. "No. No one could have got past her."

"So a ghost killed them," said J. D. "One of the Three Nephites carries a ten-gauge shotgun."

I glared at Alma. "Maddy might have been in danger. You shouldn't have sent her out to spy on them."

"My daughter can take care of herself."

"What if the killer were up there already?" I said. "Waiting to shoot them when they came up? He might have shot at her."

"None of our brethren would shoot my Maddy."

J. D. circled his fingertips on his crown.

For sure and certain, he'll rub himself bald before we catch this killer.

"I have considered already the possibility that the murderer was up there waiting for them," said J. D. "He heard the alarm and knew the deps had once again come back to put one of his brothers in jail. He made his decision and started walking or riding to the deps' camp. It takes him an hour to get to the camp and he sits behind that cedar, waiting another half an hour for the deps to arrive. Many in town are capable of killing in the heat of anger, but I know only one man in town capable of that kind of passionless forethought: Brother Franklin."

I shook my head. "From what I hear, he's too good a shot. It was a butcher job done on those deps."

"Even a good shot might be careless in his haste." J. D. spoke to me with condescension I hadn't heard him use with anyone else.

"But you just said he killed without passion. So which is it, that he used passionless forethought or he shot carelessly in haste. You want to have it both ways at once, whichever fits your theory."

"Rachel!" he shouted. "Be silent or leave us and wait outside!"

I folded my arms, burning inside.

"I was going to suggest that maybe I have misjudged all of you? Are you capable of killing and then lying about it?" No one spoke and J. D. shrugged his shoulders. "I've been thinking of another problem that makes it all impossible. Why shoot them at their camp?"

"Because of the rim," said Alma. "He could shoot them as they struggled up that last steep slope to their camp." Clearly he had examined their camp, maybe during one of the times the deps had gone to Hamblin to persecute polygamists there or to Eureka for instructions.

"But the killer didn't do that," said J.D. "He sat on the flat and hid behind that cedar. I can't imagine why. There are several better places to hide in the canyon and shoot the deps as they passed. Riding up to their camp, I noted five places where someone could hide and shoot from less than six feet. No chance of missing."

"But this person was crazy with anger, ya?"

"Then why do what he did? Why not hide at the corner of a building and shoot as they passed? Why not hide in the cemetery and shoot as they rode by within a few feet as they went toward the canyon?"

"Nothing makes sense."

"At least we know something."

"What?" Brother Stewart stared at J. D.

"None of you committed the crime. Too much is impossible. Still, I wish you hadn't lied to me, wasting my time."

The bishop shrugged. "I must protect my flock."

Alma cleared his throat. "So we're dealing with a person who doesn't think things through clearly, but can sustain anger for an hour and a half."

I unbuttoned my coat and stood to take it off. "You have thought only of men in the Principle. That description might fit a younger person. He could have been a child of a polygamist, angered because his family was persecuted."

J. D. seemed surprised. "I hadn't thought of that."

I felt a flood of gratitude at his words that I immediately shut down. I still relied on his praise and that was like a crutch used by a healthy person. He had been cruel to me today and in the recent past. If only I was more independent, I would be free of feeling shame for his anger at me.

Brother Cooper looked anxious. "Who are we talking about?"

"Boys between sixteen and twenty," said J. D.

"My Charles is in Hamblin," said Brother Stewart, "visiting his grandmother, thank God."

"Abel Franklin." The bishop numbered on his fingers. "Nephi Johnson. Benjamin Pierce. Randall Cooper. My son, Carl, who was up at the sheep camp." He frowned deeply. "He was close to the mountain, but he is a quiet boy. He would never do something like this."

"My David." Brother Cooper ducked his head as if he was ashamed. "But, rather than getting angry when another man goes to prison, I think he secretly glories when another man is caught. I have tried to call him to repentance, without success."

"I cannot imagine any one of those boys killing," said Alma.

"Neither can I," said Brother Stewart.

I felt a welling up of frustration. "Like you said, J. D., maybe nobody killed them. Maybe we imagined the bodies and that was actually pig blood we saw on the ground."

"And another problem. We're left with the fact that the killer had to come down. How is it that none of you saw him?"

The bishop folded his hands on his belly. "You know the answer. I already said the answer."

"Why *would* we want to know who it was?" said Brother Apollo. "All of us wanted those deputies to disappear. In a way, it didn't matter who had pulled the trigger."

I turned to Alma. "Susan said you went for your shotgun but it was missing."

"Yes. I've started thinking that it probably was the one—" He stopped and frowned. "My Lord."

"What?" asked J. D.

Alma looked up at us slowly. "I was just saying that my shotgun was probably the one used."

J.D. nodded. "I've thought that all along."

I watched Alma's face. I knew he was thinking something else. What? His shotgun was fired and the killer probably used it. Maddy had been in the smithy giving the warning, but how long had she been there? Had she taken the shotgun when she went up the ridge? *Bloody hell!*

My soul sank within me. Could Maddy have fired on them? If she had gone up to their camp to check on them, she was closer than anyone else in town when they were shot. She must have grown up hunting birds with that shotgun. She could have pulled the trigger twice, reloaded and shot again.

"Well, we've made no discoveries." J. D. leaned forward with his forehead against his hands.

"Except that it is not probably one of us kill them. This is good discovery, ya?" The bishop's face showed his relief.

Brother Apollo faced J.D. "You shouldn't have mistrusted us. *Fundamenuim justitiae est fides.* The fountain—"

"Please, Brother Apollo," said the bishop. "We can only stand so much of this Greek."

"Latin."

"Still I think it best to say the deputies rob Brother Apollo. I see the three patches of blood when I burn their filthy quilts. I set fires on those places, ya? What else could I do?"

Alma spoke slowly. "I don't know for sure that it was my gun used to kill. Both Sister Sharp and Brother Samuelson borrowed it this week." He turned to J. D. "That could be what you smelled yesterday. Sister Sharp took it shooting wild turkeys."

"Difficult to avoid filling all the flesh with pellets," said J. D.

"She can shoot off their heads from fifty yards." Brother Alma stood and walked toward the door.

No one spoke. Then, frowning or shaking their heads, the men stood and left the chapel.

I let my breath out, knowing my whole body was tight as a bowstring.

I followed J. D. outside. "What do you think?" He shook his head and untied his horse. We both mounted.

"I don't think they're lying. I just don't have any ideas about what to do next. There's no clear track to follow."

"Look." I pointed toward Alma's house, across his lot behind the smithy. Alma marched toward his daughter, Maddy, who was coming back from the barn carrying a milk bucket, her opposite arm extended for balance. He took the bucket from her and talked to her, close to her face. She shook her head no, shook again, and again—shaking her head in his face. Then he touched her on the arm and smiled. He hugged her, still smiling.

I found tears in my eyes. "He thought she did it. He thought his own daughter shot them."

Maddy turned away from her father and ran toward the school-house.

J. D. clucked his tongue at his horse. "She could have done it. I've seen her use that gun. She is a competent shot."

"But she didn't. She didn't shoot them." I had to believe Maddy's earnest shaking of her head, Alma's clear and immediate relief. If I doubted my sense of that clear-headed and frank girl, then I couldn't trust anything.

What kind of world is this where a father would think his twelve-year-old daughter capable of murder?

That afternoon, J. D. and I sat at the kitchen table in Apollo Store. He was poring over his maps; I was staring at my fingernails. If I spoke a word, he would take his frustration out on me. Why was I the only person he would do this with? No horse or cow or sheep ever received his wrath. Why me?

I looked at him and he seemed the most foolhardy, willfully obtuse man on the face of this earth. I had until this trip thought him incapable of human mistake. The loss of him as a hero hurt like a death and at the same time it dizzied me, as if I looked through a stereoscope with one picture on the left and another on the right.

Finally, he swept the map onto the floor. "We need to ride up the canyon again. There's a mistake somewhere. Somehow the time is wrong."

"What possible good will it do? We need to talk to Maddy. Find out what she saw."

Shut your mouth, Rachel. You know rebuking him is no good.

"Dammit, Rachel. I don't need you to lecture me." He glared at the floor. Then he looked up at me. "But that *is* a good job for you. The child wouldn't be open with me. I'll ride to the deps camp and you talk to Maddy. 'Tis something you can do."

Despite my anger at him and at my own inability to keep quiet, his words burned. I folded my arms and sat up tall. "I'll talk to Maddy, one child to another."

He turned away from me, frowning and muttering, his watch held in front of him. "You claim you want to work with me, but you are constantly contrary. You show no attitude of submissiveness, which is requisite for learning."

I thought we had struck bottom in our love for each other, but something more died between us as he slammed the door behind him.

I caught my breath, sobbing once. He was wrong to trust them instead of me. It was disgusting that he had returned to his belief in the stories of the bishopric. I agreed that time made it improbable that one of them had killed the deps, but they had made a decision to fabricate a dangerous story, spirit away the horses, and bury the bodies. These were actions of the guilty.

I walked to Centre, refusing to ride sidesaddle again. Even after walking slow, I was still too upset to talk to anyone. If I opened my mouth, I would start crying. Maddy, the person I most needed to talk to, was still in school, so I sat on a rock against the south wall of the church, waiting for the meeting in the chapel, which would mark the end of our fast. Every man, woman, and child would gather. They would stand and bear testimony, reaffirming their common belief, rebuilding their feeling of unity and community. It could be a healing meeting, unless the bishop involved them all in his deceit. That would be like healing the surface of a festering wound.

After the emotional communion, they would all go home to eat. I could hardly wait. I imagined the bread with jam, the meat with gravy, the sugared apples I would consume.. The afternoon sun warmed the wall, and I dozed, opening and shutting my eyes, lazy as a toad. A bell sounded and I heard the shouts of school children streaming across from the school. David followed them out.

Nearer, a young man and a young woman walked in someone's orchard, half hidden by the trunks and branches of the trees. They held hands, and then the young woman put her hands to her face as if crying.

Love is sorrow, whatever the social form. Every kind of love is sorrow in both polygamy and monogamy.

Some polygamist men seemed little better than worms—Brother Cooper and the Brother Wheeler who had stolen Randall's maternal grandparents' life savings. But Brother Cooper would have been a bad husband with one wife, and there were dishonest men in the monogamous world. In Nevada, on the mountainside near the mine, cabin walls had been tarpaper thin, and pretty much every word spoken was heard by all the neighbors. Nobody had secrets. There were men who beat their wives regularly, a weekly pattern: work eighteen-hour days for six days, get rousing drunk Saturday night, come home after midnight, beat the woman and scare the kids, fall in bed, and wake up with a horrid hangover and a gut full of remorse. Still, polygamy seemed to increase the opportunity for some men to be idiots.

The sun was warm, and I let all thoughts of marriage and polygamy and dead deps drift away. I imagined wading in a creek that flowed with apple cider, just turned strong. Above my head a tree bore wonderful fruit as well as roast chickens and smoked hams. I started up, realizing I had been asleep.

"My young woman, this is not a good time for dozing." I opened my eyes as Sister Griggs bent over me. Her wrinkled face smiled, her eyes were bright. "Don't you think you should be scouring the town for this killer?"

"J. D. is doing the scouring on an empty mountainside. I'm done with scouring."

"I've seen something unusual. Please come."

She led me toward the western edge of town. Beyond us lay the cemetery. She pulled me behind a shed that stood behind her house and pointed. Someone walked beyond the cedars that surrounded the small cluster of gravestones—David Cooper. He looked down toward us, and we both ducked back behind the shed. When I looked again, he had left the cemetery.

"He's just visiting his mother's grave. He puts pine boughs across her stone."

"I know he does, but this is different. He looks so furtive."

"You just want some excitement."

She lifted one eyebrow. "Look for yourself, if your vision is so clear."

We heard David's steps as he walked slowly past us as we

crouched behind the shed. Once the sound had receded, I peered around the corner at his back. He looked left and right, once turning to look straight behind him. He returned inside the classroom, now empty of students.

I said, "Very furtive."

"The deps waited there in the cemetery quite often, just where he was standing."

She and I started across toward the cemetery. Suddenly I stopped and pointed toward the church and schoolhouse. "We're in plain sight of David or anybody."

"But nobody is looking."

I ducked behind the shed again, feeling giddy with excitement, sure that any second we'd discover what J. D. couldn't. Then I saw how silly it was to playact at being a Wells Fargo detective. I joined her in the lane again.

She grinned and clutched my hand. "We'll just wait a moment."

"Do you think David is the deputies' informant?"

"He has the motivation. But he shunned them like the plague. I don't think he liked the deputies any more than anyone else did."

A few people in their Sunday dress—women, men, and children—walked past us toward the church. Sister Griggs nodded and smiled. A man led a girl along the street, and I recognized her as the one holding hands with her boy. The older man whispered in her ear, his face angry. Hopefully, he was her father, but he could just as easily be her husband.

A buckboard arrived—Naomi and her parents coming over from the store. When the wagon came closer, David came out of the school and walked along the main road, as if he hadn't timed his appearance. Seeing him, Naomi smiled, her cheeks dimpling, and it was as if the sun rose behind the screen of her face. She reached down to hold his hand as he walked. As soon as the small party was safely inside the doors of the church, Sister Griggs and I walked briskly toward the cemetery.

"I haven't had more fun since I let those misguided young boys loose from under J. D.'s nose."

Snow covered the stones and grave mounds; the only green was the live pines and cedars, and the clumsy wreath on one grave— David and Randall Cooper's mother. Sister Griggs stood next to the stone. The inscription read: *Choose ye this day whom ye shall serve.* I knelt in the snow and peered into the pine boughs.

Sister Griggs leaned against my shoulder, examining the stone. "What is it we're looking for?"

"Probably nothing." A ceramic pot, which still held the dry stems of flowers, stood on the top of the sandstone monument. Under one edge of the pot a crescent of stone showed, clear of snow. I lifted the pot and found two slips of paper.

Sister Griggs leaned across my shoulder as I spread them out on her knee. They were two maps. I heard footsteps behind me and turned to see Maddy crossing the stile into the graveyard. I slipped the papers inside my sleeve.

Soon the girl stood near the tombstone. "What are you doing? Brother David was here and now you." I started to pull the papers out of my sleeve; Sister Griggs took my arm, preventing me. "David has been a good teacher. He makes me want to learn. But he doesn't seem much happy now."

"He's focused on getting married," said Sister Griggs. "That's enough to make any man sad. And Naomi's parents don't approve of him. Double trouble."

"Do you think he could have helped the deps? I know he hates polygamy. He has told me so." While Maddy spoke, her eyes flicked back and forth across the tombstone.

Smart girl. She knows we're hiding something from her.

"Has he told other students about his beliefs?" asked Sister Griggs. "If he has, he'll lose his job."

"No. He trusts me." She stared at Sister Griggs and me. "But if he put Saints in prison and tried to harm the bishop, he should be punished."

Sister Griggs patted her arm. "None of us know for certain he did those things." We only suspect and it's un-American to condemn before a proper judgment. Now we need to get to the meeting. All of us."

Walking down, I thought of the papers in my pocket and also of J. D.'s frustration at his own bewilderment. I found myself smiling, not really a cheerful smile, but more a baring of teeth.

Maddy, Sister Griggs, and I walked out from behind the cedars and back into town. "The night the deps were shot, how far up did you go?"

"I watched them until—" She looked back over her shoulder.

Hearing a horse behind us, I turned and looked up at J. D., astride the big black gelding.

"J. D." My fingers touched the papers in my pocket.

He grunted, hardly looking at me.

I wanted to take them out and show him what Sister Griggs and I had discovered while he had been wasting time on the mountain, but I kept my hand still. They were my clues and he didn't deserve a share in them. He rode on past us. I turned to look for Maddy, but she had disappeared.

Stragglers hurried along the snowy streets. Brother Cooper's four wives arrived together, a dozen children behind them. Just as we arrived at the front gate, the bishop helped an ancient man down from a buggy.

J. D. stood on the front steps of the church, frowning at the people as they entered. Brother Cooper's first wife struggled up the steps with two children in hand; her three sister wives followed. The bishop rushed ahead to hold the door for the four women.

I glimpsed Maddy as she ran up the stairs ahead of Sister Griggs and me. Once inside, I saw that she crossed the chapel to sit with her father. J. D., as a high councilman, sat at the front of the chapel with the bishop. Sister Griggs and I found seats to the side near the door. From there, I could turn and see the faces of most people in the congregation. Everyone was somber; no one smiled or joked. It felt like a funeral—one where the dead might rise at any moment and terrify the congregation. A woman in the back wept in her seat, making a soft whimpering sound. Her sister wife tried to comfort her. David sat with Randall across the chapel, a good distance from the rest of their father's family. Naomi sat with her mother and father, closer to me and Sister Griggs.

The bishop stood at the front of the chapel and announced the song and prayer. The congregation sang "We Thank Thee, Oh God, for a Prophet." I slid the two maps inside my hymn book then opened it so that Sister Griggs and I could scrutinize them. The first map was nearly identical to the one I had found in the deputies' tent. Only this map had three X's, one to the north of town—certainly the bishop's house—one which I judged to represent Brother Cooper's lot, and one far outside town on Apollo Store. Words under each X said respectively, "In the kitchen cupboard," "In the smokehouse," and "No hiding place." The second map was a larger scale than the other; there was an arrow to the south of town. "Follow the tracks to your deputies' horses." Both notes were signed Joshua.

Sister Griggs' leaned close to my ear. "Joshua. Choose ye this day. Joshua fit the battle. The walls of polygamy come a-tumbling down."

"He didn't give them a note about where the deps were buried."

"Maybe he's like us and doesn't know."

I found myself shaking with anger. Then I remembered Sister Griggs's words about making a proper judgment. I wasn't sure who else it could be, but I had to keep an open mind. I suspected David of informing on his brethren, because he had motivation to harm polygamists. But I would save my anger until I knew for sure and certain. I glanced at him. His face seemed perfectly innocent. He watched Naomi, who turned to him and smiled.

"We should find out first whether he did leave the maps."

Sister Griggs nodded and touched me on the arm. I leaned toward her. Her whispered words tickled my ear. "Loose tongues could bring harm to David, possibly by the one who has killed already."

"He has broken trust with every person in town. He tried to get the bishop sent to prison."

"If he did this sin, he deserves a chance to leave town and never come back. I think he is not stupid enough to stay around if we tell him what we know."

"He'll have a hard enough time persuading Naomi to go with him."

Sister Griggs nodded. "Poor girl."

I considered how to tell David in a way that would shock him into a confession. What if I drew a map nearly like his, but with an X the school house? What code name could I use? Delilah? The Queen of Sheba? Esther? I shook my head. The easiest way to force a confession was to confront him with the maps. Give him a chance to explain.

Sister Griggs frowned. "It bothers me. Rachel, why is he leaving maps when the deps are dead?"

"Maybe he hopes more deps are coming. Hopes or knows. Maybe he sneaked down to the rail line in the night and telegraphed that they should come."

"He couldn't do that. Everybody in town knows that Brother Franklin has the equipment locked in a box, so nobody else can use it."

David sang with vigor, sharing a hymnal with Randall. If he was guilty, he had no right to force his beliefs on others. If it was true, he was as bad as the deputies. He had helped send to prison men who obeyed what they believed was God's commandment.

The deacons passed the sacrament. As the bread, emblem of Christ's body, passed down the rows, I examined the faces of those around me. Some stared out the window; others sat with their heads bowed or opened their scriptures. Two boys whispered in front of me. Nearly everyone in town was there. The bread came to me and I took a piece and chewed. It drew the saliva so sharply that it hurt.

All around me, people took the bread and chewed. I wondered what David would do. If he let the tray pass by him, it could be a sign of guilt, of his unwillingness to eat damnation to his own soul. As I watched he ate the bread with a calm face.

The murderer, who had sinned against God, was almost certainly in the chapel. His act, like a boulder dropped in a pond, threatened the peace and unity of every person in town. I wondered if he would eat the bread and drink the water. I turned in my seat and scanned the rows. It would be a moral act to discover the murderer, bring him to justice, make unity again possible in town.

My stomach growled and I wished again I had sustenance to make clear thought possible.

Perishing, distracting hunger!

After the sacrament, the bishop said that anyone could stand and bear testimony. A woman rose, resplendent in a white home-made dress; she was perhaps five years older than Naomi and I. She said, "I bear testimony of the Principle. The politicians have branded celestial marriage one of the two pillars of barbarism, but the pillars of barbarism are prostitution and adultery. Both of these drag women, daughters of God, down in the dirt. In gentile communities we find lasciviousness and also superfluous women. In the communities fashioned by God's children, in Zion, no life is wasted; all are made part of God's family. Only by embracing the higher law can our villages, towns, and cities be saved, lifted up like the city of Enoch, for righteousness. We cannot back down. We must not let this difficult time sway us from God's purpose for us."

It was close to what I'd read in editorials by Emmeline B. Wells in the *Women's Exponent*. When I had read her words, I thrilled to the idealistic possibilities of polygamy. Now I wondered whether the suffering was worth it.

I watched David, who shook his head, his face grim. Naomi's mouth was the flat line of anger that marked her as her mother's daughter. The woman in the white dress sat down again next to her sister wives.

Finally, Sister Griggs stood and shuffled to the front of the chapel. The bishop shifted in his seat, frowning. *How can one small woman make men in authority so nervous?* I thought. When I was old, I wanted to be like her.

She gripped the pulpit, her head barely showing over the top. "I hear some say that all gentiles, our own two deputies included, deserve to die. That's God's option to judge, not ours. Only he decides when we should leave this life. We have struggled in this community and now we fear it may be destroyed. We are all diamonds; some are polished, some are rough. But we're *all* struggling. And when we meet at the entrance to heaven, will our savior say, 'You only hated gentiles, not your fellow Saints, yes come in to heaven, take your reward'? No, he will judge us rightly. God is the god of all, Gentile, Saint, dep, and sinner alike." She turned from the pulpit and moved back to her seat near me.

A tall, gaunt man in white shirt and ironed bib overalls stood next behind the podium—Brother Franklin, the man with the huge four-gauge shotgun. He cleared his throat, glaring out at the congregation, but said nothing. Finally he spoke. "Like some of you, I imagined those deputies dead. Longed and hoped for their deaths. Sister Griggs, those were kind words. Maybe too kind, too soft.

I say if thine eye offend thee, pluck it out. We grovel for gentile clothing, gentile styles, gentile habits of mind, and gentile money."

And gentile guns like your four-gauge, Brother Pious Franklin. I knew my own weakness was gentile Hereford cattle.

"If we could remove this pestilent infection from our midst, we would prove ourselves before God. We would be redeemed of him. But—and this is the great mystery—God seldom approves of violence. On the one hand, God told us through his prophet to drive them out. On the other hand, he says that in most cases we should avoid violence. My mind is too weak to sort it out. But God's prophet has given us a way out of this difficulty. He has told us that if we would never buy gentile clothing, never drink in gentile bars, never dig in gentile mines, never love gentile women, then we would be shut of them. And if we do as he says, and build our own resources, save our own wheat, when the times of turmoil come, when the rest of the country is thrust into a famine more severe than that in Egypt, we will be the means of salvation for the children of Israel, wherever they may be found from across this great nation." He returned to his seat, his mouth turned in a sour frown.

A thin woman stood. Her hair had once been dark but now was streaked with gray.

"Who's that?"

"Sister Sharp. Alice Sharp. Her husband's in prison."

"The one who can shoot the heads off wild turkeys?"

"The very woman." A man seated in front of us looked back and frowned.

"These are troubled times." Sister Sharp couldn't speak clearly because of emotion. "I hope this rancor doesn't destroy Centre." She sat down.

Another woman stood, tear tracks streaked her face. I didn't know her well but I remembered Brother Apollo calling her Sister Pearson when she had come into the store once. "We are damned to hell. This is God's judgment upon us. Brother Franklin is right. We must destroy the gentile among us. We should be celebrating that those two demons are gone. This will mark the beginning of Armageddon." As she spoke, her voice grew louder and louder. "After this day, war will be poured out upon this nation until all of God's enemies will be destroyed."

At best, it is a misreading of scripture. At worst, the words of a crazy woman who wants to make us all crazy with her.

I saw that tension marked the face of every person present, breathed through each testimony. They all knew that whoever had killed was sitting with them in church, hiding his sin. Or was it a heroic act? The chapel was nearly silent; even small children felt the tension. Men shifted in their seats. The women stared forward, worried.

Others stood and spoke but I hardly heard them. I wanted to face down every person in town. I wanted to discover the pattern of each life and determine how that weave of community had been disrupted by the killing. Perhaps one day someone would invent a lens that would open the soul to human vision. Maybe angels had such eyes.

Finally, people finished talking. The bishop stood and gripped the pulpit. "Before I pray to end this fast let me say this one thing. Many of you brothers and sisters have suspicions that you think is knowledge. Some of you have heard shots in the night that could be Brother Cooper killing weasels, ya? For all you know, these deputies, after stealing from Brother Apollo's store, decide to flee to California. You must believe me when I say this: there is a wide gulf between suspicion and knowledge. Some of you think you know and you think that I am wrong to talk this way, but listen for a little while.

"Soon, more federal deputies will come to persecute us. You must make no mistake about this. And they will use our own words and thoughts against us. They want to destroy God's Church. Now, do we say our suspicions or do we keep them to ourselves? No Gentile will judge us fair. Every Gentile, but most especially that devil Deputy Marshal Danby, will find the way to use our talk against us. He and other gentiles only want to harm God's children, to prove we are what the gentile newspapers say we are. This we cannot allow to happen.

"So I say we should keep our silence. We should not talk about what we have heard or have not heard, what we have thought or have not thought, with any Gentile. We do *not* say our suspicions to gentiles. We must allow the gentile marshal to discover for himself any crime or no crime. We may not lie, but we may keep silent. This keeping silent may open a narrow doorway to escape the trouble from these two deputies disappearing from our town. It is a miraculous doorway."

Not for the first time, I found myself angry at his clever duplicity. He would make everyone a part of his deception, possibly destroying the soul of every person who accepted his logic. He would do more damage to the town than the deps had.

"Now we have another danger: thinking evil of our neighbor, thinking our neighbor has done evil, maybe in the Principle or out of it. Only God has a sharp enough mind to divide between sin and good. Only he can cut between right and wrong in this confused thing. I make this fast to put what is past in the past. We must forget about the fate of these evil deputies and move on. We must forget about this matter, ya? Now I pray to end our fast."

He bowed his head and clasped his hands. "Father Got, we gather before thee, thy faithful saints, to say, like the prophet Joseph in jail, when will the cup of our suffering be full? When will thou cease giving enemies power over us? Thou hast allowed two coyotes to nip at our feet, chew on our bodies, and now they have gone. Is this your deliverance for us? I pray that anyone in this town, who has any grave matter on his conscience, that he will feel that he can come to me, so I can share his burden, that he carry alone. Now, we will break this fast. I pray that we can put this behind us that our town may be unified. In the name of Jesus Christ. Amen."

After the prayer, Sister Griggs left the building, muttering and frowning. Most of the other people sat silent and stunned in their seats. Sister Sharp stood and grasped the bishop's hand. Others left the building, the Coopers first, the wives in a row, followed by their children. Alma shook his head, turning his hat in his hand, and J. D. gripped the bishop's shoulder, speaking earnestly to him. The bishop looked like an old man.

I walked toward him and J. D. Never before in my life had I approached him with such bitter reluctance.

"I will be the scapegoat. I have chosen this. Only at the judgment bar of God will I know what I have done is good or bad." Then he saw me and his face grew angry—probably because a woman outside the councils had heard his private confidence. I turned away from him and walked outside onto the front steps. Men, women, and children stood in clusters talking. I glanced around for Maddy, but could see her nowhere.

The bishop stepped out and everyone stopped talking and watched him. He looked up at the sky. "Got is hearing me. A heavy snow will cover all the tracks." Then he walked toward his house.

One man, who had been arguing with others in a cluster near the front gate of the church, turned and made an angry gesture toward the bishop's back. Everyone was angry and frightened, making it even harder for J. D. and me to discover the killer.

David emerged with his father's family. It would be difficult to talk to him alone until after everyone ate, but I also knew I should not put off confronting him. Naomi finally walked from the church and joined her mother in the buckboard. I couldn't see

Brother Apollo. Sister Apollo looked over her shoulder toward the church, her face set in anger.

Despite his hours spent earlier, riding up and down the canyon, timing and rethinking, J. D. had discovered nothing and was in an evil mood.

"There's something we're not seeing."

"Sure, there is. It's the perishing killer we're not seeing." But that didn't help his mood. I again felt a pang of guilt for not telling him all I knew. But not so guilty that I actually showed him the maps.

He turned and walked along the lane toward where the largest group of men stood talking. I watched them as he approached. They stopped gesturing and their faces turned grim. He would get precious little information from that group. Still, he stood in the middle of them, beating with words against the wall of their faces. Foolish man.

I needed to talk to Maddy, so I turned toward the smithy, but I decided she was probably at home, breaking the fast with her father and sister. I'd get nothing out of her with her father around. The next person I wanted to talk to was David, so I turned back toward the Cooper lot. I knocked on the door of the main house, but the large woman who answered said that David had left on his own horse, heading toward the school. I walked through the two rooms of the school, but he wasn't there. I found foot tracks leaving the school and heading toward the cemetery. I followed them but they went past the gravestones and on up the canyon.

I was weak from hunger and didn't know how far he had gone. It could be an hour before I found him. I looked at the tracks, then back at Apollo Store, where Sister Apollo would have food cooking. I turned that direction and walked back through town. A few specks of snow whirled down, advance scouts of the coming storm.

CHAPTER 16

Naomi and I worked on dinner in the underground kitchen. I was weak and famished, but also emotionally drained because of the tension between J. D. and me. Grating wizened apples for Brown Betty, I could hardly keep from biting into them or stuffing the peelings into my mouth. I knew the food would make me feel better about everything. I had promised myself that I would avoid nibbling until the meal was ready and all those at the store could break our fast together. I would do the pious thing. Maybe if I did that, God would put my world back together.

Not perishing likely. I don't think God works that way.

The aroma from a venison roast filled the kitchen. Sitting across the table from me, Naomi mixed biscuits. Potatoes boiled on the stovetop. Neither of us spoke, both sunk into private thoughts too tangled for words. The maps seemed like leaves of hot metal burning in my pocket.

I knew that my evidence would drive the young lovers out of Centre and change their lives in ways that would make them unhappy. It would probably also ruin my friendship with Naomi. I wished for a second that I had turned it all over to J. D. when I'd had the chance outside the church. But the clues were mine, mine and Sister Griggs's.

J. D.'s pig-headedness, David's duplicity, and the bishop's sermon about the safety of silence had all made me so angry that I felt dizzy. The town of Centre seemed woven about with lies.

Even Brother Apollo, the most honest, warm-hearted man I knew, was tangled in the web of deceit. I was forced to revise my idea, conceived as I dozed in the sunlight against the church house, that the institution was less important than the character of the people in the institution. In Centre Town, polygamy had exaggerated and intensified deceit, contention, and unrighteous dominion over the will of others. I knew that what the bishop was doing was wrong. For Brother Apollo taking a second wife was wrong. Naomi had told me that, after the fast meeting, he had slipped into Sarah's cabin instead of coming home with the others. I had almost told her then about the maps, but Naomi had been so perishing furious that I decided to wait for a better time.

I tried to imagine my own town in such turmoil and confusion. I believed that J. D. and the other leaders of Rockwood would never let such a thing happen. Or would they, threatened by crisis, turn crafty and imperious, like Bishop Peterson and his councilors? As I had walked toward Apollo Store, people stopped talking and turned toward me, anger, fear, and confusion in their faces. The bishop had intended the fast meeting to endow the people with the certainty that their fate was in God's hands, but it hadn't worked. Putting a lid on a boiling pot just makes it boil harder.

Naomi stood above the bowl and cut lard into the mixed dry ingredients. Imagining the biscuits slathered with butter and honey, I nearly drooled. I thought of pouring hot drippings across a thick slice of roast.

"Did I put in one or two teaspoons of salt?" Her first words in over fifteen minutes startled me.

"I wasn't keeping track of your spoonfuls. I was thinking that I'm hard put to offer up a righteous fast to God with the aromas in this kitchen." I growled and made biting motions toward the oven.

Naomi didn't smile. "Too little is better than too much." She put the bottle of salt back on the shelf. She stirred the ingredients with a wooden spoon and then added a saucer of clabbered milk.

"Naomi?" When she turned to me, I shrugged my shoulders. "Nothing."

Naomi walked to the door. "I wish Papa would give up on me being a queen in heaven. Today he asked me, 'Do you want to serve as a handmaid to every other woman in God's kingdom?' That's why David and I will have to move to another town. Papa *still* wants me to marry the bishop or somebody important here in Centre or in Hamblin. Brother Cooper tried to walk me home from church because Papa told him I was interested in joining myself to a family in the Principle."

I shuddered. "That lecherous old goat."

"He can't even support one wife. Why would God make him a king in heaven just because he has made many women miserable?" The juice from the apples smelled sweet as heaven. "It's so confusing that Papa married Sarah."

"Sarah chose him over Randall."

"Randall never spoke to her, or to anybody until it was too late, and then I think he's only talked to you and me, so it's not as if Papa stole her from Randall. I've decided that he married Sarah more out of sympathy than a desire for kingdoms. He believed she'd probably never get married. Marrying her was the best kindness and the worst cruelty, both at once. Confusing."

"So your love—a love to one man—is clear and never confusing?"

"Of course it isn't clear. I just don't want the Principle. I want David."

I stood and began removing plates from the drying rack. I carried them into the dining room and set the stack at the head of the table. I paused, leaning forward, palms down on the old wood. Then I walked briskly back into the kitchen.

"I need to talk to you about David."

"At least *he's* of one mind. He hates every aspect of the Principle." She stood and greased a wide tin sheet.

"Would he send his brethren to prison?"

Naomi's eyes widened. "If you start such a rumor, it will be the end of his teaching. The brethren would drive him out of Centre today."

"Would you go with him?"

"Of course I would, but that doesn't mean I want to leave my home if I don't have to. He's willing to stay here. He just doesn't think it will work." She covered the biscuit dough with a damp cloth. "He has talked about teaching school in Eureka, where there would be little prejudice against someone who doesn't favor the Principle, but I don't want to live in a gentile town."

"But you would leave your home if he insists. I guess that's something I wouldn't do."

"You haven't been in love yet." Naomi turned to face me. "If you say this suspicion to anyone else, we'll have to go. I will have no choice in the matter."

I turned away and stood in front of the stove. I fingered the tiny maps in my pocket. I could easily thrust them into the fire. But what would I say to Sister Griggs? And I couldn't keep this secret from J. D. for long. Perhaps I could tell him that because Mormonism is such a liberal government, they could afford to be generous even to heretical souls like David. J. D. would say that kind of thinking was like crippled stock and should be cast off. I decided at that moment to talk to Naomi before I showed the maps to anyone else.

"I think of you sneaking out in the icy cold with David. I think you'd get enough talking and flirting done at school."

Finally, Naomi smiled. "I'm past the stage where I'm happy with talking and flirting. I wanted serious hugging and kissing. I want to have children with him. Anyway, we're too busy at the school to talk much about *us*. We have a signal for meeting. He sets a light in the window of the school and when he blows it out, we meet at the bridge."

I stepped forward, puzzled. "But the night of the storm, you didn't go walk with him, did you?"

"You know he had a meeting with the bishopric that night. He told me that when he finished he would go home to bed."

"What if he used the lantern to signal the deps to come to the meeting and carry away the bishop?"

"You're not making sense." Naomi frowned at me. "What are you saying?"

"Look." I pulled the maps from my dress pocket and smoothed them out on the table. "J. D. and I found this one in the deps' rucksack. And Sister Griggs and I found these two on the head-stone of David's mother."

"What are these?" Naomi bent over the papers.

"Maps. Sister Griggs and I believe they are designed to show the deps where—"

Naomi let out a long breath. "These are the hiding places of the bishopric. So these were never acted upon." She paused. "Just because someone used his mother's headstone doesn't mean—"

"We saw him at his mother's grave. Look at the signature: Joshua."

Naomi just shook her head. "This proves nothing. I will ask him myself. I have invited him to dinner tonight so we can an-nounce our engagement." She gathered the slips of paper and put them in her own pocket. I held my hand out for them, but Naomi shook her head.

"I can't believe you suspect David."

She rolled the dough out on the tin and cut it vigorously with a butter knife, crosshatching and spreading out the biscuits.

"I hope your father will be easy about your engagement. I wish you luck."

I opened the oven and put in the Brown Betty next to the roast. A flood of aroma filled the kitchen and my mouth watered again. I looked with longing at the steaming brown meat.

"You say you wish me luck." Naomi's voice was hard. "But you accuse David of deceit." She held a fistful of spoons, and when she sat at the worktable, she let them clatter from her hands. "Are you jealous of me? Is that why you want to ruin my life?"

I looked at my own hands. As Naomi said the words I realized I *was* jealous of Naomi, being loved by one man. *But that isn't my motive here. My motives are for pure justice.*

"You may marry Ezekiel." Naomi's voice was loud in the small kitchen. "If you marry him you may be happy because you've never known real love." She strode out of the room.

I watched the swinging door. I felt my own anger swell, but at the same instant I knew Naomi was right. I might marry Ezekiel. I might choose to grow old living in a household with enough to eat, next to J. D.'s house. I could raise cattle and lucerne to feed them. I could become a solid citizen of Rockwood community and at least a marginal citizen of God's kingdom in heaven.

I might become like J. D. We might be friends again if I married the man he wanted me to marry. I would be giving up part of myself, but every woman gave up part of herself when she married.

Naomi would have a very different life. Because no Mormon town would put up with a school teacher who preached against the Principle, David and Naomi would have to move to a gentile town, isolated from the constant brotherhood and sisterhood of the Church. If they continued as teachers, they would live on the edge of poverty, sustained only by the grace of the children's families.

I swept the apple and potato peelings into the slop bucket. Then I found a cloth near the water bucket and wiped down the table. Finally calm, I sat at the table.

Nothing but hard choices faced me.

Naomi desired one man for herself—one man for whom she would cook and clean and bear children. I considered my possible sister wives. Sophia was overly pious and strident as a goose. But she was an excellent weaver and sold her cloth for a high price. Abigail was as bossy as the head cow in a herd, but she kept the household in an orderly manner.

I knew that if I kept my mouth shut when I was inside and if I worked outside as much as possible, taking care of the cattle, horses, and sheep, then I could fit into that community of women. I could even be happy, especially living across the street from J. D. Somehow Ezekiel wasn't in the picture. We women would share the man between us, but most of the time we would be free of his authority and embrace. I could easily live that way even though I didn't believe in polygamy, even though I had viewed firsthand its defects. Naomi was right; the two of us were not alike.

You're a candle bent by every breeze. Make up your damn mind!

"Hell's bells." The tradition was to break the fast together, but I could no longer wait. I took a raw biscuit, hardly warm, out of the oven and laid the dough directly on the stove top, flattening it out with my fingers. I had seen my birth father cook food that way. After a few moments, I flipped it over, again lifting it gingerly with my fingers. The cooked side was black. I grimaced as I considered that I had in this small way reverted to my Nevada character, grabbing food when it was there, disregarding the culture and restraint taught to me by J. D.'s first wife, Mary. Soon the bread was black on both sides, although likely still doughy in the middle. But I scooped it onto my hand, juggling it as I crossed to the table, where I dipped the scone in the butter and then the honey. I stopped my hand when it was an inch from my mouth.

"Dear God, I pray as I end my fast that the violence in this town doesn't destroy it and that my revelation to Naomi won't destroy her. And that I may in the future more fully deny the natural and carnal man that is so strong within me." I sat at the table, wolfing down huge bites of the black and doughy flatbread slathered in butter and honey.

Sister Apollo insisted on waiting dinner for her husband. The food was ready, biscuits and Apple Betty sitting out on the kitchen table.

"Cold and moist is better than burned," she said bitterly. "But the roast will do for a few minutes more."

After we had waited for a quarter hour, Brother Apollo still had not returned. Brother Cooper, who hauled orders between the small desert towns, had come to the store with his wagon, and J. D. was helping him load flour and other supplies for Rockwood and Simpson Springs, where a few soldiers were stationed.

I walked into the storeroom, intending to speak to J. D., say I was sorry for getting angry at him. When I walked up to the wagon, he nodded toward me as if I was a stranger. I turned on my heel and left him to stew in his own juices. Donning my coat, I walked outside and into the barn to help Randall with his chores. I heard him above in the loft, muttering as he threw down hay for the horses.

"Randall, who are you talking to up there?"

"The devil."

"Is he listening?" I climbed the ladder and stuck my head through the opening.

"He always listens. It's God who doesn't heed me." His face was twisted with anger and he gripped the fork like a weapon. He paced back and forth between the top of the ladder and the huge barn window. "He's with her now. It's an insult to Sister Apollo, and to me."

"With Sarah?"

"Yes, with her. In the middle of the day."

I clambered up into the loft. "It's not likely they're—" Then I saw his face and regretted even saying that much. I walked forward and touched his arm. "Randall, you have to get over her. She's not going to leave Brother Apollo, no matter what."

"What are you? Are you my new mother?" He grasped the fork with both hands and lowered his forehead against his fists. "Sarah and I have loved each other since we were children. He just felt sorry for her so he married her. He has no love for her."

"Maybe a form of love."

"It's pity. I love—loved her."

"Did you talk to the deps about more than Brother Apollo? Did you and David tell them where some of the brethren hide?"

"Me and David?" He glared at me. "He—he wouldn't do that."

"He damn well may have. I think he helped send some of his brethren to prison. Did you do the same?"

"No. I mean, I told only about William Apollo." He walked toward me, his face twisted with anger, the pitchfork still gripped in his hands. "You must be stupid or lying to think that David would do that."

I stepped back, anxious that he might suddenly thrust the tines into me and just as suddenly feel remorse. I imagined that the same anger could have prompted him to kill the deps, but I knew he had done no such thing. Even now, he frowned down at his hands, his fury suddenly gone. He was not capable of the sustained wrath that would have lasted for an hour as he ran or rode toward the deps' camp.

Even though my fear of him died as quickly as his anger, I thought it unwise at that moment to attempt arguing him out of his trust for his brother. There was no benefit that could come from such persuasion.

We stood in the window from where we could see the town, cemetery, bishop's house, and higher on the hillside, the schoolroom from which David had probably signaled the deps. Randall pointed toward someone crossing the bridge. "Speak of the devil. What's he coming here for?"

"Naomi's invited him to dinner. And to announce their betrothal."

"Oh, Brother Apollo won't like that." Randall shook his head so that his sandy forelock slipped down over one eye.

"But he's not here, is he?"

"No, he isn't." Randall's face turned so sorrowful that it nearly made me weep to see it.

When David showed up, nervous, to ask for Naomi's hand, he'd find a couple of surprises: Brother Apollo absent and Naomi upset because of my accusation.

Then Randall swore. A buggy had caught up to David, who turned and watched it pass. Those inside the buggy didn't even raise a hand to greet David. Soon I could see it was Brother Apollo and Sarah, sitting side by side. David stood in the road considering, then he shook his head and walked on.

Randall threw the pitchfork at the wall of the barn. It stuck for a moment, the tines quivering, then dropped to the floor. He rushed down the ladder, and I worried that he might fall. Once safely on the ground, he jerked open the back door to the barn, and I heard the crunch of the snow as he ran across the barnyard.

When I came out into the lane, Brother Apollo was handing Sarah down from the buggy, which he had apparently borrowed so that he could approach the store with dignity. Sarah was still dressed as if for church, wearing a blue and white pinafore and a bonnet. She looked anxious, as well she might. *Don't worry, Sarah, you won't have to be anxious for long. This is going to be a dammed short visit.*

CHAPTER 17

"Randall," Brother Apollo called.

I pointed toward the fields. Brother Apollo turned and they both saw him leave the road, trotting in a wide circuit of his brother. "Randall! Damn his hide. Where is he running off to now?"

I walked quickly forward and took the horse's head. Brother Apollo held the door for Sarah. They disappeared inside. I led the horse into the barn and took care of him, and then I sprinted toward the store, nearly running into David. "Tonight is not a good night for asking for anyone's hand in marriage."

"But I am determined not to wait longer. I went to the mountain to pray and I have confirmation to go ahead and ask to marry her."

He started down the stairs.

"I found the maps you left on your mother's tombstone."

He turned toward me. "What?"

"I found the maps you left for the deps. Sister Griggs and I saw you go up to the graveyard; then we went up and found the maps."

"I didn't—" He shut the door and looked around, even though there was no one in sight. He took a step toward me. "What did you do with them?"

"I gave them to Naomi."

"Damn you!" He turned and rushed down into the store.

I called after him. "David! David, I need to talk to you." There was no more doubt that the maps were his.

Following him down, I found Brother Apollo and Sarah sitting in chairs set against one wall. No one spoke. Brother Apollo stared at the floor between his knees, so he didn't see me and David enter. Sarah's chin quivered with disappointment, embarrassment, and probably fear.

J. D. still helped Brother Cooper load his wagon, and the two men constantly glanced over at Sarah and Brother Apollo.

David stood in the middle of the floor. "Where is Naomi?"

"David," said Brother Apollo. "What brings you this way?"

"Naomi has invited me for dinner."

"What?" Brother Apollo seemed unable to focus on what David was saying.

David said, "*Impavidum ferient ruinae.*"

Brother Apollo just shrugged his shoulders. "It didn't go so well. I said to her, 'Gwyneth, I've brought my wife, Sarah, so that she can break bread with us.' She told me to turn around and take Sarah home. Then she left, wouldn't listen."

Sarah leaned forward. "I could do that. I could go home. Maybe today isn't the best time."

"I could take you," said Brother Cooper.

"You stay." Brother Apollo patted Sarah's arm. "We will pass through this straitened gate." But he didn't seem to have confidence that what he said was true.

I glanced at David, whose face was a mask, his lips pressed into a thin white line. He turned away from Brother Apollo.

I walked toward the dining room. Sister Apollo sat at the table where J. D.'s useless maps were still spread. Naomi stood behind, her arm around her mother.

"She's not moving in here." Sister Apollo had been crying, tears running down the wrinkles in her face, and I thought about Sarah's smooth, unlined skin. "He can exercise his priesthood all he wants elsewhere, but *not* here. *Not* in my house." She nearly stuttered in her anger.

"David is here." Suddenly I smelled the faint scent of burn. I rushed across the hall into the kitchen and jerked open the oven. A flag of black smoke rose from the door.

"Oh, no." Sister Apollo was close behind me. "The roast." The three of us looked down at the tray, which was smoking black. "We've overcooked it. We were all distracted and let it burn."

"At least the biscuits are all right. And the Brown Betty."

"Cold." Then her face softened. "This food will fit our mood: burnt roast and cold biscuits."

"We can slice off the burn." I took a couple of padded cloths and lifted out the roasting pan, placing it on the wooden preparation table.

"It will be dry and tough inside."

Naomi stood with one hand on the swinging door. She was clearly divided, wanting to go to David and wanting to comfort her mother.

Sister Apollo leaned against the wall. "I need to decide what I can bear. I've said she will not sleep here. But should she not eat here, now that we're all married before God?" Then she laughed, a short, unnatural bark, quickly replaced by her frown.

"I can take care of this. You go talk to them." I nudged her toward the door.

"Yes. It's all out in the open now. We must talk." Naomi led her to the door. "I need you, Naomi." The two women disappeared down the hallway.

I began sawing away the burnt part of the roast. I ground some coffee and placed the pot on the stove. We all needed that disobedient comfort.

Soon, Naomi came back; her eyes were dark, brooding. "He had no right. But Mama is so practical and reasonable. They're making the best of it."

"Tell me what she said."

"She told Papa that he was wrong to take a second wife without her permission. That any marriage had to involve the good will of every person, and he and Sarah had neglected to secure her good will. He said he had tried. Mama said he hadn't tried to talk nearly hard enough. She found out from her friends in Relief Society that he was courting Sarah. And when she complained, he still didn't try to talk; he just made proclamations. She said that making proclamations in Greek and Latin isn't talking."

"She is a Christian woman."

"'So what should we do?' Papa said. Mama said she would try to develop friendship for Sarah, but she would be the one to invite Sarah into her home, not Papa." Naomi uncovered the pot of potatoes and then poured off the warm water into the slop bucket, using the lid to hold the potatoes in. "Papa said it was his home, too, and Mama said they needed to respect her wishes in this matter even if they respected her in nothing else. She said she could more easily bear having Sarah here if she had control over the visit. Then she said that Sarah should never stay overnight here."

"He agreed?"

"What else could he do?" Naomi smiled briefly. "Then Mama invited Sarah to dinner."

"And David?"

"I had no chance to talk to him." She looked up at me. "You are determined to force us out of town?"

"Naomi, please. Sister Griggs found the maps with me. I can't keep this a secret."

"You expect me to thank you for what you've done? I will have to move away from the town I love. You thought I'd be happy?"

Naomi lifted a crock of milk, turning so sharply away that some slopped out the top. She poured a little across the potatoes, stirred it in. Working in silence, we soon had the food prepared and the dining room table spread.

"All right. You get Mama and Papa and the others."

Brother Apollo, Randall, and J. D. stood near the stove in the large southern room of the store, talking. David sat across the store from them, his face a mask of anxiety. Sarah and Sister Apollo were nearby, examining together the bolts of cloth stacked on shelves against the wall. Sister Griggs sat on a trunk, smiling at the others. "I've come for dinner. I have money to pay."

"It's ready." I wondered if every meal I ate in that dining room would be fraught with tension.

"I couldn't stay away, when all the excitement is here."

Brother Apollo was talking. "The sheriff in Hamblin says a theft of goods by agents of the federal government should be looked into by the federal government."

"Useless," said J. D. "Useless, foolish prevarication."

"This means Deputy Marshal Danby will investigate."

"I think he'll see through this plan of the bishop's," I said.

David turned suddenly and tripped over a keg of nails. "Of course he will. This is a despicable lie."

"I heard you say Marshal Danby," said Sister Griggs.

"That man is like a devil." Brother Apollo brought his fist down on the table so hard that the silverware clattered.

"I warned you," J. D. said to him. "I was certain no good could come from this fabrication. Danby is too smart to be fooled by such a ruse."

"I've always thought the bishop an intelligent man." Sister Griggs folded her hands in her lap. "I must change my opinion."

As I entered the kitchen, Sister Apollo touched one hand to her hair, before a small mirror hung there, which gave a wavering reflection. Naomi held her arm around her mother's waist.

Sister Apollo forced herself to smile. "Who would have thought that I could bear this day?" She lifted the biscuits into the basket and carried them to the dining room.

Everyone stood around the table, and then Randall rushed in, his hair sticking out in all directions. Brother Apollo insisted that Sister Apollo sit at one end of the table, he at the other, just as they always had. "After all. We are the head of this family. Husband and first wife."

Sister Apollo stared at the fork she held in her hand, but then she smiled, a scant curve, thin and quick as a breath. He held the chair for Sarah, directly to his left. Naomi sat on her father's right, with David next to her, and I found a place on his left. J. D. sat at Sister Apollo's left. Randall glared at Brother Apollo and took a place next to Sarah, opposite Naomi. I hoped he could control his anger. Sister Griggs watched everyone, grinning like it was Christmas morning.

The room was silent except for the sound of eating. It reminded me of the first part of the dinner with the deputies, the room full of tension but nobody talking yet. I stuffed a biscuit whole into my mouth, chewed it while I buttered another.

J.D. cleared his mouth before speaking. "A second storm is coming."

"The bishop's been praying for one." No one seemed to notice the irony in my voice.

David opened his mouth to talk, but Naomi shook her head sharply.

Sister Griggs chewed and swallowed a bite of roast. "Delicious. But I do like the brown, fatty part on the outside of a good roast."

"The brown fatty part is black as sin." I could hardly speak through my mouthful of meat.

Sarah looked toward Sister Apollo. "Still, I can't remember when I've eaten better."

Sister Apollo smiled and looked at her plate. I couldn't tell whether it was a sarcastic smile or whether she had worked through to serenity. "Your compliments are too strong. We shouldn't ignore the fact that it is badly burned and very dry."

Brother Apollo opened his mouth several times as if priming himself to speak. Finally he succeeded. "This feels like Thanksgiving, with all our loved ones gathered about in peace and bounty."

Everyone stared at him as if he was an ostrich that had suddenly appeared at the table.

Randall turned red in the face. He opened his mouth again but said nothing. Finally he left, carrying his plate with him.

"Please have another roll." Sister Apollo passed the pan to me and I offered it to Sarah.

"Thank you," said Sarah to Sister Apollo. "I can't stop eating even though I've had more than my share."

David cleared his throat. "Naomi and I have decided to marry."

The room was silent. Brother Apollo put down his fork and stared at his plate. David cleared his throat again. Brother Apollo sighed and his face quivered as if he were going to weep. "I will honor your decision." At last he lifted his eyes to Naomi.

After dinner, Naomi and David disappeared. Brother Apollo drove Sarah home, and J. D. left to talk to the bishop. I helped clean up and walked out into the store, seeing the lovers sitting head to head next to the book shelves. A lantern stood above them, casting shadows across the large room. The maps lay open on Naomi's lap. Her face was distorted by fear and anger.

As soon as he saw me, David stood and walked toward me. "After the lies are spread, I will lose my job. I had intended to leave someday, but not so soon, not like this."

"I will spread no rumors. *Is* it a lie? I want you to tell me. You're lucky someone even-headed like me found the notes. You would have lost your life if someone with a murderous heart had found out before Sister Griggs and I did."

"Who have you told?"

"Only Sister Griggs. And you and Naomi. I will tell J. D." I pointed to the maps. "'Choose ye this day whom ye shall serve.' You've chosen." I was surprised by my own anger. "You've chosen to serve our enemies."

Naomi stood, shadows flickering across her face, and the maps fell from her lap; one slipped back and forth through the air like a falling leaf.

"Was Randall involved?" I needed to know.

David shook his head." Not Randall."

"He told them about Brother Apollo's plural marriage."

"That was all he did. And that did no good."

I stood face-to-face with him. "You sent men to prison."

Naomi moved forward as if to step between us. But then she just lifted her hands to her mouth and stood next to David.

"They sent themselves." He put his arm around Naomi. "There's something you don't understand. As a people, we will suffer the wrath of God. Worse than happened to these two unfortunate deputies will happen to us." He spoke in bursts, almost like Randall did when he was beside himself with anger. He gestured in my face. "Polygamy is an unnatural state. The prophet is a righteous man, but the yoke given to him is heavy. Soon he will throw it off or God will move on without him."

I stared at him. "I agree that it's an unnatural state. But no more unnatural than many human arrangements. You don't have the right to force somebody else's choice. Do you really believe the prophet will change his mind about obeying God's law?"

David's voice had become unsteady. "The scripture says the wheat and the tares will abide together for a time, until the day of my coming. It's not easy to see what is wheat and what is tare."

I shook my head. "But you believe you can discern well enough to send your brethren to prison. How can you quote scripture defending yourself?"

"The bishop, too," said Naomi. "Is it true you would have endangered him?"

"I will hide nothing from you." He took Naomi's hands. "Maybe I was inspired by an evil spirit, but I want to put an end to polygamy. The more men who are sent to prison, the more pressure is on the Church to abandon the Principle. Then we will all be free of this curse, and God's kingdom can roll forth like the rock cut out of the mountain without hands."

"Every burden is what people make of it. Whether you're happy about polygamy or not, you don't have any right to destroy the lives of people who believe in it. You seem to feel no compassion for the wives and children of the men in prison."

"Of course I feel for them. I'm not proud of what I have done, but it was necessary." He turned to Naomi. "And you will come with me?"

"How can you doubt that?" She leaned toward him and grasped his hand.

His whole body relaxed. "I would like to leave tonight if possible."

"We must at least finish one last day of school. We need to say good-bye to the children and give them a reason for our leaving, or they will be unhappy."

David frowned, rubbing his cheek with one hand, his eyes on Naomi.

"Naomi," I said, "he's in danger if he stays here."

"No one would harm him. They may disagree with what he did, but no one would harm him."

"Someone has killed. If that person finds out that David has been sending his brethren to prison, he might be very angry."

"Someone has killed strangers. Everyone has known David since he was a child."

David looked at Naomi. "I would like to go tonight."

"I want more time."

"You would endanger my life? We can leave on the train if we hurry. Please, Naomi. I'll go to my house and pack a few things, and then we'll go. We can be married in Eureka."

"Eureka. The gentile town. I feared we'd end up there."

"I won't be able to teach in a Mormon town." He kissed Naomi and rushed past me and up the stairs. "An hour. We can walk down and wait for the train."

I reached for Naomi's hand.

"Don't touch me or speak to me." Naomi strode toward her room.

I slumped against the bookshelf. I shook my head, tears filling my eyes. I had told myself that I hated force, but hadn't I wielded a kind of force to make David act as I believed he should?

Perhaps ten minutes later I heard something, a regular sound, nearly as faint as my own heartbeat. Then I realized it was the warning sound of Alma's or Maddy's hammer. I took the stairs two at a time. From the lane, I saw a group of men on horses only a quarter mile away, riding toward the store. Clearly a posse of deputies.

"Damn. Perishing damn. We're in the boiling stew now."

I knew J. D. would hear the warning but wondered whether he was smart enough to get himself out of sight. The deps had probably come at the sheriff's request, to investigate the purported robbery. If Danby was among these new deps and if he was as smart and mean as his reputation, he might show his power any way he could—by arresting known polygamists such as J. D. I looked toward Centre. David was about halfway there, just crossing the bridge. I could see no sign of the buggy with Sarah and Brother Apollo inside.

I rushed down into the store and found Sister Apollo. "Riders." I tried to catch my breath. "Federal deputies."

Sister Apollo frowned, one hand to her mouth. Then she slumped into a chair. "So soon? I thought we'd have a few more days." She stood abruptly. "William. He is so stubborn in what he thinks is right. Maybe he will refuse to hide."

"J. D.'s the same. I'm going across to town."

I saddled the brown mare faster than I had ever saddled a horse. The deps were only a couple hundred yards away. I jerked the cinch tight, mounted, and trotted along the road to Centre. Across the delta, I saw men and women standing near their front doors looking toward the cluster of riders coming across the flat. A man strode around the corner of his house, probably heading toward one of his hiding places. A cluster of women moved along the street, looking back over their shoulders.

Turning in the saddle, I saw that the deps had ridden into the space between the entrance to the underground store and the barn. They were out of sight for only a few minutes and then they reappeared, riding along the road toward Centre.

As I entered town, I saw Brother Franklin run toward his home. The streets had suddenly become empty. I didn't see J. D., and I discovered that all my anger at him had melted before my fear for him. He'd only be in prison for six months, but he might not see it that way. Someone so used to violence might do something stupid when the deputies tried to arrest him. The killing of the two deps was proof that people didn't always act rationally.

I directed my horse toward the bishop's house and found J. D. standing on the porch. "Go hide. I don't want you in prison also. Go up into the bishop's secret room."

He shook his head once, watching the men, eleven of them, ride up the hill into town. I realized I could be a danger to J. D., mistaken for a young wife. If I stood apart from him, maybe he'd be safe. Half a block away, Brother Alma came out of the smithy with his shotgun. Then he reconsidered, perhaps realizing the foolishness of a single weapon with eleven deps, and turned back inside. I hesitated then lifted my chin and stood next to J. D. I was his daughter; only the guilty need seek hiding places.

Well, we are also the guilty.

Alma walked toward the bishop's house and arrived just as the deputies passed the first houses.

From that rise, we could see all of town. At the far edge, the school door opened and Maddy burst out and raced along the main street toward her father. "Alma!"

CHAPTER 18

The eleven deps rode in three rows of three with a lone man in front and one behind; most of them propped their rifles upright against their thighs. The rear dep turned halfway around in his saddle, scanning the houses and outbuildings behind them. Someone slammed a door, and they all turned toward the sound. None of the riders were as young as the dead ones; several were as grizzled as J. D.

One, obviously the leader, dismounted and stepped forward to face the group of Mormons gathered on the bishop's porch. Like Alma, he was tall and thin. I turned and looked toward the school but couldn't see well enough to know whether David was watching. Somehow he had known they would come, and that was why he left the maps to the bishoprics' hiding places. I vowed to prevent him from helping anyone else to prison. I also felt an urgency to help J. D. discover the murderer. To do one I'd impede the law of the land, to do the other I'd endanger my own people. My head felt that it would explode from fear and contradiction.

The leader stepped to one side of the door. His face was intelligent—something like pictures I had seen of Abraham Lincoln, long-faced but without the beard. Stark, black hair made his face seem pale.

"J. D. Rockwood." A wry smile twisted his lips. "You range far from home whenever there's mischief." He had an accent that I couldn't place—Rackwood instead of Rockwood, fair instead of far. His accent was not foreign but rather cultivated. He would not be out of place, I decided, attending an opera in San Francisco or Denver. "Certainly, you came to hunt down my deputies for this robbery."

"I—I came to return a stolen horse and to purchase a birthday dress for my wife at Apollo Store. The rest of this—," he shrugged his shoulders, "—came after." He frowned. I had never seen him so discomfited.

"When did you come?" His voice was hard and sarcastic. "And you're still here. What complexity in this simple crime has held you here so long?"

I watched J. D.'s face stiffen. Wisely he said nothing. This man, who must be Deputy Marshal Danby, was as dangerous as a damn snake. Any second he could ask his men to put J. D. in handcuffs. J. D. would not defend himself and so he would go straight to prison. I imagined him dressed in the striped clothing of other polygamist convicts. Prison wouldn't humble him or make him change his devotion to his wives. Worse things could happen. For example, some fool, maybe even J. D., might resist arrest.

"Alma Wright. You hammer with a strange rhythm."

"I warn the community when scavengers are about."

I could hardly move my eyes away from Danby, who had a kind and sincere face but was called devil by every Mormon in Rush Lake Valley. I shook my head at the disjunction.

"Yes. I can hardly blame you for your resentment. Few citizens are so secure within the law that they don't fear those sworn to uphold it. In your case, you're caught between the rock of your religion and the hard place of the federal law. Should you Mormons obey *your* God, who is an Old Testament deity, or should you obey the Christian God?"

"He is the Christian God!" said J. D. "He is Christ. The laws of this country are not the laws of Christ."

Shut your yap, J. D.! You can hardly afford this argument.

Danby smiled, half nodding his head. "I'm in a quandary similar to yours. Do I exercise my natural sympathy for my fellow man or do I hearken to the voice of duty? We are all in a muddle, and the balance between justice and mercy is seldom achieved."

He said the words ironically, as if he sorrowed that life was so unfair. I decided he was moved by none of the viciousness of the small, murdered dep. Even his jokes and insults were calculated for their effect.

"You deps have showed my brethren little mercy," said Alma.

"As I said, the balance is difficult to achieve. Supposing I called on a member of the bishopric here in town. If I had the—ah—good fortune of finding one of them home, I'd know because of his position that he is a polygamist." He scanned the crowd. "I'd know that Karl Peterson or Mahonri Cooper or Heber Stewart or the man who claims he was robbed, William Apollo, is a polygamist. And he'd know that I knew.

"Now, polygamy is against the federal law of these United States of America, but not against the law of your God." He watched J. D. "The difficulty is proving him a lawbreaker. If I searched his house, I imagine that I wouldn't find more than one woman, one tired woman with about ten or fifteen children, half of whom call her 'Auntie.' Thus we see the problem of justice. But I didn't come to discuss the ways that religion and government confound each other. I came to say that we are not adversaries in everything. While we will pursue any lawbreaker, we've ridden here primarily about the matter of property, apparently stolen by my former deputies."

"That was Brother William Apollo, the man you already know everything about." Alma spat the words.

"Yes." Danby frowned straight into the blacksmith's face. "We talked to his wife briefly as we passed his store. She said he was here in town, although I don't see him now. The news of this theft came to me after William Apollo and Karl Peterson rode the train to Hamblin and talked to their religious leader about this matter. Together they talked to the sheriff, and even though he is a Mormonite, he knew his duties and turned it over to the federal officials. Strange that this crime had to be reported in person, rather than by telegraph. And that the man reporting it required the counsel of two levels of church leaders." Danby walked to his horse, but then turned back. "Oh, could someone please tell me where my misfortunate deputies were camped? Even though they've fled, we may use the same spot."

Maddy stepped forward. "You follow the tracks up along the creek."

"Tracks? I thought they fled the night before the storm." He watched Maddy, who backed up.

Alma spoke. "We—someone went up to visit their camp since they left. We wanted to make sure they were gone."

The marshal stared at Alma. "I'll wager you did."

"The tracks of their horses went off south." Alma opened his mouth but shut it without speaking again.

"They went off south? So they escaped well before the storm." Danby, frowning, appeared perplexed. "And J. D. Rockwood has made no effort to track them down?" He mounted his horse. "I want you to understand that we'll be looking into their—ah— disappearance carefully. I mean to say that we won't be doing anything arbitrary or unlawful."

"Of course not," said Alma. "You don't need to when the law authorizes unconstitutional and un-Christian behavior."

Danby tipped his hat. "I leave matters of the Constitution for politicians and lawyers to work out and matters of Christianity to my minister. I just enforce the statutes as they read."

J. D. fumbled with his hat. "I have worked to uncover this matter."

"I'm glad to hear that. Perhaps you can share information with us."

"Perhaps. Perhaps later."

"You may tell the men of this town to consider their hiding places well. We have come to look into a robbery, but we will not shut our eyes to other illegal behavior." He turned to J. D. "Because you are sworn as a justice of the peace, you stand to lose most by finding yourself among the camp of law breakers. As the scripture says," he mounted and, grinning, wheeled his horse, "'Choose ye this day whom ye will serve.'"

He and his men rode through the streets of town, which were as empty as if all the residents had been lifted to heaven. They used the same formation as they had used before, three abreast, one ahead and one behind. A dog burst around the corner of an adobe house, followed close by a black-haired child. The boy looked up open-mouthed into the barrels of the guns. Then a wail came from his lips; he turned and ran home, shouting "Mama, Mama, Mama," the dog right behind.

"It will take a miracle to keep Brother Apollo from being accused of murder," said Alma.

The deps rode along the edge of town and toward the cemetery, without wavering to left or right. I trotted up the lane to keep them in sight. Alma kept pace with me. The deps paused a moment near the grave of David's mother. Even though most of the horsemen aligned themselves between the grave and town, I thought someone dismounted and examined the gravestone.

They would certainly see the tracks in the snow—mine, Sister Griggs's, David's, and Maddy's. I wondered: *What will they make of that tangle?*

The deps soon remounted and continued up the canyon, scanning the sides of the ravine. The rear dep kept his neck craned backward. These men would not be surprised.

"Wolves." Alma's mouth curved down in a profound frown. "It's just like in Illinois and Missouri. Those who are supposed to protect us are first at the carcass."

"If that storm doesn't come soon," I said, "they're going to discover the bodies of the deps."

Alma looked at the departing officers angrily. "We are in God's hands." We walked down the street toward the others.

"I am now implicated in this charade," said J. D. "I despise being bound by my brethren to lie for them."

"Nobody forced your hand in this." Alma turned and walked toward the bishop's house, followed by J. D.

"But if I say all I know, it will now do more harm than good."

"I'm glad you see that. Finally."

J.D. pressed his point. "I warned the bishop this would happen."

He seemed so petty, clinging to the fact that he had foreseen trouble. Most anyone could have seen it coming.

I watched the backs of the two men. It was the first time in my memory that I had seen J. D. waver concerning the best course of action. No matter how difficult the situation, he always knew exactly what to do. Had I been blind to his flaws? There was a whining note in his voice that I had never heard before. Had it been there all along and I had just never heard it? It felt strange to still love this man who no longer seemed like a hero to me.

Alma turned toward J. D. "I wonder how much your warnings have to do with wanting to keep your position as a justice of the peace."

"We may all land in prison and not for obedience to the Principle. 'Tis more essential than ever to find the killer."

"No! Now's the time to be very, very careful." Alma turned to Maddy. "You go back to school. I'll watch and give warning if they come back down this afternoon."

The girl's face fell and her father touched her arm. "They are too many and too seasoned for you to follow without being seen.

These men are nothing like our foolish deps. I want you where you'll be safe."

Our foolish deps? The new danger has made the old one seem acceptable.

One thing I knew: now that Danby had come, because J. D. was a polygamist, his acts would be hampered. I would have to step in and do what he couldn't. I followed the two men toward the bishop's house. All over town, women and even a few men were doing the same, walking out of their houses and toward the bishop's. He opened his front door as Alma and J. D. walked up to him. A dozen people stood in the yard, including Brother Cooper with two of his wives.

"What do we do now?" asked Sister Sharp.

The bishop hesitated.

"You need to tell them something." Alma touched his arm.

The bishop stepped forward but stayed well back in the shadow of the porch. He glanced continually toward the canyon, even though the deps were out of sight. "You must all go back home. I could hear Danby. I believe the informer has been active, so I urge those brethren who are married in the Principle to find new places to hide. This is the time for silence, ya? Let them find what they can find."

He paused, but no one left. "Go now." He waved his hands at them as if he were shooing chickens. "Go to your homes."

He waited until most of the men and women turned away then spoke more softly. "Not you, Brother Cooper. We must talk, all of us in the bishopric. Alma, would you bring Brother Apollo? And come to me with him. You too, Brother Stewart." He turned to J. D. "I want you to be with us. I want you working with us or leaving town. And since you won't leave, I want you in this meeting. It's no good you acting alone, ya?"

The bishop turned and held the door for Brother Stewart and J. D. When I tried to follow, Bishop Peterson smiled and swung the door to block me. Without thinking, I put my foot in the doorway. He looked down and applied more pressure.

"You're hurting my foot."

"Then you must remove it from my door, ya?"

J. D. touched the bishop's arm and pulled open the door, blocking the doorway with his body.

"Rachel, there is a time and a place for all things. And dealing with a murder is not for a woman. Please understand this. This is not for you."

My whole body clenched, muscles tightening so that I couldn't move, couldn't breathe.

J. D. backed up and shut the door in my face.

Damn him to hell. Damn him to hell. Damn him to hell.

I waited a minute and knocked on the door. Susan answered. "The men are shut up in the kitchen. They are not to be disturbed." She swung the door shut quickly.

Anger made my muscles tight, but I discovered I could walk. I left the porch and took my own horse into the bishop's barn, taking off her bridle and saddle and putting her in a small pen there. When I emerged, I saw Maddy climbing the hill toward the school, obeying her father. I followed. I thought about telling her that obeying her father was the worst thing she could do, the worst thing any female could do.

As I walked, I breathed deeply, feeling the stretch of my lungs at the bottom of my stomach. Gradually I felt slightly calmer. I would not talk to Maddy with anger clouding my mind.

When I reached the playground, I found most of the children engaged in Red Rover or some such game, but Maddy sat with her back against a lone cedar tree in the school yard. She had been required to spy on two grown men, one of whom might have harmed her if he had found her; perhaps she had no need for play.

The thought made me melancholy. I walked toward her. Her

mouth was set. Her wild hair and her dark eyes, which warily followed the children's play, made her look like a feral child. Through
the windows of the school, I saw David and Naomi talking. The
glass of the windows distorted their faces, but I thought I saw
Naomi lift something white to her eyes.

"Maddy. I haven't seen you in a dress. Looks nice." *Like lace on
a bullwhip*, I thought. Maddy reminded me of myself when I first
came from Nevada.

"You don't believe that. I shouldn't be here. I should be watching over them deps. Alma made me come to school."

I shrugged. "I've wanted to ask you about something." I heard
the bell ring. All the children ran for the building.

Maddy stood. "I've got to go in."

"I'll walk you to the door." The branches of the cedar had been
worn bare by climbing children. "I have questions about the murdered deps."

"The kilt deps. They wasn't murdered."

"How high did you go that night?"

Maddy chewed her lip and turned away. "Quite high."

"How high?"

"I kept even with them all the way up." The corners of her
mouth turned up slightly. "I was right above them and they didn't
even know it."

"You saw them and they didn't see you. You are a clever girl."

Maddy glared at me, and I regretted my condescending praise.

"You know it was a blizzard. I heard their voices below me;
that small, mean dep shouted all the way up, he was so angry at
missing the bishop again." She glanced toward the school door. "I
have to go in now."

"When did you turn back—before or after the shots?"

"It was cold."

"You didn't answer my question."

I had to keep reminding myself I was talking to a school child. Maddy stopped walking and faced me. I looked over at the door and saw David waiting on the step.

Suddenly I heard the pounding of horse hooves on the lane inside town; Brother Apollo trotted up to the bishop's house. His face was flushed red and his mouth was a thin scar on his face. He dashed inside without knocking.

Maddy stepped close to me. "I went on up. I wanted to make sure they bedded down in their tent and didn't turn and go back to town. Sometimes they did that, started up the canyon and then doubled back to surprise men who had come out of their hiding places."

"Yes, that's what they often did. I don't understand how you could get close to them without them seeing you. I mean, other times, not the night of the blizzard."

"Whenever I watched them in their camp, I circled the flat and came down at them from above."

The same direction the killer might have used.

"The cover was better there; the patch of cedars comes down nearly to the flat, and they never looked that way. Their lookout was always downward toward town. They never looked above. In the dark, I could come right down close and listen to everything they said."

"So what happened that night?"

"They were angry and shouting, rushing around, so I didn't dare come as close as I usually did. But I could see their fire."

"Their fire?"

"Well, somebody's fire."

"Wait. You were above camp? Then you could see behind that cedar in the middle of the flat."

"Yes."

"Did you see anybody behind the cedar? J. D. and I supposed

that the killer hid behind the cedar. You should have been able to see him."

"Behind?"

"Your side of the cedar."

Maddy paused then shook her head. "I don't think so. But I couldn't see well because of the blowing snow."

"Then?"

"I don't think he was behind the tree. I heard voices below me, and the voices was angry and I heard the shots."

"You heard voices?"

Maddy frowned. "I'm confused about when things happened. I was even with them all the way up the canyon, hearing their voices. But then they somehow got ahead of me, or they must have got ahead of me, because they had already built a fire by the time I got above the flat. Then right after that I think there was voices and then three shots, two shots quick as the dickens, then another shot afterward. After the shots there was no other sounds. I couldn't see anything clearly. And it was quiet."

I waited, but Maddy didn't say anything else.

"Whoever killed them was sitting as quietly as you were, waiting for the bodies to bleed out before he moved them." A patient man. "Were you frightened?"

"No. I just thought it was time to leave. I was cold. I could see the body of one of the deps and somebody bending over him. So I left and went down."

"You did just right."

"I wasn't asking you if I done right."

David stood behind the girl. He put one hand on her shoulder. "It's time to start class, Maddy. How can we go on without you?"

Maddy turned and faced me. "I didn't want to know who the killer was. But now I hope you find him. Even when they were hauling people off to prison I felt safe in town. Now I don't."

A shadow seemed to cross David's face. I expected him to go into another blasted tirade about the evils of polygamy. "Mathematics. That will take your mind off murder."

I walked to the window of the schoolroom. One small girl, daydreaming as she looked out the window, saw me and smiled. I smiled back.

David and Maddy walked up the aisle between the desks. Maddy sat toward the front, looking like a demure child in her dress. David taught one group of students, circled at the front of the classroom, while Naomi worked with some other students at a table in the back of the room. Maddy had a third group, seated on the floor, working on counting small piles of something, rocks maybe.

I wondered whether Maddy was lying; perhaps she had seen the killer more clearly than she said. The girl's story made me consider again the idea that the killer had climbed the mountain before the deps instead of storming up after them, beside himself with anger.

Maddy had come up to the camp about as soon as the deps did. What if she had stumbled onto the killer and he had turned the shotgun on her by mistake? I watched Maddy's face which, as she taught the younger children, still looked as worried as an adult's. The bishop was wrong to think that his deceit harmed no one; every child in Rockwood was affected.

Maddy had perched shivering on the hillside within, what? a hundred feet of the killer. She could do this job, better suited for a grown person, because she was small and clever enough to sneak where almost any man would be discovered and shot. Once again, I was glad that the children of Rockwood were not afflicted with the same frequency of danger. Because it was at the far end of the valley, deputies seemed to overlook it. The children could grow like flowers, bending freely toward the sun.

I shook my head and walked away from the school building.

The entrance to the yard had been worn down to dirt by the many feet that passed in and out. Likewise, my mind seemed to have worn a similar track, and I couldn't see clearly. It still bothered me that the fire blazed so quickly in the storm and that Maddy hadn't seen the killer behind the tree. She had heard voices. Could the killer have spoken to the deps? Had he held his gun on them and talked to them before shooting? If one of the polygamists in town had built a fire, the deps would never come up on him unaware. They would have shot him from the darkness.

I shook my head as I walked down through town. Perhaps a spirit had pulled the triggers. I could imagine no other way someone could have gone up invisibly, although returning invisibly made perfect sense because no one wanted to see him. Perhaps J. D.'s joking suggestions was right—the killer was one of the Three Nephites, ancient, benevolent beings who wandered town to town across the Mormon desert. Perhaps each one of the three had fired a shot. I smiled at the thought.

Then, instead of going straight to Sister Griggs's house, I turned on my heel and walked in open sight to the graveyard. Bending over the first Sister Cooper's grave, I examined every possible hiding place for more notes that David might have placed during the night. I could find none.

Walking back down, I hoped David had seen me. He needed to know I would be wary and vigilant, so that he couldn't easily contact these new deputies, but then I remembered his "prayer" in the mountain. Maybe he had left them instructions at the former deputies' camp. I found myself at Sister Griggs's gate. The door opened immediately.

"We're up to our hips in it now," she said.

"Any little thing could turn this to bloodshed."

"With luck and prayer, it won't happen. Come inside for a cup of tea."

"Only if we can bring it back out where we can watch the bishop's house, where the important men are meeting without us. We must also keep an eye on the school, the cemetery, and the canyon."

"So much responsibility. You watch and I'll bring the tea." Soon she returned with two cups that steamed bountifully in the cold air. "This is what we women do—watch and wait while the men deliberate."

"Or act while the men deliberate. We're keeping David from planting more maps."

"That we are. Everyone is all worked up. The feeling is the same as the night we knew the first deps were killed."

"If I were the killer, I'd head for Nevada." I kept my eyes on the snowy reach of the canyon. "I'd skedaddle out of here."

"You said the killer was a calculating man, calm and careful. I'd name Brother Samuel Franklin."

Finally the bishopric, Alma, and J. D. emerged from the bishop's house. J. D. saw Sister Griggs and me and walked up the street to speak to us. I thought about ignoring him, but I was too curious.

I swallowed, but the tension was like smoke in the air. "So what's the revelation from heaven concerning the fate of this town?"

He looked at me sternly. "The bishop's talked them into waiting to see what happens. Alma suggested that we kill these new deps and head for Mexico."

At that moment, the alarm sounded, Molly beating in rhythm on the anvil, warning anyone with ears.

I stepped to the left, to a better vantage point. "There they come." The pack of deps descended the ravine, passing close to the cemetery.

Sister Griggs hobbled toward her door, holding it open for J. D. "This might be a good time to come inside for a spot of tea." She took my cup. "I predict they won't be so congenial now. The way Rachel described them, they were perfect gentlemen." J. D.

paused, frowning. "There's no use offering yourself as a temptation," Sister Griggs said more urgently.

J. D. ducked inside. His retreat was undignified, and I smiled, despite how serious the situation. I remained at the fence, watching. At the opening of the delta, two of the deps turned south across the flat.

"Those two are following the direction the bishop said the deps went when they fled following the robbery," J. D. said from just inside the door. "The horse tracks are clear as day. An idiot could follow. I tried to warn them that they couldn't hide murder."

"I'm praying for snow," Sister Griggs said from behind him. "I'm not in favor of polygamy, but these deputies have the aspect of Satan."

"Let's go stare Satan in the face," I said.

Sister Griggs flung her shawl around her shoulders. "Yes. Let's."

CHAPTER 19

The nine remaining deps rode into town with their rifles up, their faces hard.

"Self-important men," said Sister Griggs as they passed, "strutting like cocks." One of the deps turned and glared at us. "They see themselves as heroes out of a storybook."

I followed at a brisk pace behind the horses; Sister Griggs tried to keep up. Soon the older woman stopped. "I can't walk that fast. You come back and tell me what happens."

I walked back to her. "You watch the cemetery to see that David doesn't try to leave more maps." Sister Griggs smiled and turned toward her house. I trotted behind the deps' horses. I was curious what they would do, but I also felt that someone should be a witness; someone who was not a physical threat should watch to bear evidence against them if they were cruel or unlawful in their pursuit.

The two rear deps—a tawny-bearded man, wearing a red handkerchief tied around his neck, and an older man with a fringe of white hair at his collar—both watched me nervously. The bearded man turned his horse and spat a stream of brown before my feet.

"I'm harmless. You don't need to spit at me." I was angry at the insult, angry and frightened, my blood racing, but I also felt powerful. My following and watching had unsettled him.

Danby turned back on his horse and glanced at me. "Keep up. Keep up and together."

The riders stopped at Brother Cooper's front gate. The two deps in back turned their horses toward the street, while the others dismounted and walked toward the house. I slid between the horses and stood at the edge of the porch. A curtain twitched in the window of the next house over, which I believed was also Brother Cooper's house. Danby walked onto the porch.

"We have no appointment," he said to the woman who came to the door, the stern woman who had spoken to me and J. D. Now she appeared frightened. A child clung to her dress. "You will certainly tell me that your husband is not home. Still, we'd like to converse with him. We have secured a witness who will testify that he has two additional wives." He turned and pointed straight at the window of the neighboring house; the curtain twitched again. "Perhaps one of his wives is in that house."

"My sister." Her face was impassive.

"And you are sister to every woman in town. No matter. This witness of which I speak is one of your own. After all the chickens are gathered, he will testify against them."

"This witness you speak of is a worm devouring this community." She swung the door shut, but Marshal Danby put his hand out and stopped it. She opened it partway again. "My husband is not inside this house."

Danby turned back to his men. "Search everywhere." He pointed to two closest to him. "You stay out here."

Then he leaned back and watched the woman.

She stared him in the face. "You enjoy frightening me."

"I admit I've grown bitter about polygamy. I enjoy seeing the people who practice it become a little—"

She slammed the door, cutting him off.

"—unnerved."

Soon the men returned from the barnyard and the house, shrugging, frowning down at their feet.

"Well!" barked Danby. "Say where you have looked." He listened to them recite the places: barn loft, attic, outhouse, bedrooms.

"We searched the floor of every room for trap doors. We moved every rug."

Danby pointed to the smokehouse. He walked toward it and opened the door. Frowning he shut it again. Then he stopped as if he heard something. He opened the door, bending to examine the floor. Then his head rose, as he looked around. I saw him reach for something and pull up the fake floor.

Soon Brother Cooper appeared as if from the bowels of the earth. He walked toward the cluster of deps.

Sister Cooper stood on the porch, her bearing dignified. "This is not an ending, Mahonri Moriancumer Cooper. We will be here when you are released from prison. God's way will survive long after these evil men are rotting in their graves." Her voice was flat, emotionless.

Suddenly, Brother Cooper broke free and ran across the barnyard.

"No!" His wife shouted and took three steps forward. "No!" One of the deps brought his gun up and Danby knocked it down. The mounted men turned their horses back at the noise.

"Robert! He's running south."

The younger, tawny-bearded dep grinned and kicked his horse around the corner of the street. Brother Cooper clambered over his pole fence and ran straight into the dep's horse. He looked up into the barrel of a rifle.

"Thank God."

I looked back at Sister Cooper, who stood with one hand to her mouth. Now Brother Cooper walked in the middle of the four horses, his head down.

Even from the street I could see that Sister Cooper's hands were shaking. "What will we do when the bishop's storehouse is divided among so many widows?"

"He has broken the law. Tomorrow we'll take him to jail in Salt Lake City—him and the rest of the lawbreakers in town."

"He will freeze. I hope you get him to jail tonight on the train." She paused, frowning. "Is the jail heated?"

The posse rode only a short distance, stopping at the bishop's house. I followed, intent on pushing as close as Danby would allow me. The rear deps watched me, frowning.

"Marshal."

Danby turned back and the deputy pointed at me.

He rode back toward me. "Do you have a pistol in your pocket? We are doing nothing illegal."

"Neither am I. I'm your conscience, Courageous man!"

He kicked his horse and rode forward. "Beware you don't hinder our work in any substantial way."

I walked to the bishop's barn and to my horse, which I saddled quickly. I worried about J. D. and hoped he had the good sense to stay inside. Mounting, I trotted down the hill into the fields, where I pushed my horse hard. My horse thudded across the bridge and soon I climbed the opposite bank of the delta to Apollo Store. Randall came out of the barn, but seeing who it was, returned inside. Tying my horse in front, I ran down the stairs and found the three Apollos sitting in the dining room.

"The deps are coming for you."

Brother Apollo stood and then sat down again. "I have no hiding place planned."

"The loft, under the hay."

"First place they'll look," I said. "He's not safe anywhere in the store."

"I'm not budging until this is settled with Naomi."

"It is settled, Papa."

"Naomi, please don't do this thing. I gave you permission, but it still worries me. Please don't marry this man. I have a sense that you will have unhappiness from such a union. If he has begun to doubt the gospel, as you say he has—"

"Papa, he doubts polygamy—as I do."

"And the gospel? You can whittle at God's plan until only what you want is left?"

I said, "The deps won't be long in coming."

"Of course I don't doubt the gospel."

"You can't have faith in God's prophet and at the same time believe his enemies. That's like sitting in two saddles at once. *Duabus sellis sedere.*"

Sister Apollo grasped her husband's hand. "Good Lord, William, go hide. Don't be a fool about this."

He shook his head. "I will not hide from them."

"Perhaps we should feed them." Sister Apollo stood then sat again. "Perhaps we can gain by being friendly. It worked with the others." She laid her hands on the table and took them back, twitching, into her lap.

I walked up the stairs and climbed the ladder in the barn. It was no surprise that Randall was there already, looking across the delta. The two of us stood in the big window and watched the deps' horses, still gathered at the bishop's house.

"Do you think they'll find him? They've had long enough to measure the house and find the room by subtraction."

"No. They won't find hide nor hair of him." Randall spoke with certainty.

"They'll threaten his wives."

"Then they'll threaten his wives. They won't have him. His wives are obedient."

"So whose wives are disobedient?"

"You'll be, if you ever get a husband."

"Sure and certain, I'll be. I'll tell him to go to hell daily."

Randall laughed, his whole face alive.

Finally the deps mounted their horses and trotted through town. I peered at them but couldn't tell whether or not they had the bishop.

"They're coming here next. They'll put Brother Apollo in prison. Does that make you happy?"

"Don't make me happy a'tall. And I never told these deps nothing. I only told once and that was t'other deps, I mean James. I told him about William Apollo marrying Sarah. I never said nothing to the little one, the one that deserved to die. James was a good man, just confused, only different than I'm confused. We talked some whenever they come for dinner. He even tolt me he was getting married."

Randall caught the ledge above the window and leaned out over twenty feet of space. "His girl doesn't even know. Since I saw him dead, I've thought about her waiting for a letter from him, waiting for him to come home. The way the bishop has this set up she'll wait forever without word. He shouldn't have died."

"Wish David were that perishing contrite. He's done real damage to this town."

"Don't make him happy either. Today I heard him praying in his room. He was praying for forgiveness for what he done. I'm going to hell, because I have nothing but my green jealousy making me want to hurt Apollo, but David, he's different. He's an upright man—a torn-in-half man."

The deps crossed the bridge, and I saw that there were still only nine riders and one man walking in front of them: Brother Cooper; they'd had no luck at the bishop's house.

"You had reason to be angry with those deps. You sure you didn't follow them up to their camp and kill them because they did nothing about Brother Apollo?"

"They lied to me about taking Brother Apollo. They just didn't care about him. Naomi says they just wanted to keep eating here—that's why they didn't touch him."

"Randall, you didn't answer my question. Did you sneak up the canyon that night and kill those two deps?"

"No." He shrugged. "I had no reason to. I mean I had no reason to kill the one. Anybody who met the other had reason to kill him." The group of deputy marshals followed the road up out of the fields. "Here they are."

I climbed down the ladder and ran across to the store. Naomi and her father still faced each other across a corner of the big table. They leaned forward, talking earnestly, but their hands on the table did not touch. Sister Apollo sat at the other end of the table.

"The marshal has come."

The four of us waited awkwardly for a few seconds then heard footsteps descending the stairs. I walked out and found six deps and Danby standing in the first large room, waiting for their eyes to adjust. When I entered, their rifles swung toward the sound.

Without thinking, I dropped to the ground. "Don't shoot." I hoped my voice was clear and calm. "I'm an unarmed woman."

"Search the store."

"No need to search." I stood up again. My legs and arms shook. I knew I wasn't much of a fearless witness.

Brother Apollo walked into the large room, followed by Naomi and Sister Apollo. Two deputies stepped forward, reaching for him.

"Leave me be. *Frangas, non flectes*. You may break, you will not bend me. I will come peaceably."

Danby nodded. "William Apollo. I arrest you for cohabitation. Two witnesses have recorded seeing you leaving Sarah Stewart's house early in the morning."

He walked toward the door and turned at the stairs, flanked by the two deps.

"His is a recent marriage," Danby said to Sister Apollo. "You should never have allowed it."

"I didn't allow it." She clutched at Danby's sleeve. "He has the right to face his accusers."

"All in due time."

One of the deps laughed. "At the judgment bar of God."

Danby took Brother Apollo's arm. "Sooner than that. When he comes to trial."

"He has only me. Those witnesses lied. He's never been a night away from me our whole marriage."

"You have had no practice with deception, and I advise you to never take it up."

"This was the value of all our hospitality." Brother Apollo walked back and hugged Sister Apollo and Naomi. "*Dominus providebit*, Gwynneth, The Lord will—" He shook his head and followed the deps up the stairs.

Naomi stood and left the room. I heard a cupboard or chest open then bang shut. Her footsteps went down the next hall. A door slammed.

I ran up the stairs and nearly into Danby, who waited just outside the door.

"You were with J. D. Rockwood earlier at the bishop's house."

"I am his daughter."

"J. D. Rockwood's daughter. Above here in my deps' camp I saw a black fire pit that smelled wretched, like cloth burning, and in the ashes, buttons. Very curious. Why would they burn their own clothing?"

He waited, but I was silent. Without speaking, he walked toward his horse. Both Sister Apollo and I followed him out into the chill air.

"You're taking him up to your camp?" she said. "Why can't he just sleep here? Why can't all of your prisoners stay here?"

"Your place is not easy to defend." Danby faced Sister Apollo, speaking only to her. "Up on the hill we can see anybody who's coming to rescue their brethren. I hope they don't try anything. That would be a tragedy for us all. We've put up two large tents and there's plenty of bedding. He won't freeze." He turned to his men. "Let's go."

I tried to imagine why they didn't just take their two captives on the train to Salt Lake City. Maybe they wanted to establish their presence on the mountain, making sure every lawbreaker knew he was watched. Or maybe they wanted to kill any Mormon who attacked. Danby was right. Unless someone circled around from the top, through the deepest snow, the way Maddy had come to spy on the others, these deps would be in an ideal spot for defending their captives.

"Will they go to prison?" I asked.

"We'll wait and see. It would take a Solomon to sift truth and lie in what I've heard today." He paused. "What is that boy's name— the one you were standing with in the eaves of the barn?"

"Randall!"

"Randall!"

We waited but he didn't come.

"I can't worry about him now. But that boy knows something I'd like to know. And I'd like to know what J. D. Rockwood is here poking and prying into. Because wherever he goes, he pokes and pries. I ask again: if he was after those thieving deps of mine, why is he still here, even though they have gone?"

I stared back, blinking my eyes innocently, trying to adopt the blank look Susan had perfected.

"Maybe he needs to join us as a prisoner in our tent on the mountain."

Despite my unhappiness with J.D., I hoped he would stay inside Sister Griggs's house.

Danby mounted and I watched the deps ride down into the fields. Brother Apollo and Brother Cooper walked between the horses.

I hoped that all the prisoners would get a chance to go to trial and not be shot trying to escape. "Run," a dep might say. "Just meant to throw a scare into you. Now run, before we change our minds." Then they would shoot the prisoners in their backs. I doubted that Danby would stoop that low, but I couldn't be sure.

I walked into the dining room but then heard the sound of voices further back, in Naomi's room. Sister Apollo sat on the bed, her face empty, while Naomi packed her clothing.

"Don't go with him, Naomi," I said.

"She didn't listen to her father nor to me, and she won't listen to you."

"He is a deceitful man." I took a breath, knowing I would anger my friend, but believing that Naomi needed to hear it. "He will be unsteady in more ways than this."

Naomi pointed to the door. "Go. Leave me alone." She shrieked the last.

I turned and walked through the store and up to my horse. The deps made their slow way back across the valley. The dep on foot kept the rear, sometimes walking backward and peering across the desert, making sure no one followed.

I rode behind them, slow enough not to worry them. Why had I tried to persuade Naomi not to marry David? Was part of it simply jealousy of their love?

Everybody in the whole perishing universe, me included, seemed inclined to know what was best for someone else. The deputies and David wanted polygamy stopped. The Mormons wanted the world to adopt their ways. Everybody was a preacher. And everybody hated the unconverted.

CHAPTER 20

I followed the deps until they turned up the canyon. Then I rode through town to the school. Inside, I found David packing books into a canvas bag.

"Look!" I pointed out the windows of the schoolroom. "Look at what you've done! You think you'll endear yourself to your future wife by putting her father and your own in prison?"

"This is a logical fallacy. It's called blaming the messenger. They broke the law. I didn't. Even my father broke the law."

A faint smile slipped across his face, and I had a sick feeling, looking at him.

I stepped forward until we were face to face. "I could run out now and tell everyone in town that you are the informant, that you are responsible for sending their brethren to prison."

He didn't back down. "But you won't, because that would do nothing except give sorrow to the woman I love."

"You think you're doing right?"

"I know I'm not, but I'm doing something. I'm not just standing back and letting the Church go to hell because I wouldn't act my conscience, even if it's a divided conscience. I will do all I can to stop polygamy. Now, you've made it so I have to work from the outside doing it. I'll write for the *Tribune* or some other anti-Mormon paper. Are you happy about what *you've* done, forcing me to act outside our community?"

"No. Nothing has been clear in this."

"Right. Nothing is clear, but we still have an obligation to do what we can."

I turned and walked out of the school. Now that the marshal and his deputies had disappeared, women and children started walking back into the streets. Molly sat on the ridgepole of the smithy, looking back toward Apollo Store. Out on the flat, a small buggy moved quickly toward town. I wondered why the alarm wasn't sounding, and then I recognized the weekly mail cart that ran between Simpson, Rockwood, and Centre. From Centre the mail went on the train to Hamblin or Salt Lake City.

J. D. walked toward the smithy from Sister Griggs's house.

I glanced at the enclosed mail cart, which, instead of stopping at Apollo Store, kept on and was crossing the bridge in the meadow. Molly still watched it. Then I heard Molly's shrill voice just as the bishop came to his front porch and turned toward the canyon, peering up with one hand over his eyes. The alarm sounded, either Maddy or Alma beating on the anvil, but the bishop remained where he stood, facing the canyon, watching for the deps to come streaming back out.

I started walking toward him. "Bishop!" He didn't hear.

The mail cart passed quickly through the edge of town.

"Bishop!" I called again, running toward him. He turned and stared at me, then looked back up the canyon. "Bishop! The mail cart." Finally he turned, just as a man leapt out of the cart. The dep crouched and leveled his rifle on the bishop, who turned toward his porch.

"Not one step," the man called from below. "You'll be dead before you reach your door." Another deputy leapt out of the cart and scanned the rest of town, watching for any threat to the man who had his gun trained on the bishop.

I heard the sound of hoof beats, and from the canyon came seven horses, running hard, Danby on the lead horse. Three saddles were empty. Danby's rifle was out, grasped in one hand. Above town on the ridge two other deps stood, their rifles also out.

The two men who had hidden in the mail wagon walked up toward the bishop, one facing forward, one back, both wary.

Brother Sheffield, who carried the mail, climbed down from the wagon. "I'm sorry. They held a gun on me. What could I do?"

Danby, still riding hard, shouted, "Move! Move away from the house." The bishop stepped off his porch and took one step. He glanced back at his door, clearly wondering whether he could get to the door before he was shot.

"No! Don't do it." Everyone but the man with the gun turned to stare at me.

I saw movement behind the church, a man—was he Brother Franklin?—crouched with a gun.

I screamed. "No! The bishop will die. Many of us will die."

Everyone stared at me. Blood pounded in my head, and I thought I might faint from fear.

Danby arrived, his horse blowing froth from its mouth. He rode between the bishop and the porch and levered his gun once, pointing it directly at the bishop's face. One of his deps held another gun on the bishop from the opposite side. "Get on!" Danby said, and in the same breath shouted, "I'm squeezing tight on the trigger. If anyone shoots at any of my party, my partner and I will both shoot and your bishop will die."

The bishop slowly climbed on the empty horse. The two deps who had arrived in the mail cart swung themselves onto their horses, and the group swept away toward the canyon.

"Quickly. Faster. Faster."

Before anyone could move, they were above the cemetery and into the canyon.

In the lane below the bishop's house, J. D. stood with three women who had stepped out to watch. Soon Brother Alma and a few other men gathered. Brother Franklin came from behind the church, carrying his rifle.

They stared at each other with blank faces. "Our bishop is gone."

"The whole bishopric."

"We can't go through this again," said Brother Franklin. "I wish we could just take him back from them."

A few others gathered, men and women walking from their houses.

David walked past me with his suitcase.

I glared at him. "You've just taken away their hope."

"No. I am not to blame." But his face was twisted with anger and, I hoped, shame.

Alma ran toward the crowd. He stood on the bishop's front steps. "We can't let them take the bishop. They have put too many of us in prison."

Doors were opening and others, men and teen-aged boys, gathered in the street. A few of them held rifles or shotguns. Sister Sharp joined them, clutching a pistol. Snow had started falling, first a little then more and more. A sign from heaven, but of what?

Brother Franklin stood shoulder-to-shoulder with Alma and spoke to the gathering people. "We have stood for as much as we can." Others in the group shouted their agreement. Several of the women shuffled their feet nervously.

Looking into the men's faces, I saw they were working themselves up to a stupid anger. I wondered whether I could slow them, give them time to reconsider, if I revealed what David had done. He was halfway across the delta, walking toward freedom with his future wife.

"What should we do?"

"We should take him back," said Brother Franklin.

The others crowded around him and Alma. Some clenched their fists, their faces growing more and more angry. Once J. D. burned an old shed. It had started slowly but then burst into an inferno within half a minute. The crowd seemed the same.

I clambered onto the far end of the porch. "You're talking yourselves into a mistake," I shouted, but no one was listening.

"How many of us are there?" Brother Franklin stood on the lower rung of someone's board fence. "At least twenty of us with weapons. There are only eleven of them. If we move fast, they will not be ready for us."

"They are seasoned soldiers." J. D. tried to force himself to the front of the crowd.

Maddy came from the smithy and stood near her father. She grasped his sleeve and pulled him down the steps and to the edge of the crowd. She spoke to him, her face earnest. Her father shook his head. Brother Franklin spoke angrily and steadily to the men. Even Sister Griggs had walked down the lane from her house. Molly came from the smithy, wobbling on her slender legs. She held a steaming mug, protecting her hand with a checked dishtowel.

"Not now, Molly. How can you think I'd want it now?"

"Maddy said to bring it."

I stared at the small girl lifting the cup toward her father, so incongruous among the men with their guns. Molly had been bright enough to watch the mail cart suspiciously before anyone else had even noticed it. I wondered if the two girls sent the coffee to slow their father down, make him think before he acted.

"Alma." She lifted the cup higher, snow falling all around her.

J. D. faced Brother Franklin. "You want to start another Missouri? Another Illinois? You want that?"

"No, but we don't want them to destroy us either. We can no longer afford to be peaceable cowards."

Alma smiled down at his daughter. "Thank you, Molly. I'm sorry I was sharp with you."

"I made you coffee."

Brother Alma extended his hand for the mug, but Molly yelped and dropped it. The black liquid spilled on the snow.

"It was burning my hand." She frowned up at him.

"That's all right. That's all right, Molly, my sweet."

I stared at the deep splotch across the snow. I looked up and saw that all the men were staring at it also. I wondered if it made them also think of blood spilled on the snow. I hoped that dark sign would make them reconsider what they were doing.

Then Brother Franklin spoke, his face grim. "It's time to stop hiding and feeling guilty. We can use my four-gauge. They can't stand against it." He turned and walked toward his barn. "With that weapon I am the match for ten men."

J. D. held up his hand. "No." The men hesitated then followed Brother Franklin. "No." He stood in front of the men, some of them teenaged boys. The group simply flowed around him. The men seemed to march with the regularity of soldiers.

I knew if they weren't distracted quickly, there would be more bloodshed. J. D. ran in front of Brother Franklin, and turned, blocking his way. I knew that J. D., whose anger toward people came as quick as the strike of a snake, might kill a Mormon who contradicted him. He had once killed the thief of one of his horses.

"We have listened to the lies of gentiles long enough." Alma turned toward the smithy. "Brother Franklin, I'll get my shotgun."

"I have a weapon," called Sister Sharp.

Brother Franklin slapped Alma on the shoulder. "You're the strongest. You must help pull the four-gauge. We have plenty of guns."

Alma turned and followed the crowd.

"Those deps will kill half of them before they're forced back down," J. D. said to me. "They have no hope coming from below." He ran after the men. "Stop! All you'll do is get yourselves killed."

I stared down at the stain of coffee on the snow. It was as dark and dramatic as a revelation. I thought again how much it looked like the blotches of blood on the deps' flat.

I wrenched myself away and followed the men across town to Brother Franklin's barn. They talked angrily to each other, shaking their clenched fists in the air. "Listen to me!" My voice was weak and they didn't hear me, didn't turn from their purpose. "I have something to say about how the first deps found all the hiding places." My voice was lost in the clamor. The words seemed weak, useless.

When they arrived at the barn, Brother Franklin swung the doors open. His wife and children stood together on their back porch as the group of men wheeled the four-gauge across the barnyard. "They cannot stand against this weapon."

"Brethren, hear me." J. D. stood between the men and the street, his hands held out toward them, palms down, in a peaceable motion. "Half of you will be killed. All of you will be arrested as insurrectionists."

I imagined the mountainside covered with bodies. Nothing could happen that was more horrible than that. Every woman in town would be bereft, would wail in her sorrow.

"The government has driven us to this. The territorial officials are the criminals."

The group of men nodded and murmured. "Yes, the government is to blame." Their faces were twisted with anger, which I knew had been so long held back that it would certainly burst out in a flood. I also knew that if someone didn't stop Brother Franklin, or distract his followers, several of the men of Centre would die. They were intent on hauling that engine of violence up the mountain, that gun that could bring down a cluster of ducks at once. I was desperate to stop them.

At the edge of the group of men, I swung off my horse and ran to J.D.'s side. I decided to turn their anger onto David. Even if they did him harm, one man dying was better than half a community dead.

"Not now."

I pushed my face close to his. "Tell them David is the informant."

"What?"

"This is the first skirmish in a holy war," said Brother Franklin. "Let it begin here. Remember how we dealt with Johnston's army when they tried to send soldiers to subdue us before the Civil War?"

Men were nodding. He certainly knew how to work a crowd. "We said we'd torch every building if they stopped in our Holy City. Brother Brigham showed them he would sacrifice everything he'd worked for and move again if they threatened our liberty. Well, now our liberty is being threatened again."

He strained at the tongue of the small wagon. "Help me. It will take too long to harness a horse, and my horse couldn't pull this heavy cart up the side of the ravine anyway. We'll pull it ourselves. It's the fastest way to finish them off. Show them we won't be persecuted."

Alma hooked a singletree into the front of the tongue and he and a short burly man strained against the weight of the wagon. Other men pushed from behind and the gun rolled up the lane.

J. D. was shoved back. "Wait! Wait!" He trotted after them, his hand held up in entreaty.

I ran after him. "No, J. D. Don't go with them!" But he didn't listen.

Brother Franklin worked the crowd. "We'll end this."

"Damn deps!"

"Can bear no more of this!"

"If I have to rot in hell for it, I'll see them dead."

The men rushed up the street behind the huge shotgun.

"David Cooper told the old deps about all the hiding places." I screamed, my voice shrill as a child's. "He sent your brethren to prison. He betrayed you."

Brother Franklin turned. "Even if what you say is true, David is not the problem. These infernal deps are the problem. The territorial government is the problem." He turned back to the gun, pushing it from behind.

I wondered whether anyone could talk them out of their anger. Without something dramatic, they would never stop long enough to listen. Their blood would be spilled; more blood would blacken the snow.

They started up the lane that led to the canyon and I followed, not knowing what to do next. J. D. was in front of them, talking in their angry faces, falling behind, circling like a yapping dog, but without effect. Their backs disappeared into the shadow of falling snow. Soon it would be dark.

I shook my head. Blood in the snow. Snow swirled down, just like the night of the murders. Snow came into my head, soft and white, making it impossible for me to think clearly. I thought about the dark blotch of coffee. Molly and her father had walked toward each other. I remembered his smile, his hand reaching out. The tea had spilt like blood across the snow.

Then the story of the deps' shooting turned around in my head. The killer had walked from the fire toward the deps, reaching out his arm in the flickering firelight to shoot them. That made sense of the blood splotches and the distance between them and the fire. The killer had not come up over the rim nor hidden behind the cedar tree. He had been sitting at the fire, waiting for them. And they would trust him because he had helped send his brethren to prison.

I turned and walked briskly back to where Sister Griggs waited at the church.

"They knew the man at the fire. David built a fire and waited for them to return."

"What? You're confusing me."

"David built a fire. He was there waiting when the deps came up. He built the fire and they thought he was their friend. He probably had his gun covered with his overcoat or something, so they walked right up to him. He lifted the gun and shot them."

"David killed them? That makes no sense. Why would he want to harm them? He was in favor of what they were doing."

"I'm sure. Even if it makes no sense, I'm sure."

I looked toward the darkened windows of the schoolhouse; David had left with his satchel. By now he had reached Apollo Store. Getting Naomi? The men were passing the cemetery. I could run after them, shout in their faces: "David is the killer!"

Would they listen any better than they had listened to J. D.?

"Rachel." Sister Griggs tugged at my elbow. "What will you do?"

Maddy walked from the smithy, tears streaked her face. "My father will die! He's in the front. He will die."

I shook my head. What proof did I have, proof that would convince the men that David was the killer? A splotch of black in the snow proved nothing. My speculations proved nothing, unless I could hear it from David's lips.

I turned to Maddy. "Go after them, Maddy. Try to talk to J. D. and your father. Tell them David killed the two deps and that he's going to leave town. He's going to get away." Maybe the shock of the news would at least slow them down, perhaps make them think. If they once thought, they would abandon their blind rush.

"David couldn't be the killer. Why would he?"

"Just believe me! Now go! Run!"

Maddy ran up the lane toward the mountain and then disappeared, swallowed up in the storm and the gathering dusk just as the others had been. Soon she would catch up to the men and boys surrounding the four-gauge. Would anything she said stop them, prevent them marching with their faces grim, their rifles and shotguns held ready?

Standing in the falling snow, I knew that David might be able to stop them with a confession that he was the killer. I doubted he would do it, but it was the only thing that might make the mob pause. Also it was not good that Naomi should go with him, ignorant of what he'd done. Naomi should should have a choice. And he should not simply slink off into the dusk. Instead, he should face the people whose lives he had damaged. Did he also deserve to face their wrath, perhaps pay for his crime with his blood? J. D. would say yes; I knew his attitude concerning blood atonement: that some crimes could be paid for only with blood.

I turned and ran toward the smithy where I had left my horse. I feared that soon I would hear shots from the mountain, not just three but dozens. Half the town could fall tonight.

Across the fields and desert, falling snow blurred the horizon between sky and ground. I passed between the houses, and a few women came out onto their stoops, their faces torn with worry.

Sister Griggs called to me from behind. "Rachel, didn't you tell me that Alma's shotgun might have been the one used to kill the deputies?"

"J. D. thought it was the most recently fired."

"Where is that weapon now?"

"I don't know. David's gone. Sure and certain, I'll never catch him."

"The train hasn't come yet. I've been listening."

What I had to do, and do quickly, was find David and confront him. What he would do in response, maybe even God didn't know. As I rushed up to my horse, the poor mare turned her head as if to say *What now?* I swung myself into the saddle and urged her away from the church. Ahead, a woman appeared out of the dusk—Sister Apollo.

"Naomi is leaving me alone. My Naomi is leaving." She put one hand to her throat. "She wants to say good-bye to her father. I suppose Marshal Danby wouldn't let him come down." She turned left toward the cemetery and canyon. Her face showed her hopeless despair, stripped of husband and daughter in one afternoon.

"Is David with her?"

"Yes. I don't understand why I'm not happy for her. He's so ardent for her to leave quickly, it frightens me, I guess."

I leaned down and touched Sister Apollo's arm.

"Go!" Sister Griggs motioned me forward with her hands. "I'll take care of her." I turned the little mare toward the fields and kicked her into a trot. I couldn't see Apollo Store because of the darkness and the falling snow. I thought about what Brother Franklin hoped to do—bring the four-gauge to bear on the flat—but from what position? If the townsmen came up from below, the deps could lie along the rim and mow them down. The only open perspective would be from above, but the men would have difficulty dragging the cart up that steep hillside.

And Danby would not wait patiently until the Mormons established a position of advantage. Coming from the canyon and not along the higher ridge above the flat, the men of Centre would have to cross open space within a hundred yards of the deps. Even in the darkness, that would be dangerous. If the men were thinking rationally, all this would be clear to them.

David was leaving the town in ruin because of his implacable hatred of polygamy. Trotting my horse through the swirling snow, I knew mine was a fool's errand: David would never confess, Naomi would go with him anyway. And men would die on the mountain.

But I had to do something, and uncovering the killer was all I could do. I wasn't pure of motive; I ached to uncover the killer before J. D.

Snow stung against my face. Then I heard the long wail of the train whistle. I ducked my head and urged the mare faster.

At the store, I flung myself off my mount. It was nearly full dark now. Two horses were tied at the hitching bar and I wondered if David and Naomi had changed their plan of catching the train. Taking care with the dark steps, I heard voices and then saw them sitting next to a lantern in a corner of the store. They sat on chairs next to a cook stove, cupboard and bed, all arranged by Sister Apollo to appear as they would in someone's home.

David stood in the pool of light and peered toward me. "Who is that?"

"Rachel."

The two of them stood and faced the sound of my voice. They held their arms around each other. I could hardly bear the sight of my friend standing in the cluster of furniture as if in her first home. But I knew I could not allow David to keep his secret from her. She had to know that her future husband had helped send the men and boys rushing up the canyon toward their deaths.

"Rachel, I'm preparing to leave Centre. It's so hard for me not to blame you." Her voice had a liquid quality, telling me she had been weeping.

"This is nothing new." David's voice was soft and kind. "Throughout time, women have left their parents to cleave to a husband. And they've all sorrowed."

"You've missed the train."

"Naomi has anguished over leaving her home. Still, once she is ready, we now plan to ride to Packer's ranch tonight. We'll stay there until tomorrow and catch the train from there."

Packer's ranch was four or five miles away, north along the train line. "Thanks to you, we need to get out of town tonight." His voice, patient while explaining Naomi's feelings, turned bitter when he talked about the harm I had done them.

"All the men in town are rushing up the canyon to rescue the bishop." *Slow down sleakit beistie*, I warned myself. I knew it wouldn't be easy to get David to confess. "They are dragging Brother Franklin's four-gauge up there."

"Papa! They'll get him killed."

"Exaggeration." David stood square in front of me. "They'll shoot at each other from behind rocks and maybe one will get lucky and wound someone."

"With that four-gauge, they don't have to be very lucky. It will produce a blast that will spread to ten feet across in twenty yards." I touched Naomi's arm. "Are you happy about leaving with him? I was frightened that you had gone without talking to me."

If I just blurted out what I knew, Naomi wouldn't believe me. Did I believe it myself—speculation from a fire and the position of three spills of blood?

"I haven't gone. I'm all packed and ready to go, but I can't seem to get out the door." She smiled and sobbed once. "I'm being such a foolish girl."

"What is holding you back?" My insides felt tight as a wound spring.

Naomi looked at David. "I have only half of what I wanted. I wanted to marry David and live here, teach school with him. If it wasn't for polygamy and your meddling, I could have both."

"Yes," David said. "Our chances are ruined because people will know that I helped put lawbreakers in prison. It seems ironic to me."

"Ruined by standing up for your principles. Even if I don't agree with what you've done, I can't say you did it without integrity.

"So what are you waiting for?" The men would be a third of the way up the canyon. "If going with him was for the best, you'd be on the train by now. What does your heart say?" This, coming from someone who was a foreigner to her own heart.

David took Naomi's hand. "Rachel, speak of what you know, not what you extrapolate from your hatred of me."

"She doesn't hate you, David. She couldn't."

David leaned toward the lamp and cupped his hand above the chimney, blowing out the flame. The store became so black I could see nothing, not even shadows. If he was the killer, he might do me harm in the darkness and Naomi would never see. My whole body clenched with fear. Suddenly his hand clamped on my elbow as he shoved me toward the door.

"Naomi and I are not finished talking. Please let us finish. Please say good-bye to your friend. She will sorrow a moment longer. Then we will go in peace."

I let my breath out and my fear lessened. He had just wanted darkness to get me roughly out the door. Then I was angry. I twisted my elbow out of his grasp.

"Did you hear me? All the men in town are marching up the canyon. Does that mean nothing to you?" Then I knew what to say. "Let's go now and try to stop them. If you confess that you are the informant and that you repent of your sin against this community, they might stop."

I didn't believe he would go or that he could be effective in stopping the mob, but it was a way of giving him and Naomi both a choice. "Both your fathers could be killed in crossfire."

"No! You're not going to win in this, Rachel."

"If we did that, David would be in danger."

I had to try again. "Naomi, don't go tonight. You don't know his heart."

"She is no longer a child."

"Not a child." I heard the sound of weeping move across the store.

"Naomi," said David. "Where are you?" His footsteps moved away from me.

I tried to follow, but barked my shin against something pointed. Reaching down, I found I had run into the blade of a plow. I decided not to blunder around in the dark. "She shouldn't run off with you until she knows what you've done."

"She knows and has forgiven me."

"David, Naomi has the right to know *everything* you've done. She should sure know what you are capable of."

Please, Dear God, I prayed, *give me the speech to make him leave*

Naomi behind. Bless us that no one dies tonight. Help J. D. stop those men from killing themselves. As I prayed, I felt again the futility of my hopes.

I made myself talk. "So you're planning to set up someplace else—leave Centre. Why will another town be better than here?" Holding my hands before me like a blind woman, I moved toward the corner of the room where Naomi still wept quietly. Finally I felt the warmth of her arm.

"Oh, Naomi." I tried to hug her.

"Leave me to think. Do what he says and leave us alone."

"In another place—," said David. The sound of his voice surprised me, right at my elbow. "—we can worship God without plural marriage."

"I've thought the same," I said. "I've thought that the Church would be better off without such a confusing Principle. But—"

"This Old Testament practice should never have been revived."

Naomi pulled away from me. I heard her footsteps going across the dark room, away from David.

"But it *was* revived, wasn't it? And our single-minded leaders will *never* in any of our lives give up on it. So we adapt to—"

And then I knew why he had killed them. This is the worst thing that could happen, J. D. had said. The worst possible blow to the Principle was to have a polygamist kill a dep. And to have mass slaughter in the canyon between agents of the federal government and Mormons would do even more serious damage. All David's goals were being fulfilled.

I felt my way to the middle of the room, pushing my feet cautiously forward. Then I held still and listened. I couldn't hear either David or Naomi.

"Naomi?"

"Naomi," said Sister Apollo from the top of the stairs. I felt a rush of cold air and heard the sound of footsteps descending the stairs toward us.

"I used to think it possible to change the minds of our leaders," said David. I could barely distinguish his form, dark as a shadow across the room. "But then the bishopric conspired to lie to the law of this territory concerning this murder, and I gave up on the possibility of change in the Church. If the leaders are capable of that kind of deception, I want nothing to do with them."

He bumped into me, clutching at me. "Naomi, we need to go before someone else comes. Naomi? Please, come with me now. I will die if I lose you."

"I'm Rachel."

"Naomi," said Sister Apollo. "Oh, Naomi. If your mind is divided on this marriage—" The sound of Naomi's weeping moved closer to her mother standing at the foot of the stairs.

David let go of me and walked back toward Naomi and Sister Apollo. Something crashed to the floor.

I took a breath. "Wandering around with J. D. these last couple of days, I've thought some about this town. Laid out in squares, so perishing orderly, each house at the front of a lot, space for gardens, barns. Everything in its proper place. But sure and certain we're not orderly inside. We are bundles of contrary thoughts, just like Marshal Danby said. We're taught to obey God's prophet who teaches the Principle, but we also should obey a government that says cohabitation is evil. It's easy to say that God's law is higher than man's law, but it was God's law that said obedience to government is good. Such a tangle. We think of love as a unique bond between one man and one woman, but we force the best men to spread love between several women. It's all confusion."

"That's what Naomi and I have been speaking about. We desire a place where those contradictions don't exist."

"There's no such place on this earth." I walked toward him,

pausing halfway to listen. "Especially not in perishing Eureka. I've seen a church on the hill there, but right next to it is a bar. Wives and prostitutes. It's not just in Centre that apparently upright men perform secret evil."

"Then we'd create such a place." David's voice came out of the darkness like the voice of a disembodied spirit.

"Contradictions. You believe the prophet speaks the mind of God, but he's not listening to God. You think the prophet is the leader of us all but that he carries a yoke."

"I've given up on belief. I've decided that I can't wrestle with it anymore."

"You're leaving the Church?" asked Sister Apollo. "Naomi, would you run away with an apostate?"

"I feel like the Church left the truth decades ago."

"And I feel like you've opened my eyes," said Naomi. "I just wish I knew whether that was a good thing."

He said, "It feels that all my life I've tried to walk on the top wire of a barbed wire fence. I'm tired of it. We need to start over."

"I don't know why I'm delaying. I made my mind up about this long ago. I'm just having trouble letting go of my home."

No, that's not what I wanted her to decide. Naomi would require more than a suspicion before she would be persuaded that her love was a killer.

"Yes, yes, Naomi, we need to leave. If you're going to come with me, come with me *now*."

"Naomi." Sister Apollo's voice was so low I could hardly hear it. "Perhaps you should wait until you are sure."

"I don't have a double mind about it now. Let me get my small bag. You'll have to send my trunk along on the train." Her footsteps and David's moved back to the corner where the lantern had been.

I walked toward the entrance and stood on the bottom stairs. I could hear Sister Apollo breathing. Then her footsteps moved toward the living quarters, following her daughter. I had waited long enough; now was the time to confront him. I felt a second breath of cold air and then heard footsteps behind me on the stairway. *J. D.*, I prayed. *Let it be J. D.*

The breathing was right behind me, light, like a child. "Sister Griggs?" I let my breath out slowly in disappointment.

"The men are talking in the canyon. J. D. convinced them to stop and listen to him. Alma made Maddy come back down because he was worried about her safety."

"About time he worried."

"I just hope she obeys him and doesn't go back up. She could be shot either by the deps or her own people if she sneaks around up there tonight. The men are stopped for now, but Maddy thought they wouldn't listen to J. D. for long."

"Who's there?" asked David.

"Sister Griggs. She says the men are stopped. They're listening to J. D. If you want to prevent further killing, go help him."

"I don't want to go back. I want to be shut of this town."

"Damn these old bones."

I took a step toward David. "Someone built a fire before the deps arrived at their camp."

"A fire?" Sister Apollo's voice sounded from across the room. "I'm so tired of thinking and talking about this awful killing."

Though I couldn't see him, I could hear David's breathing. "J. D. and I found this fire pit, fresh black despite the snow that fell. What fire would last through a six-hour blizzard?" I paused, everyone in the store silent. "So who built it halfway through the storm?" I closed my eyes and rocked slightly. "The deps could have built it quickly, as soon as they came back, trying to warm themselves before going to bed. But they had wet wood and hardly any time, because they were shot only a few minutes after riding into their camp.

"When I came in from that storm, I took off my wet clothing and climbed straight into bed, but maybe, we figured, deps don't have good sense. Then we guessed that the killer had built the fire after he shot the deps, keeping warm while the bodies stopped bleeding, not wanting to get blood all over creation. But that didn't make sense because they would have bled out in a few minutes.

"Or the deps might have built it when they first came up, and the killer kept it going. These were the only ideas we could have because we were sure that the deps would be wary of any Mormon, so wary that a killer would have to sneak up on them. But the wounds showed that the shots were from close up. Who would they let close enough to kill them from such a short distance?"

I knew the words were tumbling out of me in an inane babble. "So none of it made sense. We couldn't fathom the deps trusting anyone in town, so we couldn't imagine the true explanation. But what if someone was there before the deps returned? Someone they feared so little that they would walk right up to him sitting at a blazing fire in their campsite. Who in this town of polygamists wouldn't they fear? Can you tell me, David?"

His shadow moved toward me in the doorway. I flinched back from him.

Naomi's face was a white blotch looming close in the dark. "This is so fantastic that you make me disbelieve your other claim."

"But David is so perishing honest. You admitted to informing on your brethren. Why do you lie to Naomi about this?"

"Rachel, how can you think David killed them? He's not a violent man. It was a polygamist killed them."

David was silent. I couldn't see his face, couldn't know what he was planning. The darkness was making me frightened. "Could we light the lantern?"

"I'll do it." But his voice moved away toward the hallway that led to the south room, where Brother Apollo kept the guns.

I ran forward in the dark. "I couldn't understand why at the time, but today J. D. made Brother Apollo lock all the guns in his bedroom. You'll have to break the door down to get at them." I hoped he wouldn't test the truth of my false statement. "And even if they were available, who would you shoot? Which of us women would you shoot?"

"What makes you think I would shoot anyone? This whole story is a fabrication."

I heard him return to the north room. I felt my way back to the doorway. In the dark I knocked over something slender, a broom. I took it in my hands and returned to the foot of the stairs.

"David." Naomi's voice was right at my elbow. "Say it to me. Say Rachel isn't telling the truth."

"See? You are driving a wedge of mistrust between us. Are you that jealous of Naomi's good fortune?"

"Come, Naomi," said Sister Apollo. "Come with me to the bishop's house. I'm frightened here."

"Why, Mama? I want to hear him deny what Rachel is saying."

"Yes," said Sister Griggs. "Let him speak."

"There is nothing to say. This is a—lie."

"There is one reason to kill that J. D. and I never considered—killing so that blame would fall on men in the Principle."

"Ridiculous. Some polygamist shot them. You told me that."

"You've borrowed Alma's shotgun a few times, a ten-gauge shotgun. What do you kill with it?"

"Turkeys or grouse. Sometimes deer."

"You can't hit a grouse," said Naomi. "And a shotgun is no good for hunting deer. Any child knows that." Her voice broke. "You told me you were practicing."

"You killed them deps." Realizing I was so upset that I had

273

reverted to common talk, I took five breaths to calm myself. "You killed them to stir up public anger against plural marriage." I kept my words as tight and flat as bullets. "You told the deps to wait for your signal, and you told them they could catch the bishop alone and unprotected at the church house. But the storm ruined your plan. Or did you want the deps to be killed by your brethren? What kind of news would that make, a whole town killing deps?"

A shadow moved toward me as I stood in the doorway.

"We must repent." Even though I knew he had come forward, the closeness of his voice startled me.

"David?"

"We need waking up. But maybe we never will."

"You change so quickly. Just yesterday you said—"

"I see more clearly now!"

I clutched the broom handle, a nearly useless weapon. Still, it felt good to have it in my hands. I groped forward in the darkness and touched the chairs David and Naomi had sat in earlier. I groped on the table until I found the lamp and then, miracle, some matches. I lit the lamp and saw David and Naomi, standing together not far from the door. Naomi had her bag in her hand.

The only way out of the trouble was to talk and talk and talk, but there wasn't enough time for all the talking needed. "Because of the storm the deputies couldn't see your signal. They gave up waiting and came early to the church. Then you heard the alarm and knew they'd come before they should have. I was hiding inside Sister Griggs's house, and I saw you hide behind the cedar near the bishops house with Susan. Then the others came."

I stepped forward in the darkness. "When did you get the idea to shoot them? Was it while you hid behind the church? I don't think you planned it from the beginning."

"David, what is she saying?"

"Listen to her," said Sister Apollo.

"You—you can't know any of this—can't know that any of this is true." I heard him moving still closer to me.

"So it was just impulse to grab Brother Alma's shotgun when you left the church?"

"I am not prone to impulse,"

"What then? Inspiration? You ran up to their camp with Alma's shotgun and built a fire. When they gave up on capturing the bishop and rode to their camp, you shot them both and waited until they had bled out. Then you loaded their bodies on their own horses, and packed them down here into the store. You left the horses in the bishop's and Brother Cooper's barns and the shotgun against Brother Stewart's door, laying blame at the feet of all the leaders of the Church in Centre."

"This is your guess. Your preposterous guess."

"David? Are you lying to me?"

"Joshua. You signed the maps 'Joshua.'"

"*She's* the one who's lying."

"Joshua?"

"'Choose ye this day whom ye shall serve.'" My throat filled with disgust.

"I told you we are all asleep."

"David." Streaks of Naomi's tears glinted in the lamplight.

He turned and strode up the stairs and out the door. Which way would he run? If he rode toward Eureka, he couldn't help me stop the Centre men, but if he turned up the canyon he might disrupt J. D.'s efforts to get the men to turn back. Since he had refused to confess, I could think of nothing good that could come from whatever he did.

I rushed up the stairs behind him and saw him mount one of the two horses that had been tied to the hitching bar. He disappeared into the swirling snow, riding toward Centre.

Then I remembered the shotgun in Alma's smithy. "Oh, damn. Oh, damn." Sister Griggs had asked me about Alma's shotgun, but I hadn't recognized her words as a warning. Now it was everlastingly too late to act. I undid my skirt and threw myself on my poor little mare.

CHAPTER 22

I rode after David, seeing only his tracks and hearing the muffled thud of his horse's hooves. I kept steady rein on the horse, which I could feel through my legs was nervous, ready to jump in any direction. Snow had started to fall in earnest—wet flakes that seemed as huge as lace doilies.

"Naomi," Sister Apollo called behind me. At the sound, my horse leaped forward as if she had been whipped. "Naomi, come back." I turned around in the saddle and saw Naomi running toward me.

I rode across the bridge, and the silly beast shied at the sound of her own feet on the wood. She bucked once, then slipped and fell. I kept myself on top as she went down, and then pushed myself away from her as she struggled to her feet. When I tried to catch her again, she trotted back toward Brother Apollo's barn, holding her head to one side to avoid stepping on the reins. I ran after her through the snow, finally grasping the reins when the horse met Naomi and hesitated. I remounted.

"Naomi, go back where it's warm." I turned the mare, threw myself across her back, and trotted once again toward Centre.

David's tracks led straight to the smithy, where I found his horse standing outside the open door. I should have listened to Sister Griggs and secured the shotgun.

I stepped toward the door of the smithy. Breathing hard, David's horse watched me but didn't try to run away. I didn't think it wise to rush blind up to a crazy man who held a shotgun, so I ducked around the side of the smithy door. Something fell, clanging against the rest of the scrap iron scattered inside. Then there was silence.

I thrust my head in the doorway and heard David's heavy breathing, heard him fumbling toward the corner where the shotgun was kept. Then I heard a sound, faint as a mouse, up in the eaves where Molly had sat the first day—a small scrape of shoe or knee across the boards. David apparently heard the sound also, because he dragged something large across the hard-packed floor toward the place where I remembered there was an opening into the attic.

A metallic click sounded, the hammer of the shotgun drawn back. Molly or Maddy had taken the gun into the attic. They were smarter than I was. After that all I could hear was snow falling on the roof, quiet as a whisper. No one moved; it seemed that the very earth held her breath. Then David bolted from the doorway, nearly knocking me down as he ran toward his horse.

"David!" Naomi wailed behind us at the edge of town.

He paused, and I saw he had something in his hands, but to my relief it was a shovel instead of a rifle or shotgun. He whirled his horse, and I darted into the lane in front of him. My sudden appearance startled the horse and it leaped sideways, slipping and going down on the icy lane. David tumbled forward over its head. The horse clambered to its feet and stood shaking. David twisted to his hands and knees, retrieved his shovel, and remounted, urging his horse faster up the lane.

"David!" Naomi screamed again.

I stepped back into the smithy. "Who's there? Maddy?"

"Yes." Her thin voice came from the attic of the smithy. "I thought he was going to climb after me. I thought I was going to have to kill him." I heard Maddy climb down. "Sister Griggs told me to hide the shotgun."

We went outside together, Maddy still carrying the weapon. At the top of the lane, David turned toward the canyon. Was he capable of stirring the brethren up to continue their attack on the deps?

Naomi stumbled toward us and slumped to the ground. Her mother walked behind. "Naomi, please get up. Please get up and I'll get you inside the bishop's house where you can be warm and dry." I helped Sister Apollo lift Naomi to her feet. I walked with them a few steps, and then Naomi shrugged out of my grasp.

"Don't you touch me." She leaned more heavily on her mother. I watched the two of them shuffle toward the bishop's well-lit house. Rebecca stood in the doorway. She lowered her lantern and walked toward the mother and daughter. Maddy followed in their footprints, the large shotgun laid expertly in the crook of her arm.

I turned in the direction of the canyon and stared into the billowing darkness. Perhaps J. D. had talked the men into starting back down. Hopefully they wouldn't be startled into firing on David as he rode past us in the dark. At the thought of that possibility, I ran for my mare. The mare stood hump-backed and forlorn because of the wet snow. I pulled myself into the saddle, flung my leg over, and kicked her forward. She crow-hopped, clearly unhappy about her treatment. Clinging to the awkward side-saddle, I urged her past the cemetery and into the canyon.

I realized that one of the boys or more foolish men might shoot at me if I rushed up on them in the dark. But if I slowed down, someone would die anyway. As I trotted my horse past the cemetery, the falling snow melted on my face. In the mouth of the canyon, I looked over my shoulder at the town, where lights showed in a half-dozen windows. Lights moved between the houses, women coming out to investigate Naomi's screech, I supposed. Frightened that my horse would go down and pitch me onto the icy ground, I turned to look forward again, settling into the saddle and urging her faster up the canyon.

As soon as I was away from town, the world became silent.

279

Except for the cotton thump of my horse's hooves in the snow, the rasp of my own breathing, the imaginary sound of snow falling, I might have been alone in the universe. I urged the unhappy horse forward with my hands, knees, and heels.

At each bend of the ravine, I thought I would come to the point where the path climbed to the deps' camp, but each time I knew I had farther to go. It seemed that I had been riding more than an hour, not merely the half hour it must have been. Suddenly a shot sounded, then three more, too close together to be one gun. I kicked the mare in the ribs, but the winded beast would go no faster. The only sound was her regular gasp for air and the soft thud of hooves. I finally recognized the bank and angled path, directly below the camp. Above me, cedar trees spotted the shadowy bank, the upper hillside invisible in the swirling snow.

Not far away, a man perched on the hillside, his rifle held halfway up. He looked back at me, and then faced up the hillside again, crouched low.

Suddenly, a rider-less horse loomed, sliding down with its forelegs stiff. The lone man on the hillside leaped to one side. I pulled on the little mare's reins, backing her away from the path of the crazed horse. Seeing us, the other horse snorted and bucked away from me, stirrups flapping.

"David!" I screamed as loud as I could. I forced my horse up the slippery hillside, but she refused to go. My heart whamming in my chest, I dismounted and scrambled up through the mud and snow. I passed the man with the rifle.

"Watch yourself. You'll get yourself shot. They've already killed someone. Shot him right off his horse."

"Who else is down there?" I believed it was the voice of Danby. Then more quietly he said, "Put out the fire. There may be more of them. Dump snow on that fire!"

"Damn. We're sitting ducks up here on this flat."

"Shut up!" Then he shouted. "We have no choice but to kill you Mormonites if you charge on us in the dark. One of your men is dead. I wish to kill no one. Go back to your homes."

I struggled through the snow toward where I remembered the path. My feet caught on the front of my dress and I tripped, falling in the snow. The ground was slippery and I finally just tore off the front of my dress.

I saw more men crouched behind cedars, facing up toward the flat, their rifles and shotguns held in ready position.

"Don't shoot," I screamed, panicked. "Don't anybody shoot."

I saw to my right where the men were struggling to drag the four-gauge up through the snow.

"Wait!"

Someone stepped from behind a cedar. "This is J. D. Rockwood. None of you shoot."

They had not listened to him before, why will they now? Why will they listen to me?

"Don't come up." Danby again. "We'll kill you just like we killed the first one. One of your men rushed upon us in the dark, careless of his life. He got too close before any of us saw him. But he just came out of the dark, screaming like a crazy man. Waving his gun. Go back to your homes."

The cluster of men continued to haul the four-gauge up the slope on its wagon. Soon there might be more men dead on the mountain.

"It's a shovel. The fool came at us armed with a shovel."

I struggled higher on the trail. "He is your spy! He is your own dammed spy!"

"Shoot as soon as you see movement."

I struggled forward again. A tall, thin man was at my side on the dark slope: Alma, who said, "Don't go. They'll kill you."

"We have to end this."

281

"Yes, we do. We will end this skirmish and begin a proper war."

I struggled forward and he didn't stop me. The slope was so steep that I slipped backward one step for every two. I thrust my hands forward and crawled up the last steep incline below the rim.

I don't want to die.

"I'm coming up. I am a woman and unarmed. I am Rachel O'Brien Rockwood. If you shoot me, you will shoot an unarmed woman. I am coming up alone. I have some information for you about the man you just shot. I have no gun. I am a woman and I am coming alone. I am Rachel O'Brien Rockwood and I am coming unarmed."

I held my arms above my head and kept talking, each second expecting to hear the thunder of a gun. I didn't stop until I reached the lip of the flat. Spread around me were the deps, crouched low, staring into the darkness below. Steam and smoke rose from the fire pit and a dep shoveled more snow on the embers. Snow powdered their heads and shoulders. The two tents had been pitched where the former deps had pitched theirs.

A dep stood in the doorway of the southernmost tent, his gun held ready. Voices sounded behind him, inside the tent. "Shut up," he said, over his shoulder.

Danby grabbed me and pulled me to the center of the flat, well back from the rim. "Keep sharp. This could be a ruse. She could be a decoy. The Trojan harpy. Keep your eyes below and above, both."

He pulled me back to the tree near the fire pit. "What are you here for? You took a ridiculous chance walking into the guns of my men."

I saw a body sprawled in the snow. "Dead?"

"Yes. Now talk."

I pulled loose from him and walked to the body, thrusting my fingers against David's neck. I could feel nothing. A patch of blood spread under his belly. Knowing I had but one chance, I turned toward the rim, shouting as I walked. "I am Rachel O'Brien Rockwood." I repeated the words numbly, like a chant. "I am unarmed. Don't shoot me." Danby stood in front of me, and I put my head down and darted past him. I stood on the rim so that both the brethren below and the deps could hear. "David Cooper is dead."

From the tent, I heard a cry and then the sound of a dep's hard, reproving voice. "David. My David. Let me see him." His round face appeared at the tent flap.

The dep looked up at Danby, who shook his head. The dep thrust his rifle into Brother Cooper's face, forcing him back inside. Any second a gun would go off and then everyone would start shooting. Panic gripped my body, and I knew only quick action would stop the carnage. "David Cooper is dead," I shouted again. "He rushed into their guns and was shot to death. Danby, tell these men of Centre that David was your spy. You must tell them you used him to ruin the lives of women in this town."

"You have it backward," he called out. Below us everyone was silent, I hoped listening. "Three months ago he came to me. Said that *polygamy* was ruining the lives of women in this town. He said he would leave notes for my deps about where polygamists were hiding. He wouldn't let me pay him. The poor boy couldn't stop talking about how he hated polygamy. Told me the story of how it had ruined his mother's life. That he didn't want it to affect his children's lives. He was the one law-abiding man in this town."

I shouted so that everyone had to hear. "David Cooper was the damned spy informer. He sent many of our brethren to prison. He was the deputies' informer and now they've gone and shot him. I found his notes in the—," I took a breath, "—in the graveyard, near his mother's grave. They had Joshua written on them."

I heard a sound off to the side of the flat. Perhaps it was the men with the four-gauge, bringing it to bear on the deps. "Brother

Franklin, you hold and listen. You will only do damage if you fire on these deps."

Danby took my arm and walked toward the sound. "Don't shoot. If you shoot any one of my men, three of yours will die. We've got a shotgun against the head of your bishop. Just hold still everybody and we'll make it through this with no one else dead."

J. D. called from below. "I need to come up and talk."

"You do and we'll shoot you, despite your gray beard. Your daughter is doing just fine." He stepped closer to me. "I want those notes. I want to see what message he left me about my missing deputies."

Instead of answering, I walked to David's body, which the deps had pulled back near the smoldering fire. "He was your informer but he was so divided about it that he became crazy. He loved his people but you turned him against them. Then when he came to you for help, you shot him. How will the story go in an eastern newspaper?" I heard another sound off to the side, where I had last seen the men with the four-gauge. I had to get the Mormon men off the hillside before anyone else was killed.

Danby stared at me. "Why do I have the feeling that this poor, dead man is the scapegoat staked outside the camp of Israel? I wish to hell I was shut of this whole business."

"The Mormons in this town will do nothing now. You've punished him yourselves." My teeth chattered.

"Are you sacrificing him so that we won't look for complicity?"

"He's *your* spy. Was he working with someone else?"

"No. He wasn't." He thought for a moment. "I meant complicity of the town in the murder of my deps. You're hiding something."

"Rachel!" J. D. again.

Danby watched me. "You know who killed them."

I didn't know what to do. If I shook my head, would Danby leave the town alone or would he keep sniffing at the scent of deceit until he found the truth? Suddenly I was sick in my soul at the duplicity and secrecy the bishop had forced on everyone.

I nodded.

I heard noise from below. Any second the big shotgun might blast out.

"Who?"

I pointed to the ground.

Danby shook his head. "No. He hated polygamy."

"What man in this town wanted so badly to destroy polygamy that he arranged for all this to happen?" I spread my arms wide. "He wanted carnage in the news in the hopes that it would hasten the destruction of polygamy. Who, after I accused him of the murders, armed himself with a shovel handle and rode his horse straight into your rifles trying to salvage his plan?"

"Rachel!" J. D. shouted again.

"I'm walking to the rim," I called out. "Don't shoot. I'm a woman and I'm unarmed."

"The hell you are," said Danby softly.

"Would you bring my mare up?" I said to J. D. I knew he could force the mare up the slippery hillside.

Before I could walk to the rim, one of Danby's men stood in front of me. I looked back at the fire pit, where Danby stood, head down, thinking. "Let her go."

"I'm coming down now!" I called to the men below on the hillside. I stepped off the rim and took my mare from J. D.'s hand. "I'm going to get the body. We need to get everyone off the hillside." I led the mare back up to the flat. "Don't anybody shoot." The mare didn't shy away at the smell of blood, so, apparently, she had been used for hunting. "Help me get him loaded."

Two deps lifted David's body and flopped it across my saddle. The mare snorted and danced but soon calmed down. Another dep brought rope and tied the body in place.

"We'll bury him next to his mother. The Mormons will follow me off the mountain. Don't get hasty and shoot anyone else. You do that and you'll start a war here. Where is the justice *or* the mercy in that?"

I led the horse to the rim then turned back. "But I advise you to take your prisoners away from here tonight." Danby nodded, and I led the horse down the hillside past the men crouched behind cedars.

"It's over," I shouted. "David Cooper is shot. He was the one telling the deps about the hiding places of the men of town. It was one of our own who betrayed us. Now he's dead. For sure and certain, we don't want any more dead. Let's go back home. One of our own informed against us."

I led the horse down, still shouting. "He's dead. He was the spy. David Cooper. They shot their own informant. They killed the one who put your brethren in jail. Now it's over. Now let's get off the mountain before anyone else is killed."

I filled the air with words until they were as thick as the snowflakes that still fell. My throat felt raw and I prayed it would not give out. "If you use that big gun on them, half of you will die from their gunfire, then what will happen to your wives and children? Who will feed them? Who will care for the children and wives of the men in prison?" I babbled on, knowing that if I kept talking they would not turn and charge the hill. I could lead them off the mountain with my voice.

Two men came out of the trees. "You say they shot David Cooper?"

"Yes."

He put his arm around the second man, whom I recognized as Randall.

"Papa," he yelled. "David is dead."

"He ran up on them waving a perishing shovel handle. He wanted to be dead. We don't want more dead. Let's get off the mountain and I'll tell you the whole story. Tell you why he ran toward their rifles wanting to be shot."

"My brother is dead." I seized the opportunity and led the horse farther down the mountain. Randall followed. Someone else came: Alma. The men on the hillside turned back toward town. "It would be suicide for you to attack them," I called to the men on the hillside with the four-gauge.

The second suicide of the night.

Finally, I saw them also follow me down.

"Let's return to our homes," someone called. "She knows what happened," said someone else. "She'll tell us." Behind me, I saw the dark forms coming through the snowy cedars. Snow powdered their shoulders, swirled above their heads. We moved in a line, riders and walkers, trudging down the canyon toward town.

A cluster of women stood silent in the snow just outside the gate of the cemetery. One stepped forward, clutching her hands before her chest. "Who is dead? We heard the shots. Who was killed up there?"

The bishop's two first wives stood with their arms around each other.

"David Cooper," I said. "He was the informant and he rode his horse straight up the hillside. Danby and the others thought he was attacking, so they shot him."

Sister Sharp said, "If he was a turncoat, he deserved to die."

"Yes," said Sister Cooper, the youngest wife. "I agree that it's the best that could have happened."

Sister Griggs muttered, "The best that could happen? Phooey!"

The men gathered behind the women, a circle of people. Everyone watched me, listening. Their vague guilt about a murderer still in their midst would continue to fester and grow. No longer. "He's also the one who killed the deps, James and Sammy."

The shock of it silenced the women for a moment.

"We've all been sick with dread," I called out, "that one of our brethren killed the deps and started this whole mess." I waited until everyone became silent, focused. "David hated polygamy enough that he would do anything to get polygamists blamed for the murder of federal deputies." The men were listening now. If only they'd listened before, David might still have been alive. "I don't think he planned from the beginning to kill them. He just wanted to put the bishop in jail, so the night of the first storm he told the deputies about the bishopric meeting hoping they would arrest the bishop, but when that didn't work out, mostly because of the storm, he grabbed a shotgun and rode up the canyon to wait for them. He hated polygamy so much that murder seemed the only way forward. I think he pictured the newspapers spreading all over the country the news that Mormons had killed two deputies. He thought it would hasten the end of the Principle."

"That's crazy," said Brother Franklin.

"He *was* crazy. After he killed them, he packed them on their own horses and carried them to Apollo Store, where he laid them out on the floor on a piece of canvas. He put one horse in the bishop's corral and another in his own father's pens. The shotgun he used to kill them was propped against Brother Stewart's porch the next morning. He did this all in one night. He wanted the bishopric blamed for the killing. And they fell right into his hands, trying to cover it up with this impossible story about a theft."

"This is all implausible," said Brother Franklin.

"When I accused him, when I told him this story that I've just told you, he mounted his horse and rode straight to his death. He wanted a bloodbath."

I was finished talking, and pushed through them, making my way to the edge of the group, where my horse stood. Alma wiped the blood from my saddle. I took the reins. "You are a remarkable woman," he said. "God protect the man who marries you."

I led my horse away, wondering why he had to say that—as if my future husband needed God's blessing to survive living with me. No one would say the same to a man, even though it was generally truer that women needed God's protection from the follies and cruelties of their men.

Sister Griggs caught my arm. "Naomi is at the bishop's house. She wants to talk to you." They stopped in front of the bishop's storehouse, and Alma and J. D. carried the body inside.

While Alma watched, I walked to the bishop's house. Inside, my cheeks stung from the warm air. Rebecca led me into the parlor, where they had spread a blanket for Naomi, who was lying on the couch. She had laid her head on her mother's lap. Susan sat on the floor, holding Naomi's hand.

"I heard the shots. Even inside here, I heard the shots. He's dead, isn't he?"

I nodded.

J. D. came in and stood behind me.

Naomi struggled to sit up. "We almost left. I almost left town with him. If I hadn't delayed, we'd be on the train now between Hamblin and Salt Lake." Then she sobbed, taking great heaving breaths. "If you had left us alone, we would be gone by now. He wouldn't be dead, and we'd be gone by now."

I backed toward the door. "I'll come back when I don't disturb her." I turned and left the house. Tears came to my eyes. She was right. My acts had brought about the death of the man she loved. I shook the water from my eyes. "Damn. Damn."

Standing on the step, I looked across town. Most of the homes had lanterns lit. Men and women stood in the cold lanes, talking as snow fell around them. In front of the storehouse, Alma still worked on my saddle.

Sister Griggs touched me on the arm.

"He was not stupid," I said. "He knew what would happen if

289

he ran up the hill waving something that looked like a gun. He wanted to die." I sobbed once and felt tears running down my face. "When Naomi said she wouldn't go with him, he didn't want to live. I've helped kill him."

"He chose his own death, you can't be blamed for trying to help Naomi." She led me down the hill toward her house. "You could use a hot cup. Maybe three cups. You need some comfort."

CHAPTER 23

Nearly the whole town attended David's funeral two days later. Unwilling to chance another charge on the hill, Danby and his deps had left quietly before dawn, leading the bishop and the others to the train at Packer's Ranch and from there to jail in Salt Lake City, where they would await trial.

The stake president, Rodger Hunsaker, spoke in the chapel; he had come from Hamblin to attend the funeral and reorganize the bishopric. "Time is fleeting." He was a tall, broad-shouldered man. His brown beard was streaked with white and he was thin and dignified. I had found space in the back of the church; Naomi sat close to the front, next to her mother, just behind the Coopers. "We wake as children and before we know it we're grown, often making decisions with inadequate preparation. Life on this earth is twice forty years of wandering in the desert. But God waits for us with open arms, always close, like a mother hen with warm wings."

Then everyone in town walked slowly behind the wagon that bore the casket. The procession went past Sister Griggs's house and up to the cemetery. Next to his mother's grave, a hole had been chiseled through the frozen surface. Icy chips of surface soil and the gray, unfrozen clay from deeper down had been heaped up in a long mound, which looked dark against the white snow. The green pine boughs still lay across his mother's headstone. Naomi stood next to the hole. Sarah, at Naomi's left, had her arm around Naomi's waist. Randall leaned against Naomi's right side, pressing her hands in his. Susan stood directly behind, her hands on Naomi's shoulders. Brother Franklin dedicated the gravesite that it would be unmolested. Every Mormon dedication prayer I had ever heard promised that the dead one would rise with the righteous in the first resurrection. Brother Franklin did not speak those words over David's grave.

After the prayer, the townspeople filed back down to the church where the Relief Society sisters had prepared a luncheon. Naomi, Randall, Sarah, and Susan were almost the last to leave."

"Naomi?" I walked toward them. "Naomi."

"How could I know how tangled he was inside? If I had known, I could have helped him."

"If only God made us all seers," said Susan.

Naomi faced me. "You never knew him. You may not believe it, but he had a kind heart. I've been thinking that it took years of turmoil to bring him to where he would kill. I still wonder whether I could have helped him. If we had loved each other years ago, and left here, maybe he would be all right now."

I reached out to touch her arm, but she turned away.

"Maybe it's irrational, but I wish you weren't so tenacious. You wouldn't let go until you uncovered his secret. Does it surprise you that I'm not grateful?"

I stepped back and the four friends from Centre walked together down to the church.

I leaned against a tree while Alma, J. D., Randall, and Brother Franklin shoveled dirt onto the coffin. I felt too tired even to weep. For a few minutes, I listened to the rhythmic thump; then I turned and mounted my horse, turning her head toward Apollo Store.

That afternoon at Apollo Store was torture. I would have been glad to leave and go home to Rockwood, but J. D. said he didn't want to arrive home in the dark. Naomi sat in the large room, next to the stove, table and cupboard where she and David had talked about leaving. Her face was empty. Sister Apollo wandered room to room in the underground store, her face also blank as a dead woman's. J. D. spoke to me about wrapping the dress, what supplies we needed to set aside from the store, and whether the clear weather would hold. We didn't talk about what had happened.

I wished he would say something, some word of praise because I had discovered the killer, but I was no longer angry with him. I knew now he was just another fallible man, not the hero I had seen him as most of my life. There was also distance—mistrust— between us now, and I couldn't find the words to begin talking through the barriers. Finally, he just left the store—to help President Hunsaker organize the new bishopric. It would have to be composed of monogamous men, I knew. Hardly any polygamist men were left in town.

That evening, Naomi took her bag and boarded the train for Salt Lake City, where she said she would live with her sister. "I can't bear another night in this town."

J. D. and I sat up with Sister Apollo alone in the store. "What will you do?" asked J. D.

"I'm selling out to Brother Stewart. I'll move to Payson, near my son."

I tried to embrace her, but she held her body stiff, beyond comfort. Finally, well past midnight, the warm milk seemed to work and Sister Apollo stumbled off to bed. I lay in my bed awake and thought of all those sorrowing: Naomi and Randall. Brother Cooper. I had thought that finding the killer would leave me with a satisfied, completed feeling, but I felt ripped apart.

Early the next morning, Brother Stewart and his first wife puttered around their new store, rearranging things, making it their own. I wrote a letter to Danby, enclosing the letter from James's fiancée, so he would contact her and let her know what happened. Then I finished packing and sat in the corner of the north room of the store, staring at the place where Naomi and David had held hands. J. D., who hated waiting for anyone, made me wait for him, while he talked at Sister Apollo, trying to preach her out of her anger at God. At least he wasn't trying to preach the same to me.

Around nine he gave up and we left for Rockwood, driving in silence through the bright, white desert. If J. D. seemed to be a different person, almost a stranger, I also had changed. I hardly knew myself.

I opened my mouth half a dozen times to break the silence, but each time, I just shut it again. Finally, the tension left my body. The platter of Rush Valley, smooth with snow, seemed as wide as the sky. The massive earth seemed unsusceptible to pity or tragedy.

Still we didn't speak. During that silence, I wondered if we would ever again be as close as we were when I was a child. I thought not. He had offended me too deeply by dismissing my value to him. And, even though he wouldn't admit it, it irritated him that I had uncovered the killer under his nose.

Our argument while we had hooked up the surrey was about how I could know who the killer was.

"Physical evidence solved the crime," J. D. had said. "Knowing that the deputies were shot closer than the cedar tree. That's what enabled you to figure out who the killer was."

"Talking to people, knowing what prompted their actions, helped me know who the killer was."

But now we could hardly talk. Finally, J. D. peered out from under his sheep-pelt robe. He turned to me. "I have something to say."

"What?"

"You did well."

His words felt like rubies and diamonds to me. "I couldn't have done it without you and your devotion to physical evidence."

He snorted.

"And I have something to say to you." I paused. "I've decided to stay single all my life. I'm going to work with you tracking down horses and killers. We'll become famous all across Utah territory."

"Seriously. You know I'm too old for that. And you're a woman— none of this will work. If you were a man—"

I thought, *Why do men always say too much?*

"What have you really decided?"

"I *was* serious." We rode in silence for some time. "It was a serious dream. I give it up only with difficulty. Maybe I'll marry Danby and hunt down polygamists with him."

J. D. stopped smiling.

"This time I *was* joking."

"So which is it? I'm asking what you're going to do with yourself now that you're a grown woman."

"I've decided to ask your sister whether I can live with her in Salt Lake until spring. I'm going to look the young men over."

He frowned, and finally, I touched him on the arm. My hand had been waiting for that touch.

"Till June. If I don't find anyone by then, I'll come back to Rockwood."

I smiled, thinking about my plan, and whipped up the horses because the *sleakit* mare was pretending already that she was too weary to walk. I hoped J. D. wouldn't refuse to try to talk me out of going to the city. But he smiled, a real one.

"Go to Salt Lake with my blessing, but part of me goes with you."

Then he was embarrassed and pulled the furry quilt over his head. Soon he was asleep, snorting and grunting like an old boar bear in pain.

AUTHOR'S NOTE

Rachel's story is continued in *Ezekiel's Third Wife*.
For more information, see johnbennion.com.

MORE FICTION FROM SIGNATURE

Caldera Ridge
by Jack Harrell
hardback $29.95 | e-book $9.99

Dream House on Golan Drive
by David G. Pace
paperback $24.95 | e-book $9.99

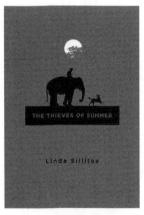

The Thieves of Summer
by Linda Sillitoe
paperback $21.95 | e-book $6.00

Murder by Sacrament
by Paul M. Edwards
hardback $23.95 | e-book $6.00